THE MURDEROUS HAIRCUT OF THE MAYOR OF BEL AIR

a psychic barber mystery

PHILLIP MOTTAZ

Not As Bad Books

The following is a work of fiction. That means it's made up, and any resemblance to real people — alive or dead — is strictly coincidental.

Special recognition to everyone who loaned their names, whether they realized it or not. Many yearbooks, phonebooks and old conversations were scoured to pull authentic sounding names. If a name sounds familiar, please know it only happened because it sounded great, and not as any comment on your personal lives.

Names are hard.

THE Murderous HAIRCUT OF THE MAYOR of BEL AIR

A PSYCHIC BARBER MYSTERY

PHILLIP MOTTAZ

AN ASK AND A WARNING...

Consider signing up for the newsletter!

Check **phillipmottaz.com** or email **phillip.mottaz.author@ gmail.com** to sign up for freebies, contests, and very, very little spam.

Or follow **@phillipmottaz** on Twitter.

Furthermore, I'd like to provide a **trigger warning**: this book contains scenes of racism and homophobia, as well as one of violence.

While I try to be a co-conspirator in the fight for equity and justice, I recognize that I make mistakes due to my personal biases. Please feel free to reach out and hold me accountable, and I promise to do better in the future.

To my friends, supporters, spell-checkers, Beta readers, ethical shoppers and all the otherwise good looking people I'm lucky to have in my life, thank you.

To my Rachel and Henry, an extra thank you.

CHAPTER ONE

"MY BARBER'S SO GOOD, it's like she's psychic."

Danica Luman's customers often spoke about her with such exaggeration, and it never sat well with her.

First, she only had her stylist's license, and though she'd been cutting hair since her mom taught her at fourteen, she had not yet become a licensed barber.

And second, she considered herself a channeler, not a psychic.

A big difference.

Psychics predicted the future, read palms, used crystal balls and scammed people. As far as she could tell — based on her experience since getting her first visions in her teen years — channelers like Danica received glimpses into the thoughts of people they touched, particularly when they touched the back of their heads. The better the grip on the back of a skull, the more vivid the images seemed to flow. At least, that's how it worked for her. She hadn't been clinically diagnosed by a doctor or anything. Her assessment came more through trial and error.

That same trial and error led her to her mild levels of success. Her mom had helped her develop a technique of always asking customers some form of "What type of cut are we doing today?" while casually touching the backs of their heads. Most times, customers took the bait; while their mouths droned on about "a little off" here and "this needs to foomff" there, their brains responded with clear images of their dream hairstyles.

Only three people knew about Danica's secret ability: her roommate Gabby, her manager Carla, and her late mother. Scared her daughter would become a lab rat if word got out, her mother made Danica promise to keep her ability a secret. Danica stuck to it, even after her mom died. It felt like a low-key secret to keep, and one that could easily be chalked up to "natural ability." She hated to think of it as a "power." That made it sound like she belonged among the B-level X-Men characters. She thought of it as a skill, one with little practical use besides picturing exactly how to taper someone's sideburns.

Danica kept her life in low-cost order, partly by design, partly because she had no other choice. She wore T-shirts and tank tops, with her ex-boyfriend's hoodie for the cool mornings. She never wore shorts, choosing straight-legged cargo pants or jeans for their durability and because they looked cool with her off-brand Doc Martins.

She kept her own hair short in a number-one buzz. No mess and low cost, her peach fuzz look served as a litmus test for prospective acquaintances: anyone not cool with a woman in short hair could (and would) screw right off. She could see people making this decision in real time, even without touching their heads. Most times these people were not the kinds she wanted to be friends with anyway. Such were the types of lies introverts like Danica told themselves to justify why they spent so much time alone. Despite living in an enormous, left-leaning city like Los Angeles where like-minded people could be found, she kept mostly to her small circle, reading and working and thinking. Besides, big groups of friends ended up becoming a herd, fueled on group think and echo-chamber ideas, none of which was her style.

She smoked for five years before stopping on June 6, 2007, and she thought about it every day after.

Monday, August 25, 2008. 8:46AM. Van Nuys, California.

The longer Danica's 1995 Honda Accord sat watching red lights, the greater the chance the old car would completely and finally break down into a million rusty pieces. Her car was thirteen years old, the AC didn't work, the dashboard dimmed when she made a right turn, and the odometer stopped working years prior. Other than that, it ran great.

As she crawled up Hazeltine to the left-turn lane, she bumped out a quick "running late" text to Carla, then noticed the flashing lights in the intersection. With one notable exception, she didn't like cops. They made her nervous. She took a breath and tried to look patient, and hoped these were not the types of cops who would see a shaved head on a woman as 'trouble.'

She looked past the row of NO TO PROP 8 posters preaching the benefits of equal rights to focus on the store-fronts on the corner. The yellow-ish office park on Sherman

Way had always grabbed her curiosity. It held a collection of odd mom-and-pop businesses begging to be transformed into Subway shops. Of all the offices, only one held evidence of anything resembling life: the private investigator's office. Its window framed a neon sign that promised "RESULTS" in bright letters.

The boldness of the sign made Danica laugh every time. The whole building seemed to be hiding from the world, yet RESULTS appeared so hopeful. She wondered who could possibly work there, how hard they worked, how successful they were at delivering any favorable outcomes, and what kind of customers would procure their services.

The cops in the intersection waved a few more cars through, but stopped Danica's Accord at the line. The wreck ahead became clear: someone's nice-looking car had hit someone's not-so-nice looking car, and spilled itself across three lanes. The screams and swears from one of the drivers rang through more clearly as well, and Danica assumed that the man in the suit with slick hair and designer sunglasses owned the formerly-nice-looking Lexus.

Her phone buzzed, then buzzed again. Danica tucked her phone under her leg and glanced at the cop in the intersection. He had flinched. He probably heard her phone. He must have. She tried to stay calm. Receiving texts wasn't against the law, but Danica's financial situation meant that she got nervous getting in its proximity.

Another message buzzed into her thigh. Three quick text messages in a row meant Gabby. Danica's roommate believed that three sequential messages were more helpful than one. She hadn't seen Gabby this morning, and Danica assumed there was an audition or early call or some other actor thing going on across town. If an emergency had come up, Gabby would have phoned; that was basic mobile phone manners.

RESULTS flickered again. She wondered at the requirements of becoming a private investigator. Were they all just failed cops? Were they failed cops who — sick of working traffic duty — rented a space and bought a sign that over-promised? And if they were mostly failed cops who had trained at a dogmatic process, would an outsider's perspective be helpful? Perhaps someone with absolutely no formal investigative training, but who had seen mystery shows on TV and considered herself, perhaps, insightful?

Her special skill gave her an ace up her fingers, but advertising herself as the "Psychic Investigator" seemed like an invitation for trouble, or at least ridicule. Nobody needed her, she didn't need the trouble. Plus the PI lifestyle likely involved licenses, permits, cards, papers, insurance and all of the other trappings of the free market discouraging adventure. It was all too difficult. Probably.

The cop in the intersection finally gave her the go. The rain held off until the last leg of her work journey. She pushed the windows up, as their motors had given out years ago, and the Accord instantly felt sweaty.

The grey walls of the strip mall on Saticoy and Sepulveda seemed even more drab in the rain. Every door had a faded red awning, and they all needed attention, especially the one above Earl's World of Curls. Earl's did just well enough to stay afloat, to fight off selling the business to a corporation, or to hiring awful people. Carla took over the business years ago from someone she would not name, and ran a tight, friendly ship, valuing word of mouth and customer loyalty. Danica was a white girl who could cut Black people's hair, and her sulky realism charmed her way into the position. The fact that she could nail a customer's style through supplemental means helped in her demonstration and she got hired quick.

Danica parked in her spot at the end of the lot, locked her door and jogged past the tax preparer's and the tarot card reader's to the Earl's entrance.

The smell of shampoo and hairspray baked into the linoleum floor welcomed her with a smack in the face. KOST 103.5 FM played low from the one working speaker hanging above the door. Beyond the cash register counter were the two stations against the mirror wall. One station had a customer (an older woman) and Carla Velez stood behind her.

Danica expected a barrage of motherly questions from her manager. "Where've you been?" "How massive was this accident?" "You can't find another route?" "Don't you know I got customers?" Carla cared about her, but she still had a business to run. Add to that the stress of trying to refinance her house, and her mood was wholly understandable.

Yet as Carla's eyes stared over her blue plastic glasses, no such barrage arrived. Instead, a strange smile brightened her face, and her dusty curls might have even had a bounce to them.

"Danica, girl!" she said. "We were just talking about you."

She followed Carla's nudging head and recognized the customer in the chair. Mrs. Roosevelt had been an Earl's regular, and was known in the professional haircutting world as a Handful. She often asked for dye jobs, and usually had big dreams for new styles every time she returned. The desperate smile on Carla's face made more sense.

Danica pulled off her wet sweatshirt to hang it up, apologizing for being late, and Carla shuffled over to her.

"I need you over there." Carla spoke in a hush. "Says she wants something like on '24.'"

"Kiefer Sutherland?"

"Her words," said Carla. She looked lost.

Danica nodded and approached Mrs. Roosevelt. The customer waved from under her smock. "Didn't mean to be disloyal. Just couldn't wait. Big plans."

"Sure thing," said Danica.

Normal social situations prohibited people — however familiar they might be with each other — from walking up to one another and playing with their hair. However, normal social rules did not apply in the shop, and Danica took advantage. She twiddled Mrs. Roosevelt's wispy hair and asked, "What are we doing today?"

Mrs. Roosevelt began a rambling babble of gobbledygook as Danica's finger tips found their place. A sullen young woman appeared in her mind, younger than everyone in Earl's by a decade. She had blonde hair in tight waves against her forehead.

Danica released her grip and said to Mrs. Roosevelt, "You're in good hands," then whispered to Carla, "It's that Eliza Cuthbert actress."

"Elisha Kush-berg."

"I think we're both wrong," said Danica. "Doesn't matter. Just look her up. Tight waves to the forehead, but not bangs. Give as much body as possible."

"You're a lifesaver."

"I owed you."

"Yes, you did. Kush...?"

"Cuthbert."

"What?" said Carla.

"Never mind. All fine. You're welcome," said Danica, and

she shooed her boss back to the customer. Only then did she notice the man sitting in the waiting area.

She held up a finger to ask for a minute and hustled to her station. She shared it with Gene, the drama queen who worked nights and told everyone else why they sucked. He and Danica had worked out a system to tell what stuff was whose: Gene kept his things in tidy order, and Danica did not. Despite owning fewer items than anyone on the Earl's staff, her things found a way to be chaotic. Old bottles of shampoo lined the area by her half of the mirror, and her sink held wet towels from the night before. Gene's towels, on the other hand, sat folded in a nice pile on top of his polished tool kit. Danica's tool kit doubled as a rack for dirty aprons.

She flattened an apron against her gray tank top. She hung her last working water bottle on the loop of her cargos and motioned for the customer to join her.

Even after seeing him take only a few steps, it seemed obvious this guy was athletic. Danica's bare arms felt even thinner when she glanced at his poking out of his nerdy polo. His face was new to her, and it held a stiffness in the jaw. He wore jeans that looked like they were ironed, and not in any way remotely cool. The man eased his way into her chair like he had entered an especially hot jacuzzi. Danica took care to spin him slowly toward the mirror for fear he might barf from all the excitement.

Just as she got him facing the mirror, the front door swung open and a tall woman shuffled inside, her impractical vest with the hood down, rain be damned. She held her purse over her hair with one hand, and a coffee in the other.

"Got a sec?" said Gabby. The audition must have been quick.

"Not really," said Danica.

Gabby sidled up to the chair and invaded Mr. Uncomfortable's personal space. "It's important."

Danica looked at Carla. She was talking to Mrs. Roosevelt, but she must have noticed Gabby make herself at home, and couldn't have been thrilled about it.

"I'm busy, Gab," said Danica.

"I got the gig. And I brought you a mocha."

Danica's antennae went up and she looked out the window. Even with the distance and drizzle, she could see Gabby's car. The recent model Prius, a gift from her parents when she moved to LA, parked right in front of the shop doors. The backseat filled with junk. A trash bag pressed against the window, next to a couple of suitcases and various shoes.

Prickles ran up Danica's neck. She looked back to her roommate and wondered if, in fact, she still was.

Gabby bit her lip.

"What the hell, man?" said Danica.

"Customer voice," said Gabby, then immediately regretted it. "The shoot starts tomorrow, so I gotta haul to Moab. Freakin' Utah."

"How long's the shoot?"

"Couple weeks."

"Looks like you packed for months."

"Maybe more than a couple," said Gabby. "But not forever."

"Okay, well, that's great. And they're paying you?"

Gabby nodded.

"Very great."

Gabby stopped nodding, and the prickles ran over Danica's neck again.

"Excuse me a second," she said to Mr. Uncomfortable.

He winced a nod and Danica pulled Gabby to the reception area.

"When?"

"When what?" said Gabby.

"When are they paying you?"

"I get paid when the shoot wraps."

"The whole shoot, or just your parts?"

She chewed her lip like bubble gum. "Whole shoot."

"So I'm guessing that's, what, like two months or something?"

"Probably."

"Gab, we need rent for not just this month, but the last one."

"This will pay for that. After the shoot."

"In two months!"

"Yes!" Gabby smiled, but it faded as she looked at Danica. "You're not happy about me making money? We need it for rent."

"Jeez." Danica pictured the pile of red-letter envelopes waiting to attack her mailbox.

"I had to do it. This is the first thing I've got in months."

"And you'll be away." Danica couldn't believe she said it. To be so vulnerable came with weird fear of being fully seen.

"I'll be back."

"Sure," said Danica.

"Y'know, I could probably talk them into hiring an on-set stylist. You could come."

Despite all evidence — high cost of living, dangerous, enormous, full of douche bags — Danica claimed Los Angeles as her own. She won it in the separation from Tommy. He took the music, her favorite plates and the TV, and she took the city. Leaving her adopted home would count as a defeat and there was no way Tommy would win that one. She shook her head.

Gabby handed a wad of cash to Danica, but she pushed it back. "It's OK. You'll need gas."

They hugged. Gabby made a squealing sound, then broke it off and handed over the mocha. It weighed expensive.

With one last pouty face, Gabby stepped outside, back into the rain, and jogged to her car. Danica turned back to her station. She could hear the Prius' familiar hum grow loud, then quieter, then gone.

Numbers swirled in her brain. She had months to plan for and past months to pay for. Even moving to a cheaper place would cost money she didn't have. The numbers gave way to plots and schemes, as though she was the type of person who could invent something to sell that would be not only desirable but on the market by September.

"Everything OK?" said the man in her chair. He'd heard the whole thing.

"Forget it," said Danica.

"Do you need something?"

She didn't need his condescending voice, that's for damn sure. She needed this guy to tip well and get out so someone else could get in and bring twenty friends.

"You're Danica, right?"

She nodded and washed her hands. "Someone recommend me?"

"Someone from work," he said.

"They say good things?"

"Yes. I understand you do," his voice lowered, "dye jobs." He said it like a dirty word.

There went the prospects of a good tip. In her experience, old people and dye jobs were notoriously bad at tipping. Her eyes ran over his tell-tale salt and pepper temples. She should have noticed it earlier.

"What's your name?"

"James."

"Don't worry, James. I happen to do the type of work you're looking for." Before he could ask, she added, "Discreetly."

James' resting glower gave a flicker of what, for him, must have been elation. Danica turned him to face the mirror and started playing with his hair, moving her hand to the "Intake Position."

"What else are we doing today?"

She planted her fingertips under the bump of his skull. He began speaking as she closed her eyes and gave the oncoming images her full attention. If she could nail the look he wanted, perhaps he would buck the low-tipping-dye-job stereotype.

She saw a dark field. Lots of grass, at night. Short hair on the sides, dark brown. A flashlight on the ground. Longer on top, flat. Someone's shoes, walking. The light pointed at the ground. Someone's bare feet. The flashlight scanned the toes. They were motionless.

Danica pulled her hand away from James' head and opened her eyes. Her sink and mirror replaced the images of the ground and grass and feet. She looked at the back of her customer's head. Some of those images concerned hair, but definitely some did not. Those were feet, and they looked like they were found lying somewhere.

At night.

And not moving.

Probably just a dream. Sometimes she intercepted dreams and nightmares. Channelers channeled. She didn't have a remote control to his brain. He seemed distracted when he came in. Uptight. Probably from a nightmare.

She grabbed her comb and found her clippers. She would do the sideburns first, as the clippers usually dulled the visions.

Not this time.

As she touched the side of James' head, she saw the grass again, clearer than before. The flashlight tracked the shoes as they walked. The beam found the bare feet once again. Some pink birthmark around the ankle. The beam rose up the leg, up the torn dark jeans. The flashlight rose to the shirt. A light blue button-down. Trim and sleek with short sleeves. The stomach of the shirt had a splotch of darkness. Dark brown. The light found the same color on the chest. By the heart.

The face stared at nothing, motionless. A young man. He didn't blink when the light hit him.

The beam pulled back and she saw the entirety of the young man, lying on the grass at night. Unnatural. His arms lay spread out. Whoever held the flashlight reached out his other hand and picked up the young man's wrist. It had gone limp.

The wrist had a blue bruise, but no pulse.

The hand released the young man's arm and it plopped into the grass.

Danica snapped off the clippers and pulled away. "These are the wrong ones. I got others. Somewhere. Back there." She fast-walked toward the office area in back, to the bathroom, and closed the door behind her.

The water she splashed on her face only made her wet. The images would not wash away. Danica looked around the dark bathroom, trying to find a suggestion or inspiration for any other thoughts, to springboard her imagination into another, safer, less-creepy place. A movie or a song or something else that didn't have a dead body lying in the grass. At night. Barefoot. Somewhere dark.

Facts were facts, and they needed facing. Her step-father's advice had always been annoying both in its delivery and, as she'd discovered only recently, its propensity for correctness. She had to understand what she had seen in order to deal with it.

The possibility that she had seen James' dreams seemed less likely due to the vividness of the images. Dreams didn't move that linearly, or repeat themselves. She could practically feel the grass crunching beneath her shoes — his shoes. These were not hallucinations or fantasies. These were memories, they were of a murder, and they were the murder memories of the man sitting in her station waiting to get his temples colored.

She pulled the bathroom door open a crack and looked at James. He hadn't moved an inch. He seemed very calm for a murderer, which meant he was either A.) not a murderer but someone whose brain carried the memories of a murderer, or B.) was so much of a murderer that he could sit calmly in a barber's chair and wait for his stylist to return from the bathroom. Neither option felt particularly comforting.

This spurred Danica's first plan of attack: running, out the back storage room, through the trash door, down the street and into the desert, never to be seen again. It would leave James alone with Carla and Mrs. Roosevelt, which didn't sit well with her conscience.

Calling the police seemed like a natural back-up plan. They were, after all, the police. They had training and resources. They could take it from here, and would probably tell her as much.

The cops were also a dead end. They wouldn't move their fat-blue-line butts without good reason, and good reason was just what Danica lacked. She had no way to prove what she saw, let alone explain how she saw it. The cops were useless.

Her best chance at survival seemed to be playing it cool and act like she hadn't seen images of a murder. Do the dye, get him out, then find out what she could. She rubbed the peach fuzz on her head, then dried her face and opened the bathroom door, super cool.

"Sorry," she said as she returned to her station as if nothing were wrong, and why would there be anything wrong? "I'll just use these. Couldn't find the other ones. The other clippers. So I'll use these. Those. Those clippers."

Super, duper cool. Danica prayed Carla hadn't been paying attention.

James nodded. He must have encountered babbling idiots often enough for Danica's performance to go unnoticed. Instead he raised an eyebrow when she put on plastic gloves.

"We doing the you-know-what first?"

"I'm gonna clip first."

"You do it with gloves on?"

"Sometimes. Yes. With these clippers. These. And I'll keep them on for later." The gloves also tended to make it difficult for Danica to receive visions, but she managed to keep that to herself.

She worked, keeping her fingertips away from his scalp. She felt Carla's eyes on her.

It went faster than any dye job she or anyone had ever done, and it came out much better than she suspected (which gave her another thing to worry about; bad work might have made for a one-and-done customer. Good work could bring this guy and his death images back). James cashed out with Carla at the register. He promised to tell more people about Danica's work. With a nod to the room, he left.

Once the door closed, Danica grabbed her phone and ran a quick search. The first thing she confirmed was that California held at least two billion people named "James." She tried applying additional criteria, then realized it would be a waste of battery and data, and that she was avoiding the obvious search choice.

She didn't want to search it. It felt like it would legitimize everything, and treat the visions as something that had truly happened. Or would happen. Maybe this man had made plans, had picked a victim and had focused on it so much that he was trying to manifest it, like an evil version of The Secret.

Danica had never been able to see the future, so — as gross as it seemed — that meant the killing had already happened and nothing could prevent it.

Her thumb typed in "recent," "murder," and "stabbing." She added "night" and "Los Angeles," and "young man," then submitted.

A sad ton of information appeared. Domestic disputes, a high-speed pursuit involving a knife and a few hold-ups. Everything seemed to have happened in the last month, and with varying degrees of gore. She limited her search to the night before, then expanded to the night before that, then to the full week.

Nothing useful came back.

"Congrats, by the way," said Carla. She sat in her station, and had been for quite some time, silently watching Danica try to manifest a person's identity from thin internet air. She held a small rectangular box on her leg, about the size of a necklace.

"Congrats for what?"

"Barber certification."

"Hold on," said Danica. "You cashed the guy out, right?"

"What guy?"

"That James guy."

"Yeah."

"Did he pay with card or cash?"

"Card."

"What's his last name?"

Carla tapped the box with her fingers. "That's supposed to be personal information."

"Come on."

"You can get it when you close the register out."

"I don't close tonight."

"Then you won't get it," said Carla. "What's this about? He doesn't seem like your type."

"I just need to know."

"Why?"

"Just need to." Danica recognized the expression on Carla's face that this crap was flying nowhere, no how. Not without reasonable explanation.

And since Carla was one of the few people on Earth who understood Danica's true skill set, she took the opportunity to tell the truth. Just this once.

She said, "When I was cutting his hair, I saw a dead body. A murdered one."

Carla blinked, stood up and walked to the cash register. Danica followed her. Carla put the box in Danica's hands and keyed in the code on the credit card reader.

"What is this?" said Danica, turning the box a bit. Inside, something made a thud.

"It's for you."

The credit card reader spit out a receipt. Carla read it, then said, "You're not gonna do anything stupid, are you?"

"I don't think so."

"But you aren't. You gotta be careful. Don't just..."

Danica waited for the end of the sentence. It never came, though the sentiment got delivered.

"I'll be careful. Super careful"

Carla read from the receipt: "James Van Owen."

Danica repeated the name. "Thanks." She held up the box. "I haven't passed yet, you know."

"I thought you did."

"Take the final this week."

"Open it anyway," said Carla.

She did. Inside was a straight razor. Danica had used one casually, but without her certification, she couldn't use it to make money. The handle had a nice weight, and the silver blade sat fresh and clean.

"Keep it in your station for when you pass." Carla gave a glance toward the mess. "Know what? You can keep it in mine."

CHAPTER TWO

Same Day. 5:32PM.

The late-night liquor store on the corner of Hazeltine and Oxnard attracted exactly the type of people who needed a late-night liquor store, and it was the only non-apartment building on the block. Across the street stood Island Estates Apartments, Danica's home for nearly three years. Island Estates looked like the kind of place where the lock on the front gate didn't work. Every time she came home, Danica felt fortunate that it actually did, and made sure it re-latched.

Apartment 213 sat above the laundry room and faced the pool under perpetual construction. With such lavish amenities, the two-bed-one-bath set up still demanded more rent than a single girl with a low-paying job and an AWOL roommate could afford for very long. The apartment reminded her of this, even in the presence of The Idea. The Idea had come to her on the drive home from work, while trying not to think about what she'd seen in James' mind. She tried to look for a path away from The Idea and found none.

Gabby hadn't gutted apartment 213, but her absence left a mark. Each item still there seemed lonely. It reminded Danica of when Tommy left. Random stuff cluttered in the corners, too large to take, or too unnecessary. It left her with unnecessary things to keep track of. Most of that stuff ended up going to Goodwill, except for the gray hooded sweatshirt Danica had on at this exact moment. Some people might see the sight of a ditched girlfriend wearing her ex-boyfriend's clothes as some sign of weakness. Some people might be right, but Danica saw it as retribution. She remembered how often Tommy had worn it. He seemed to love it. In his haste to clean their place out of music and movies and snacks, he'd left his favorite sweatshirt, so she wore it like a trophy from a weird kind of victory. She claimed the sweatshirt as she had the city. Tommy had let them both go, and they became hers entirely. Even when Gabby had invited her to leave LA, Danica couldn't leave because it meant relinquishing her winnings. To Tommy.

She walked through the depressed living and dining rooms, down the empty hall to her own bedroom. It had always been decorated in a kind of barren fashion, with only a small bed, old bedspread and sheets, and a plastic dresser. Now, in line with the rest of the apartment she could no longer afford to keep, it felt completely miserable.

Worse, it offered little distraction from the images of murder floating around in her memory. She tried to think of ways to sell some items on Craigslist, or find something to clean (which shouldn't have been difficult), yet the images stayed with her, as did the nagging questions, and, of course... The Idea.

Her phone's battery blinked "19%," the result of a day of

desperate searching for anything resembling anything to do with James Van Owen.

She sat on the bed, then laid down. She left the lights off, and let the street sounds around her arrive without interruption, in hopes that they might lull her to sleep and forget all about The Idea and everything around it.

Yet someone was dead. Violently so. There must have been news about it somewhere. Maybe someone had gone missing, or the police had actually found the body and were hot on the trail of the killer. And that information could lead to the fruition of The Idea, which meant it was too crazy to even consider.

She dropped her phone on the thin carpet and gave it a rest. She didn't know anything about James Van Owen. He could be in the movie business; chances were really good in this city. He could be a career cinematographer, looking for acclaim and fortune by dedicating himself to authentic images, no matter how horrific. He could even be a writer working out a scene. One with no characters or dialog and looked a lot like a memory. Maybe he worked it over in his head to get every detail perfect, so that it seemed to the audience like it had really happened.

It looked real, even in her memory of his thoughts. Too real not to be.

A toss, a turn. The room grew darker around the edges, with the only light coming from the alley lamp through her window. She needed money, or a plan to get a cheaper place, or a better career, or a more lucrative career.

Focus could help her with all of these things.

Focus on the important things.

The tasks at hand. Distractions, no matter how exciting they may seem, would not help. And The Idea was pure exciting distraction. She told herself to leave it alone, that this had been none of her business to begin with. Act like a normal person. A normal person — even one with access to some kind of inside information like this — would let it go. They ignore stuff all the time, even when those things are terrible. Why should she be any different?

Grass in Los Angeles had always been a curiosity to her. The entire city had been built on a desert, yet (almost) the entire city fought nature and tried to grow grass like they lived in Oregon. Seeing grass wasn't unusual.

Seeing a lot of it, and so lush as in that memory, was unusual. The body must have been somewhere that could afford a lush, full, well-watered lawn. It reminded her of home in Illinois.

'The body.' The melodrama spun her out. The dead body.

She had no proof. She knew only what she had seen and should let it all drop, no matter what it was.

Which was a dead body. There, again, it came back. A body, one which had been violently encouraged into that status.

She rolled onto her arm and stared at her dull wall. Her breath came back at her as it bounced off the cheap paint.

The clock said it was late, and she decided to reason with herself. If she couldn't sleep, she could still dream with her eyes open, and so her mind followed things through. This wasn't a distraction. This was trying to sleep by working things out.

If it had been an actual dead body, and if that body had been murdered, then someone did the murdering. And that someone was probably the same man she had helped conceal his age through unnatural coloration products earlier in the day.

Therefore — keeping everything very theoretical and

removed from any personal involvement since it was none of her business — therefore, if that same man with the well-done dye job had been the murderer, he was free.

Therefore someone was likely upset. The police were in the business of helping victims and survivors with resolving those problems, but they had no inside information. Not like her.

The victims might have been the owners of the lush grass. The boy might have been an heir to something, a relative to some well-to-do's.

The Idea returned again, so forcefully that she sat up. She lay back down, cursing a bit for allowing herself to go so far as to think such an idea as The Idea could be possible.

Then she sat up again. Though it took all evening, The Idea had finally won. The Idea was crazy, and depended on a lot of chances being taken, a lot of "if's" turning into "sure's," mostly from the cops. Yet The Idea clung to her, setting deep roots. It demanded consideration, and she gave in.

If all her reasoning and therefores turned out to be true, and if she could find a police officer who didn't push the issue of how she came across this information, but just went with it based on the fact that it was true and could help solve a murder....

If she found a way to make those things happen, then The Idea would come to fruition.

She hadn't spoken it out loud, yet she felt like she jinxed The Idea just by thinking of it. It would not leave her alone.

The Idea was: maybe there is a reward.

Information on a crime — not only a crime, but a murder — had to be worth something. And information on the perpetrator had to be worth even more, to the authorities and to the victims. And if the victims or survivors could afford the kind of lawn that she'd seen, they would likely be in a financial position to honor her services.

With this, her brain felt settled, ready to rest. She would try tomorrow to help society and put herself on the path toward a possible reward, and a way to survive another month or two in Los Angeles.

She rolled over again, convinced of her plan and in her need to sleep.

She lay awake all night.

CHAPTER THREE

Tuesday, August 26, 2008. Morning. North Hollywood.

Freddie Ford was a cop and one of Danica's regulars. He'd started coming into the shop a few years back and made it a habit, despite the fact that he lived somewhere on the other side of the 405, near Reseda. Based on their monthly interactions, Danica had gleaned the following information, some of which came orally, the rest otherwise:

1. Of all the cops she'd encountered, Freddie was Danica's exception. He had been decorated for his service, and even headed a task force to explore ways to address the widely-accepted systematic racism coursing through the LAPD. The fact that he was a Black man helped and hurt.
2. He worked out of the Van Nuys division.
3. He called people by their full names, but called Danica "DL."

4. He had a severe distaste for American football.
5. He loved Danica from the moment she first cut
    his hair.

Most of these gleanings had ebbed and flowed over the course of their relationship, and Carla always made a point of it when the cuts ended, since Danica had made the mistake of sharing the most embarrassing of the gleans with her. At that time, Danica's relationship with Tommy was still in swing, and she'd never been a cheater. And even after it ended, she felt rushing to Freddie would seem too weird. He'd wonder how she felt the way she did, how she had been so certain of his feelings, they'd get into it and it would fall apart.

Taking all of that into account (except the football point), Danica drove to the North Hollywood division of the LAPD. She told herself she needed the cops, not A particular cop. She thought of Freddie for the entire drive.

Danica felt stupid for looking up office hours on the LAPD website; they probably had a 24-hour night desk, since "crime never slept" and all that. Tuesday traffic brought her to the parking lot off of Burbank Avenue a few minutes after 8:00.

Despite her earlier blast of decisiveness, she still had no idea what story to tell them. She reminded herself to play concerned citizen and report a concern. She had information about a dead body.

Someone might listen.

She found a spot beyond the second fence. Even the lot gave her the creeps. The rows of matching patrol cars in the side lot were flanked by a row of sickly trees trying too hard to appear orderly.

Her dislike of cops didn't come about as some kind of

rule; she merely distrusted them. Their processes and procedures seemed to promote a kind of Boy's Club loyalty, which to Danica acted without thought. This topic came up exactly one time with Freddie, and the feeling of polite disagreement steered future conversations away from such touchy subjects.

She moved toward the front door. Invisible walls seemed to crawl closer to her with every step. She stared at the doorway.

It opened. A female police officer with dark features and hair pulled into a tight pony tail stepped down the steps. Despite the loaded weapon at her side, and despite the sexist assumption that a fellow-woman might give her a fair shake, Danica thought this cop could be "nice." With no better starting point, she moved toward her, quickly so as not to lose her nerve.

"Can I help you?" said the cop. Her nameplate read GUTIERREZ, and she scanned the parking lot like she was in a hurry.

"I have a concern to report. I'm a concerned citizen and I want to..." Danica paused, and with no chance to say something non-stupid, finished the thought with, "report it."

"Front desk." Officer Gutierrez jabbed a thumb at the doorway. "Can't miss it."

"It's just," said Danica. She stepped in front of Officer Gutierrez. Danica's hands went up to stop her. She held them back from touching the police officer just before making an even bigger mistake than coming here in the first place. Danica stuffed her hands into her pockets, then realized this might look like she was trying to grab a weapon, so she took her hands out and held them against her jeans, palms out. Unusual, but safe.

"Are you OK, miss?" A good question for anyone paying attention to Danica's behavior.

"My information has to do with, um, a possible murder." In case Danica's own brain couldn't register just how dumb this sounded, the officer's face offered a clear measure. She blinked at Danica. She didn't laugh in her face, but her eyes looked curious.

"Front desk is still your place," she said. She put her hands on her hips, right above the loaded pistol she had been trained to handle.

"It's not anyone I know. And I think I might know the person who... did the murdering."

To be perfectly honest with herself, this exchange went as well as Danica could have ever reasonably hoped. She hadn't been arrested, and given her behavior and speech patterns, that wasn't out of the realm of possibility. This cop was listening, and she'd yet to ask how Danica came to find this incredibly sensitive and valuable information.

"Danica?" It was a man's voice. It sounded familiar, and for a split second, she doubted herself and thought she'd misunderstood Freddie's workplace location. But this voice had a different kind of familiarity. The deepness had less warmth and humor than Freddie's voice, or any other man Danica had strictly platonic feelings for.

She and Officer Gutierrez turned toward the lot to see James Van Owen, smile on his face, walking from a parked car. He wore a different collared shirt than the first time she'd seen him, though in the same style, and Danica's heart stopped functioning properly when she saw the badge on his belt.

"Was just telling this woman about the reception desk, detective."

"I can take her, Gutierrez," said James Van Owen through his calm half-grin.

Officer Gutierrez took the cue to exit. James Van Owen motioned toward the door with one hand, and put his other hand on Danica's shoulder. Just to make everything clear.

CHAPTER FOUR

9:09AM. Inside the Station.

The cop at the reception desk glanced at the door when it opened, then returned his focus to his phone when James' hand waved him off. They walked too fast to be stopped anyway.

The position of James' hand on her shoulder and his strides pounding the floor sent a very clear message: "We're walking this way." And so they did.

They cruised through the bullpen and she looked around for any friendly looking cops. She would have settled for any cops, but saw none at their desks. Too early. This had been a huge mistake. To enter Cop World and expect any insiders to help her had been naive. To enter Cop World and expect any insiders to help her by going against one of their own had been completely idiotic.

James opened a gray door on a wall of gray doors and gave Danica a half push. If she hadn't been so full of terror at the thought of being stabbed in the stomach, she might have dwelled on the fact that actual police interrogation rooms look a lot like the ones she'd seen on TV. She sat on the metal chair without being told.

"Thought that was you," said James. "Recognizing profiles is kinda what I do, and I clocked yours right away."

He stood taller than at Earl's. His arms folded across his chest like a scolding teacher. And his face sat with the scowl hanging around his eyebrows.

Her only way to handle this man, she thought, was to treat him like an angry animal. No sudden movements, limited and non-aggressive eye contact, and keep something between them at all times. She placed her hands on the table. She glanced at the door, then around the room, then at James, then back around the room. He leaned against the only exit.

"I'm just gonna ask you a couple things. And I need you to be honest with me." He hadn't looked at her when he said this. James looked up, toward the top of the doorway, the comprehension of this strange situation lay beyond his reach and understanding.

"Sure," said Danica. Her palms felt sweaty. She tucked her right toe under the chair. If she had to bolt, she'd need some kind of starting block. She could be fast if motivated.

He shifted his weight. The glint against the handle of his gun flashed, and he looked her in the eye. She looked away, then back again. His stare continued.

The moment arrived. She could tell. It would happen here. She would have to fight a trained police officer and survive long enough to escape, or for another better cop to hear her and come to her rescue. Her toe tensed against the floor, locked in the starting block. She stared back at him, and expected to see similar resolve in his eyes.

Instead, she saw an expression closer to nervous fear. He

couldn't have been afraid of her; what kind of crappy murderer was this guy?

He opened his mouth, then closed it. Then moved to the table, leaned on it and said, "Can you tell?"

She froze, but her toe relaxed. She looked him in the eyes, and then at the side of his head. His fingers ran through his temples.

"You can, can't you? You were supposed to be good at this." He folded his fingers on top of his head and spun away from her. After a breath through his teeth, he turned back, no less calm.

And yet to Danica's inexperienced eye, no more murderous. She blinked and blinked again, then leaned forward on her elbows. The pleading in James' eyes came through clear, mixed with desperation. She had seen these types of looks many times in the shop, from people looking for some kind of hairstyling miracle.

"You're talking about your hair," she said.

"Of course I am!" He kicked the table leg, then threw his hands down, like a first grader upset to loose his ice cream. "I knew I shouldn't have tried this. The guys are gonna crucify me. They know."

"They don't know."

"They do."

"It looks good."

"You have to say that. You have to say it looks good. You're biased."

"It looks fine."

James leaned on the table again, his head sunk with a thunk. Danica took a good look at her work. It really had held up, if only for one day. The dye had taken hold, and so, too, had the realization that James was not a murderer.

"You saw him," she said.

"Saw who?"

"Nobody. Nothing. I meant to say... you're a police officer."

"A detective," he said into his hands.

"And you solve crimes?"

"Unsolved ones."

"Nasty ones?"

He dropped his hands and showed the confusion on his face. "Yes?" He stood straight and took in a deep breath. Then sat down. "You didn't come here about my hair, did you?"

Danica shook her head and relief sunk into her bones. James didn't kill anybody. He was just some nervous moron who cared about his looks. Like everyone else, except a cop who might have seen something terrible and, also like everyone, had trouble letting it go.

His eyes fixed on hers. "Why'd you come here then?"

She opened her mouth.

"I saw something when I cut your hair. I can do that. I can read people's minds. Though I don't like to be called 'psychic,' when my fingers touched your scalp, I saw into your mind and what I saw was a dead body. It looked like it had been stabbed, it was at night, and you were standing over it. And I thought maybe you had done it, at first. But now I don't think that. I think you're working on solving that case, or you were just called in when they found the body. Either way, I want to help. I can help you. I'm sure of it."

Those were the words Danica *wanted* to say. She wanted to present herself in a bold manner as to impress and intimidate this vain police officer into gawking at her, absorbing her information, and — in the face of her unflappable confidence — consider applauding her courage. He would become convinced and understand her situation. And then, when the message of her proclamation finally settled into the deepest section of his heart, he would ask her to join him in solving the crime, all without questioning the validity of Danica's claim. The conviction in her voice and the nobility of her position would be enough.

However, she did not say any of those things, therefore avoiding any of those possible outcomes. Instead she said, "I was hoping you'd recommend me to more people. For cuts. Every little bit helps." Even these words were delivered with the slouch of a scared quitter.

James Van Owen looked her over good and hard. "You're sure it looks OK?'

"Absolutely."

"Then sure thing," he said.

He prattled on. Danica usually avoided small talk outside of the shop, but this particular case allowed her a chance to mentally kick herself for chickening out. She came so close to opening herself up to someone for a greater good, but couldn't see it through. She'd wrap up this encounter with some added dose of humiliation by giving away coupons to a few cops.

James escorted her around as he handed them out. He endured a little joshing from his fellow officers. Their homophobic jokes reminded Danica to be grateful for not having brothers.

She handed a coupon to a blonde flat top then looked at the exit. She hoped it would swallow her and spit her back into her apartment so she could start day-drinking this morning away.

"This your girl, Jimmy?" said the blonde flat-top. "You gotta look good for the media, right?"

James touched his hair. "Shut up, Reed. She does good work."

"Sure sure, anything from the big Hollywood Star Cop."

"It was one time," said James. He leaned to Danica. "I got interviewed. Everyone's gotta do it once in a while."

"Yeah, but this jag took to it like a fish to nature. Like he's going to the Grammy awards or something."

James' cheeks burnt red. "Everyone's gotta give statements once in a while."

"About what?" said Danica.

"Homicide," said James. Like she didn't know already.

She played it up, impressed. "Anyone famous?"

The flat-top named Reed laughed again. His spittle landed on his desk. "You gotta go through his publicist, lady. 'Statement?' Listen to you. Next thing you're gonna be chasing TMZ and dating Jennifer Aniston or some whoever. Jimmy and Jen. 'Jimmy-fer!'" Danica could tell Reed thought this remark was an unimpeachable burn, awkward silence be damned.

"Is it online? The interview?"

James seemed surprised by the question. "Isn't everything?"

He gestured to the door, and Danica took the cue, with ideas flashing across her mind. How close was James to this case? Had he been assigned, or did he have a personal stake? Could she work with him? Could he work with her?

He continued. "Sorry about freaking out back there. I'll tell Freddie you did good."

"Freddie recommended me?"

"Of course he did."

Of course he did. But back to the real situation, the murder: "Do you have any leads? Are you following up on suspects?"

He reached the door, and leaned a little closer. It might

have been friendly if it hadn't carried such an older uncle air to it.

"Don't worry about it. Not your concern."

He promised to pass her name again just before the door closed.

Two steps later, the condescension set like cement. He stopped short of patting her sweet little head and telling her not to trouble it with such problems. If he had let her know a few details, maybe she could have seen how out of her depth the whole thing really was, and she'd walk away by her own volition. Instead, he talked down to her. So James had no one to blame but himself for practically begging her to obsess over the case.

She opened her phone and retrieved her old searches. A quick edit to her criteria: "Jimmy Van Owen+murder+stabbed+Tuesday."

She hustled to her car as the search ran. A few links appeared. One from the LA Times looked the most promising:

SON OF DRAKE ALBERTS FOUND STABBED TO DEATH.

By Lily Gradzhyan.

The body of 21-year-old Drake Alberts III was found Monday morning on the lawn of the family's Bel Air, California estate.

According to police, the young man suffered multiple stab wounds, though time of death has yet to be determined. His body was discovered by the early-morning grounds crew. "The circumstances of how and why this happened are certainly suspect and we'll have to look into every possibility," said LAPD detective Jimmy Van Owen. "The investigation has just begun."

The heir to the prominent Los Angeles family, Drake Alberts III had started what was to be his fifth and final year at USC. While his studies as a business major consumed most of his time, some say he found friends in many places.

"He was a sweet boy," said Keith Beckett, Associate of. "Full of promise and life. He will be sadly missed."

The Alberts family released a statement through its publicist asking for prayers and peace during this difficult time.

Any other time, Danica might have laughed at the grammatical error around listing a USC professor as only "Associate of," but this time she wanted to resemble something like a professional. The article ended with a citation promising more updates, and that some details had already been edited since its first publication.

If James and Flat-Top Reed had succeeded at anything, it was in solidifying her instincts; the cops would be no help. They would not welcome her assistance, even if they knew about her abilities. She could have entered with all the scientific evidence, ordered and laid out to perfection, and they would see her as only a woman. At best, a hairstylist.

Outsider help held more promise.

CHAPTER FIVE

10:30 AM. Van Nuys again.

She faced the office park, ignored its faded awnings and dead businesses and looked at the one office showing any signs of life. The one advertising RESULTS.

Compared to the police force, this was more her speed. She realized she was an indie-level band, hustling for any opportunities she could find. She didn't need the corporate radio of the cops, nor did she need the giant investigation companies downtown, with their huge glass skyscraper offices, fleets of cars and business cards. She needed an indie-label, working out of some guy's garage. Someone with experience but integrity. She entered the office door.

A waft of "indie label" mixed with squalor attacked her nostrils. The walls of the reception area looked like it had been painted with old cigarettes. The ceiling hung low, and sagged lower in the back corner near a skimpy door. Extension cords ran from the base of that door, keeping it slightly ajar, and snaked along the wall to the receptionist's desk.

The white woman behind that desk acknowledged Danica by holding up a hand as if to say "Hold it." Her attention was on the phone in her ear, and she withheld eye contact. Dark hair tucked up off her neck and framed her squat face. She looked sweaty and wore a durable blouse of undeterminable age.

Looking at this woman's hold-it hand, Danica felt she'd made a mistake. All those times she'd driven by and daydreamed about the office park, about RESULTS, all washing away by the cold reality sitting behind that desk.

She turned away from the finger and scanned the walls. A few pictures hung there, next to newspaper clippings of various criminal cases. One photo showed a group of men shaking hands with a former mayor. In the center hung the framed license of Malcom F. Fine, private investigator.

A loud swat jolted Danica's attention back to the receptionist's desk. The woman's face was pale, and her eyes wide awake, staring at a newspaper pressed against the desk. The receptionist pulled it up and the guts of a bug stuck to the front page, and straightened the nameplate she'd knocked over in the battle. It read M. HOWARD-MAC CLOUD.

"Got an appointment?"

"No."

"Name then."

Danica gave it.

"What's your problem? I mean," the receptionist caught herself in what appeared to be some rare instance of politeness fighting its way to the light. "You know what I mean. Why are you here?"

"I'd like to talk to Mr. Fine."

The receptionist nodded. "About?"

Danica's eagerness to get to work had cost her research. She didn't know if private investigators offered tips to newcomers, or if they had any kind of mentoring program in place. The face before her held a good indication that, even if such programs existed, they would not be offered kindly.

"I need some help," she said. "With a case." Using jargon finally seemed appropriate. To come off as someone who had information, given the setting, it felt right. Plus it was honest.

The receptionist's face found a new kind of hardness as she sighed. "I'll see if he's available." She leaned over her computer and hit the keys. It looked like how a kid plays "office," pressing buttons in such quick succession that they must have created only gibberish.

At last, the receptionist looked over her wire frames and into Danica's eye-line. But only for a moment. A ding from her computer yanked her eyes back again.

"Through there," she said. She pointed toward the door with the extension cords.

Danica pushed the door open and entered an office by way of walk-in closet. She stayed careful to avoid the extension cords, which — once inside — grew into a larger collection. They wound up the wall and out the back window. Danica barely had enough room to fit through the door as it pushed against a chair, which in turn pushed against a small, cluttered desk.

"Just a sec," said a voice. It came from behind the desk, and sure enough, in just over a sec, a man popped into view. He had flat black hair, like a naturally-grown toupee. His smile showed wrinkles in every corner. He wore a gray windbreaker despite the fact that his closet office felt even hotter than the reception area, and it was hot in there to begin with. His chest made his cotton dress shirt look tight, but not from working out. He tapped his stubby fingers on the edge of his desk, next to a cellphone belt clip that held no cellphone.

When he stood, he became only slightly taller than when he had been sitting. He held out a sausage of a hand.

"Malcom Fine. What can I do for you?"

Danica shook the hand. He motioned to the plastic chair stuck between the door and the desk. She squeezed herself into it.

"I need some help."

"OK. I figured."

"I recently came across some information and I think you might find it—"

"Wait a sec," said Mr. Fine. His attention went to his laptop computer behind a pile of papers. The rest of his desk was covered in pencils and calendars. Danica discerned three distinct-ish piles, each as unruly as Mr. Fine himself.

"Maggie," he said. "I'm gonna max out on Pantages winter."

"I wouldn't," said the receptionist.

"We have enough."

"Barely."

"I'm doing it." Mr. Fine typed on his keyboard with his pointer fingers. "The Amex?"

No answer came from Maggie.

"Excuse me. Be right back." He stood again, squeezed between his desk and the wall and bopped out of the room. He apologized when the door bumped her shoulder.

She watched them speak in low tones. Though she had no precedent for comparison, the world of private investigation already felt strange and exciting. Everything was bizarre, with coded messages and shorthand to help with snap decisions to solve sudden emergencies. Real life or death type stuff. She turned away and resolved to get used to such things, if she, in fact, pursued the hobby herself.

In that spirit of taking this hobby more seriously, the notion emerged to gather insight on her peers and sneak a peek at his laptop. A breach of trust, certainly, but if he didn't want her to learn the inside scoop on how to thrive in this world, he shouldn't have left it open and unlocked. She leaned around the desk, just hoping to see a glimpse of some dark-web-style site giving dish on the whereabouts of this person and that.

Instead, she saw a webpage for Ticketmaster. A timer in the corner ticked down with "only 4:13 left" to make a purchase. Mr. Fine's online cart held a season of tickets for the Pantages Theater's *Broadway in LA* winter season, and time was, apparently, running out. Real life-and-death stuff.

She returned to her seat and Mr. Fine returned to the office. He carefully kept his tummy away from Danica and put himself back on his side of the tiny desk. A couple hunt-and-pecks more, and he said, "There. Just wrapping something up and I'll be with you. Coffee?"

"I'm good," said Danica. She looked at the back of Mr. Fine's laptop, then to the man himself. She watched him enter information from a credit card. "I can come back another time."

"It's fine. I'll multi-task."

Her steam had left her stride. She struggled to recover her rehearsed speech. "I recently saw something. I mean I got some information."

"Uh-huh."

"About a crime."

"Uh-huh." He nodded, but Danica couldn't tell if he

meant the nod for her or for how well his purchase was going. "Who do you wanna find?"

"No, it's not like that. I mean, it could be. But the information I saw—"

"Right, uh-huh..."

"I think it could help solve a mystery and that—"

"We don't really call them that."

"Call what that?"

"'Mysteries.' Not sure why, but we don't."

"OK."

"You a PI?"

"Um... yes," she said. "I am. And I came across some valuable information. I've seen your sign while I've been... around... and thought you might make something out of it."

"Uh-huh. From where?"

"Sorry?"

"Where'd you get this information? And why aren't you doing anything with it yourself?"

"Well, it's not normally my line of—"

"What do you do? Normally? What cases? You look like you have a lot of experience." He said 'a lot' with sarcastic emphasis.

"I don't have as much experience as you. Doing all of, you know..." she watched Mr. Fine gargle down some water from a bottle, then set his eyes on the screen again, "...doing what you do."

"Sure, sure, okay."

"Are you actually—"

"Almost done. Alllllllmoooooooooost... done. It's done, Maggie!"

Maggie made a noise from the reception area, then another whack of the newspaper against her desk.

"Maggie doesn't care for bugs," he said, turning what appeared to be his fullest attention toward Danica.

"Are you actually a private investigator?" she said.

"Absolutely. Got the license out there, did you see?"

"Right, but do you, like, practice?"

"Yeah."

"Recently?"

"Yes. I think so."

"But all this?" Danica waved at the computer.

"I survive. I'm a survivor. I am a professional investigator, but that's not very steady and sometimes not very lucrative. So I gotta make ends meet by taking other opportunities."

"You scalp tickets."

"I don't 'scalp tickets.' I'm a broker. I broker tickets."

"For a jacked up price?"

"What do you do?"

He wanted to change the subject, and it worked. The question startled her. It came bold and flat, with accusation behind it. "Is that important?"

"You're not a PI." Another flat accusation.

"Yes, I am. I told you."

"I know what you said. You come here to do what? Team up with me?" She opened her mouth, but he cut her off. "'Cause PI's don't do that very often. If you were a PI, besides using the right terminology and being an adult, you wouldn't be sharing information with anybody, least of all with me. You'd be out collecting your check. You don't know how to make a dime off of this whatever-it-is you got, so you're here looking for my help. So I'll ask again: what is it that you do?"

"I cut hair."

"A fellow survivor. Like me!" He smiled. "You do what needs to be done, to get things done. That's good."

"OK. So my information is about a murder."

His smile turned upside down. "You cut your own hair?"

"Yes. Sometimes."

"You eat it?"

"...Huh?"

"Well? Do you eat your own hair?"

"No. I don't. Why the hell are you asking me this?"

"You cut other people's hair. Professionally?"

"Yes."

"You got proof. A Yelp page or something?"

"I don't think so."

"If you do, and you need it cleaned up, I can help with that, too."

"What do you mean 'cleaned up?'"

"We get people who leave negative reviews to reconsider their comments."

"That's what you do? On top of scalping and some PI work?"

"Among other things. So," Mr. Fine shrugged. "What's your answer?"

"To what?"

"Do you eat your own hair?"

"No!" She considered kicking down the desk, but knew Mr. Fine would likely sue her for doing so, as he had probably helped others do in one of his other careers. Or he would damn her with a two-star review.

"I'm here, as a professional, to ask your advice."

His demeanor switched to chipper. "Let's get some details about your case. Who should I find?"

"No, not like that."

"It's about a murder," she said. It came out on its own. She hadn't wanted to blurt it out like that, but her cards had been called. Their poker game came to a head, and she added: "Of Drake Alberts III."

At first, all Mr. Fine said in return was "Wow," followed by a deep stare, and then, "And is there a reward?"

"There could be?"

He smiled. "What else you got?"

"A couple news stories. And I made contact with one of the cops who saw the body."

"OK, OK." He smiled.

She smiled.

"So, Mr. Fine: what should we do?"

"You're gonna want to work every opportunity and contact you have. See if you can find a crack to slip through and get some more info. Family members, friends, anyone like that. You should write this down."

He offered her a pen and ringed notebook. Both appeared used, but she accepted them.

"Look for patterns and opportunities. Nothing is too small at this point. You can't sell the legwork short. You gotta put in the miles. Then, after a while, you'll solve it. Good luck."

Danica's grip on her pen went tight. "Hold it. Me?"

"You what?"

"I'm supposed to do all that?"

"Yes."

"But... I'm not a PI."

"But you wanna be."

"I just said that so you'd listen."

He laughed. "A lot of good that did you, huh?"

"So you don't you want the case?"

"No."

She sighed. "Why the hell not? You're the experienced

professional! Couldn't you use the money?" She waved her arms at the splendor of Mr. Fine's closet.

"Yeah. I'm a professional, and I don't have time to chase down one-time jobs where there *might* be a paycheck at the end. Look, buzz cut, no offense, but you're not in this for the long haul. I don't mentor people, and even if I did, I wouldn't do it with a hobbiest."

He dialed back the nastiness from his voice and added, "I believe you have information, and I believe you when you say it's good. If it's that good, make it happen."

"I don't have real resources. I got Google and Facebook searches."

He pointed to one of his paper piles. "I just put a guy away for robbery and it all started from a public Facebook post. His own, mind you. Not the brightest guy. I made some connections, found the victims, offered my services and — boom! I'm in. They were so grateful, they gave me a little more because I delivered so fast."

"'Cause you had the answer already. That's like cheating."

"Point is the world is an open book. Everyone's got a phone and an ego. Stuff, information, is everywhere. All's you gotta do is find it." He pointed at her. "And when I say 'you,' I mean you. Not me."

She stood, taking the cue for an exit. To become a full private eye, she'd need time and resources. Mostly time (which she did not have), but resources (which she even more did not have).

Malcom stopped her. "I can tell this isn't what you wanted to hear. You can call me again if you like."

"I'm not gonna do that. I can't do any of this."

"OK. But if you ever need me for anything else you think I might provide, I probably do."

She nodded. He almost sounded genuine.

"Is this what you would do, if it were your case?"

"If it were me," he said, "yeah. I'd look for opportunities and make connections. Sometimes it's all who you know."

She opened the door. "That's the same bull they tell actors.

"Are you an actor? 'Cause I book extras if you're looking for that kind of thing."

CHAPTER SIX

10:55AM. Earl's.

"I don't want to hear about it." Carla stood at her sink, cleaning combs. Danica had never seen anyone clean so many combs. She did it when she needed to think. "It's too dangerous. I don't think you should do it, but if you're gonna do it, I don't wanna hear about it."

She grabbed a brush and pulled the hair free.

"And the cops don't want your help?"

Danica said, "They're all set, according to them. They got their ideas, their rules and they're gonna follow them. They don't want any help, no insider tips. Least of all from me."

"And this freakin' dirt bag PI-ticket-scalper jerk-off won't take it either?"

"Nope. Not without a guaranteed paycheck. Which I cannot do. He won't come near it."

Carla scrubbed another comb. "You sure you don't need to clean nothing in your station?"

"Nope."

"'Cause I'm not doing it for you." The comb in Carla's hand had been scrubbed before, and recently. Lots of thinking was happening for certain.

Carla offered a few more suggestions, and doubled back to the one she'd already considered: that Danica could try to look up a bigger private eye firm. She somehow managed to not laugh in her face. It was a bad idea, but it still had to be explored. The times had become desperate, so no stone could afford to remain unturned.

"And you think you can just step out and say, 'Hey everybody, I'm a private investigator. Gimme your evidence'?"

"I can look around at least. Nobody else is gonna do it."

Water and soap and sponges made noise in lieu of conversation. Danica watched her manager mull and mull some more.

"Can I be honest with you?" said Carla.

"Have you been dishonest so far?"

"I just gotta tell you the way it is."

"Which is?"

The comb scrubbing stopped and the water turned off. "I think I have an idea that could work."

Danica sat up, her station chair spinning her onto the floor. "Give it."

"It's just someone you could talk to."

"Sure. Anybody."

"Don't worry. She's licensed."

"Oooookay."

"And I know there's still a stigma around this stuff. But it's freakin' 2008, so we need to get past it. It's about healing and opening up about ourselves in a safe environment with a trained professional."

Danica shook her head and waited for better descriptions. When Carla offered none, she put two-and-two together.

"Are you talking about a psychiatrist, Carla?"

"She's great. I've been to her lots of times. After my divorce, and beyond that even. She's really, really great."

"I do not need a psychiatrist."

"There's no shame in it."

"I know."

"I've been talking to her. All this refinancing stuff, and the bank stuff. And I've been looking how I can buy a place and can't find one—"

"I don't need a psychiatrist. Thank you." Danica didn't want to come off unappreciative of Carla's offers. Despite a suggestion that proved both unhelpful and condescending, her manager did care for her.

"I should just let it go," said Danica.

"Probably."

"It's gonna go nowhere."

"Yeah."

"Safer, too. To let it go. "

"Very much. I'm kinda glad to hear it, Dani."

She looked at her station. It did look pretty damn messy. More than usual. Some foreign power — probably guilt from shutting down her friend's advocacy for well-meaning psychiatric help — moved Danica's hands toward the tower of dirty towels, and she actually started straightening them up.

This Drake Alberts kid had been killed. The police seemed like jocks trained to hold weapons and make jokes. The only people who likely cared were Drake's family and friends. Who might, by all accounts, be rich. Rich and grieving, and waiting for help that would not come.

The image of Drake's body had come from the cops.

Directly, in fact. Danica had no more information than they did. What did she have that they didn't?

A fixation on the event, a weird desire to solve an unsolved puzzle, and one powerful — though limited — psychic ability to see into people's minds.

She couldn't do anything about it. Not while working a day job that she desperately needed. Most everyone who knew anything would be available during the daytime. She had conflicting schedules.

Danica stopped folding the towels (which she wasn't doing well anyway) and said, "I think what I need is a change in work shifts."

"You wanna work nights?"

"Just for a little while."

"We might be able to do that. Gene would have to OK it, but we might be able to make it happen. Forever?"

"No. Just a couple weeks probably."

It was Carla's turn to stop cleaning up. "Any plans?"

"Maybe."

"What kind?"

Danica put her hands on Carla's shoulders. "I think I can do it."

"What? Detective work?"

"It's just one case."

"You're saying 'case' now?"

"I think I can do it."

"I said I didn't want to hear about it!"

"I'm being helpful. There's something that needs my help."

"That's just it," said Carla. "It does *not* need your help. They have people involved and they said they do not need your help. They're the pros. With training and life experience and guns and dogs and stuff. Compared to your zero years of training and your zero amounts of everything else, I'd say they can handle it without you."

Carla spoke the truth. Danica didn't know the first thing about gathering clues. She didn't know if 'shaking down a perp' was actually something that happened or something that only happened in movies. She had no invitation to this mess.

"You don't have to come with me."

"Good. I won't."

"All I want from you is to work nights."

"Gene works nights. You'll have to convince Gene."

"Gene won't mind."

"Gene will mind."

Gene probably would mind. He was older than Carla and set in his ways, with a solid routine. Danica rarely crossed his path, and when she did, she remained careful to avoid getting him riled up. Gene had been raised tough and stayed that way. He did not enjoy being asked for favors.

"I'll convince him," said Danica. "I'll get Gene to trade with me for a week."

Carla folded her arms. "If this kid was murdered, then you're dealing with some dangerous stuff."

"I only want to help. Find out who did what, point the cops in the right direction. That's it."

"And maybe get some reward."

"That, too. But that's it."

"You'll never get Gene to switch."

"But if I do?"

"You won't."

"But if?"

She threw her hands at her smock pockets. "Then I suppose I can't stop you."

Danica hadn't felt her cheeks smile in a week. Not like

this. And she hadn't jumped for being happy in her entire life. All this added up to her hugging her manager. It was returned.

"Where you gonna start?"

"Not sure."

"You know anything about the victim?"

"A little."

"You'll do great." That one came out sarcastic.

Danica opened her mouth to speak, but got scared. Then said it anyway. "It would be more convincing if it came from you."

"What would?" Carla pushed out of the hug.

"Switching with Gene."

"Dammit, girl."

"You're his manager."

"Yours, too, I thought."

"Please?"

Carla scowled and scowled some more. Then nodded, while maintaining the scowl. "You have to promise to be careful."

"I promise."

Carla tossed her hands around again. She'd given up. "Gene's on tonight. I'll ask then. And don't you freakin' think about asking to switch tonight. He's got his gig all set up and there's no number of dead rich kids he'd switch for."

Danica agreed.

The day shift got busy, and stayed busier than Danica hoped. New customers found their way to Danica's station faster than usual. Trash cans needed extra cleaning out. Floors couldn't get swept enough. If she didn't know better, she would've sworn Carla had tried to keep her extra busy to prevent her from thinking about Drake Alberts III.

She made it to her final hour and took a longer-than-normal bathroom break to jot down some ideas. She kept things as simple as possible: "gather information," "find people connected to Drake," "search for clues." She re-read her short list and thought it looked like a first draft of a first-grader's How to Be A Detective paper. "Search for clues?" She had never felt like a bigger phony. Was she going to buy a trench coat, too? Start smoking again (that idea got more consideration than she liked to admit).

With her list exhausted, she re-read the Times article. First, her faith that English classes weren't a total waste of time got restored when she saw the grammatical errors had been cleaned up: it read simply "Keith Beckett" with no dangling participle about his title.

Second and more importantly, she gained a few more simpler-than-simple-but-still-needed-to-be-written-down,-and-at-least-her-list-was-longer ideas: "look for patterns," just like Mr. Fine said. If and when she found more information and met people connected to Drake, she could look to see what patterns emerged, then present a more substantial case to the Alberts family.

Whoever they were. The whole notion became as certain as a lottery ticket.

After the drive home, Danica's notebook contained her closest drafts at fool-proof plans for using her unique capabilities to solve the murder of Drake the Third.

Plan A: Walk around the city wearing a picture of Drake Alberts III on her chest. If anyone looks like they recognize the picture, touch that person on the head. Since everyone will likely stare at a bald woman with a dead kid's face on her chest, expect to touch everyone on the head.

Plan A got crossed out. Stupidity wrote Plan A, and Danica — being a confident adult fully capable of handling extraordinary challenges — was not stupid. Not anymore.

She was a smart person, full of innovation and originality and ideas and plans.

Plan B: there was no Plan B.

Aside from cutting hair, her powers (God, that word) had never been much use. She had a powerful ability. One with major limitations, that could neither reach beyond her own grip nor sense where to even find those things to bring them within her own grip.

But it was still a power. One. One stupid power, that didn't guarantee the discovery of any hard evidence. A power, which, historically, had only served to bring her embarrassment and misery.

CHAPTER SEVEN

Saturday, February 12, 1994. 7:46PM. Central Illinois.

She was fourteen, with puberty in full swing, when Danica attended her first boy-girl dance. Despite the fact that dances of all kinds were moronic, she went with some friends who happened to believe that dances were the greatest thing on Earth, and that this particular dance — the Valentine's Day Sweethearts Sock Hop — was the most important moment of their entire lives. This meant that the rest of their lives would be universally boring and terrible, but she held back on saying it out loud.

Danica's mom wanted her to wear a skirt. She wanted to wear jeans. They settled on a jean skirt with dark tights. She wore a sweater of her mom's choosing, and she agreed only because it could be easily removed upon arrival at the dance.

Someone's dad drove the gaggle of girls to the high school gym, and once there (and after removing the sweater to reveal her second favorite "Halloween" T-shirt), Danica concerned herself with the punch bowl area. She tied the sweater around her waist and anxiety made her sweaty. She tried to look busy by helping people with the punch cups, stopping after realizing these were young adults with years of cup-handling experience. She checked the gym's wall clock and determined the next two hours would be slow going.

Danica had long-for-her hair then. A kind of boy cut with curls over her ears and no bangs. She sat against the wall, her curls barely visible over the punch table.

One from this gaggle — Jill Swanson-Samuels — ran to her. She babbled something about a boy, and how that boy had asked her (Jill Swanson-Samuels) to dance, and that the boy had friends who were also asking people to dance, including Danica. Before she could insist that her duties as self-appointed punch-bowl manager were far too important to be neglected, a boy named Travis appeared at the table, looking right at her.

Any other night and by any other circumstance, Travis qualified as conventional. He had dirty brown hair and boring eyes. His face was composed of acne and a crooked smile. When 2008-Danica looked at old yearbooks, she would marvel at how 1994-Danica could have ever thought Travis was the most beautiful thing on two feet. But in that instance, to that fourteen-year-old self sitting on the gym floor, in the lights and with the Richard Marx-inspired soundtrack, he was. He asked her to dance and she agreed. She stood, put the cups on the table and followed Travis to the dance floor.

Thinking back on the moment, she couldn't remember the exact song playing, but at the time it was perfect. Danica and Travis held each other at arm's length, his hands on her hips, hers around his neck. The pull of that perfect song she forgot drew them nearer and nearer. They had nothing interesting to say to each other, so they said nothing. Danica's imagination wandered as she stared into those dull eyes. She looked away to keep from staring, but returned again. She thought about a future with this boy, about moving to a house, maybe to a city with more than one gas station.

Nervous, she twiddled her fingers. The song, whatever the title, gave her confidence. Her fingers rubbed his neck. He smiled. She moved her fingers into his hair.

And then it happened. The darkness of the gymnasium vanished in a flash of light. For an instant, bright technicolor shapes blasted at her. She blinked, dropped her hands to steady herself. Travis said something, maybe about her being OK, but kept swaying back and forth.

She had gone someplace else for a moment. Her stomach lurched like she'd driven over a speed bump. She held her head and offered some excuse about standing up too fast (two minutes earlier) and put her hands back around the neck of the boy she could totally marry. Her fingers, again, found his hair.

The blast returned. This time, she remained wherever it took her. She saw the gymnasium, full of the same people as she'd seen moments ago, only slightly brighter. She was moving. Slowly, toward the table with the punchbowl. She saw Jill Swanson-Samuels, babbling toward the floor. She moved closer and saw herself, the fourteen-year-old Danica, in her "Halloween" shirt with her boy cut curls, sitting on the floor.

Thoughts of alternate dimensions and wormholes didn't line up; she was seeing the recent past, from the point of view of someone else. From Travis's eyes. It felt like time travel to see herself from someone else's perspective. The dizziness grew more comfortable as she gained inside information.

Then she looked at her jean skirt. She watched herself stand up, and looked at the sweater tied around her waist, the T-shirt, then back to her legs. She looked herself up and down in a way beyond mere socially-pressured insecurity in a mirror. This was full-on male gaze, and it kept landing below her skirt. And on the back of her skirt. Vision Travis snuck a peek at Vision Danica to see if she was looking. When she wasn't, he looked at her butt again.

His eyes rolled. He looked at Jill Swanson-Samuels, first in the face (for a nanosecond) then at her body (for far too long). He checked her out with even more leer.

Vision Travis looked to another boy standing behind the girls. Jill's suitor. This boy motioned toward Vision Danica and made a thumbs up with his tongue sticking out. Vision Travis nodded, then stuck his own thumb in his mouth and sucked it up and down. The other boy laughed while oblivious Vision Danica and Jill Swanson-Samuels continued talking.

Dancing Danica — the fourteen-year-old who had just experienced her first honest-to-God vision — removed her fingers from Travis's hair and stopped swaying. She became fully present, back among the bad decorations.

"What the hell was that?" she said.

"Huh?" said Travis.

"You thought you'd get to third base with me at the Sweetheart Sock Hop?"

"How'd you... no. What? No." Travis didn't even convince himself.

"Dancing's over, jag-bag." Danica pulled herself out of Travis's grip.

He grabbed her arm. She yanked herself away, ready for

a full-fledged storm off. But she moved too slow, and heard him say "Freak."

She turned back to face him, walked close and flicked her finger into his crotch. She hit something stiff-ish, then turned on her heel and resumed her storm-off. Travis made a sound like a whimper.

Danica reached the door without looking back to confirm whether Travis had fallen to his knees. She waited out the remainder of the dance in the parking lot by the school's one handicapped spot. Her mom heard the whole story that night.

For her remaining high school years, a reputation of weird hung around her, and Danica reveled in it. Screw the hicks. From then on, her access to their secrets — even if she didn't use that access — put her on the fringes. She accepted her place and dug in deep.

———

Twenty-eight-year-old Danica stepped onto her Island Estates patio. The management company had promised personal patios, and had technically not lied. They didn't specify the size of the person who could fit on these personal patios. "Like personal pan pizzas," Gabby had said. The personal-size personal patio could sit one human with some comfort, as long as that person did not suffer from acrophobia or claustrophobia. A plastic lawn chair fit with enough room to lean back against the sliding glass door and smoke. When she used to smoke. Now she only thought about it.

The prospect of a reward seemed like a fading dream. She was an outcast, just like high school. She didn't know the family involved. A bunch of well-to-do's too good for her by a mile. She'd have to know them — or be known *by* them — to get in good enough to earn — maybe even convince them to offer — a monetary reward. Just for helping. The infinitesimal amount of research she'd managed to squirrel away had already led her to assume they'd join Travis Whatshisname in that "freak" label.

Too many things needed to be lined up, and she hadn't come close to starting. Even with a unique ability to look into someone's mind, she'd still only seen what he *already knew*. It wasn't like she saw some other piece of the story, or a part from another angle or caught any glimpse of anything more than James already knew. She knew what he knew, and no more. Giving up made sense.

Unless.

Travis Whatshisname had been her first successful (and unprofitable) glimpse into someone's mind. It had given her a taste of another angle on the same story, however tiny. So far with Drake the Third, she'd seen James Van Owen's angle. She didn't have a way to find the killer right away, so that angle was out the door. There were no other angles to consider.

Unless she counted Drake the Third's point of view.

And she could.

And unless she touched his hair.

Which she also could. Maybe.

A plan arrived, quickly and with few details. It came so fast that Danica didn't have time to write it down or contradict it. But if she could reach Drake the Third's body — possibly at a morgue, which would be a difficult trick... or maybe at the funeral, which would require becoming close with the Alberts family, which wasn't impossible... As a student? Yes. Posing as a fellow USC student was doable, and she could find some other twenty-somethings to fall in with who were going to the funeral... Somebody had to be going, and she could go with them.

Or even that Keith Beckett teacher guy who had spoken so highly of Drake, she could find him, find out some more...

— IF all this helped her to get to the funeral, she could reach Drake the Third's body. And touch his hair.

And see Drake's angle. See the killer's face.

She had very little time to accomplish any or all of this. The funeral had probably been set, and it wouldn't be too far off in the future.

Her phone dinged with a Carla text:

"I did it. Gene says he'll swap. He'll take your time tomorrow. You are welcome."

The personal-size patio became a little more cozy.

CHAPTER EIGHT

Wednesday, August 27, 2008. 7:01AM.

The morning's mission: reconnaissance. The Alberts's house being the only location she knew so far, she would start her work there. Get some idea about who the people are, who Drake was, where he was found. Time permitting, she would make a trip to USC to gather more information and initiate Operation: Late-In-Life-Freshman, or possibly Operation: Interview Keith Beckett, but that seemed like a stretch.

She chose practical clothing befitting someone with such missions:

- Loose, carpenter-style pants.
- T-shirt, grey, turned inside out to hide an old stain.
- Socks. Standard.
- Adidas sneakers, currently serving as her "nice shoes."

Her haircutting travel kit lay open on the kitchen table. Carla's old kit, given to Danica after her first month at Earl's. "Everyone freelances," she was told. Danica tapped it open and tossed in her notebook and pen. The shears inside looked dull, but they still cut through her confidence.

"What the hell am I doing?" she said to the walls.

The walls gave no answer. They didn't have to. They had already told her too many times about her place in the world, and going after big rewards and solving mysteries wasn't it. Every time she thought long enough about the case, her inadequacy reminded her of everything else. She had no contacts, no disguises, no aliases. Did she expect to charge into these places today and get answers in a gift bag?

She snapped the go bag shut and put the strap over her shoulder. If anybody asked her who she was, she was a barber. Or would be. Almost, if she passed that last test.

The Accord behaved itself on the 405 and landed her smack in Bel Air, one of those communities Danica normally avoided. Any time Danica had gone to this part of town, the self-imposed pageantry of the place riled her up. Despite being part of Los Angeles, it seemed like it begged for a divorce.

She crossed a large pseudo-gate entrance to the city within the city and managed to keep her eyes from rolling out of her skull. The first set of houses carried the same haughty air. Lots of fountains, lots of trees, and of course lots of grass. Like these people invented the stuff. As she ascended with the incline, the houses seemed to be grown out of the mountains. Money found a way to carve down the land. Neither desert nor gravity could stop the filthy rich.

The street twisted and she checked her map. The farther into the hills she drove, the more spread out the houses got. A couple more turns and the neighborhood washed away. Around her were large fences and empty sidewalks.

After another right, she saw the first pedestrian since Westwood. Wearing a summer-weight suit (very white), the man (also very white) walked a long-haired dog. She might not have noticed this man at all if he hadn't been entirely alone on the sidewalk. He looked to be in his sixties and damn near distinguished. His trim white beard helped his chin point a little higher.

Danica pulled to a stop on the corner and the man actually waved to her. Maybe she'd misjudged this place.

He pointed his bony finger at the "NO PARKING - STREET CLEANING" sign.

Never mind. The place was exactly how she'd judged.

The streets around the Alberts' home enjoyed so much street cleaning it felt like a conspiracy against parking. It surprised Danica that a cleaner truck wasn't on the streets 24/7. She finally found her way down the hill and parked at a cul-de-sac, near a three-story house under renovation.

The house stood tall, framed between two trees, with a long porch wrapping around one side and green shutters around every window. Its red door was simple but for the ornate top window arch, which had frosted roses emblazoned into it. It looked like someone's dream house. Except for the general disrepair from non-occupancy, it would have sufficed as anyone's American dream, a real two-kids-and-a-dog type of place. The yard needed a trim, but Dream House Dad could probably handle that. Piles of old chairs and desks made heap on its driveway, as did a small heap of broken stage lights. Someone got wise and left.

Her parking brake locked in place, she grabbed her go bag and Tommy's sweatshirt and got out, ready to hoof it.

The walk, mostly uphill, made the sweatshirt decision a foolish one in exactly six steps. She paused to remove the sweatshirt, and a heavy-set man waddled around his yard. Danica nodded a Midwestern hello, and the man scowled.

"Nope."

"Sorry?" she said.

"Get outta here. I'm not selling."

"I'm not sure what you mean?"

"You heard me, I'm staying here," said the man. "Move on, you."

She hoped her silence came off as stoic instead of stunned, and she continued up the hill.

The hill relented and she found the fence on the corner. A security booth sat a ways away, lost to the vastness. The wrought iron, with its ivy and jasmine and greenery, protected a long, grassy lawn. It reached back to where a grand house must have been. From that corner — the southwest — with her face pressed against the fence, all she could see was roof, but it loomed over everything in its kingdom. The water sprinklers had already doused the lawn and made the fence wet, yet no drips landed on the side outside of the fence. A line of small hedges lined the other side of the fence, cresting up the hill.

Danica caught her breath. She moved to a different between-two-fence-posts vantage point, then back again. She couldn't pinpoint it, given her limited information from James' mind, but she had a good feeling that she was staring at the spot where Drake the Third's body had been found. She remembered James' steps. They seemed slow, as if going down an incline. That put the body somewhere near this, the southeast corner.

She kneeled on the sidewalk and pulled her go bag around to grab her notebook. She scribbled a few notes. Drake might have been running away, but there didn't seem to be any escape from this corner. He could have been cornered, chased from the house or the entry way. Or he could've been strolling about and been caught by surprise.

An engine fired. A green Gator crested the hill, coming

from the house, with two men in gray uniforms, long sleeves and hats. The back of the Gator carried buckets, rakes and assorted tools. They parked near the corner, the two men taking no notice of the woman with the buzz haircut staring at them through the fence.

Danica didn't speak Spanish, but gathered by their motions that something in the hedges was of concern. Several of the hedges looked browner than the others. The groundskeepers knelt and dug in the dirt.

She watched them work and wondered what it would be like to do their work on a crime scene. Did they know? There was no indication anywhere — no police tape, no chalk on the grass, nothing. Danica only knew the location because she'd been dreaming about it for two days, but these guys didn't know. Or didn't care.

From her angle of the house, she saw no windows. Since nobody could see anything from the Alberts Mansion, this corner might have been used as a trap. Someone might have seen something from the sidewalk, but that would mean someone would have actually been on the sidewalk. The killer could have scaled the fence. It had no electrical charge. She shook the bars, weighing her options on how difficult it would be to climb the wall, twist her ankle from the jump, then cover the expanse of the yard to the house and make it undetected.

Bootsteps approached from her right, and Danica turned to face the largest security guard she had ever seen. He had dark skin and squinted in the sunlight. He motioned for her to come closer and she obeyed him completely.

"Help you, miss?" The guard's stance looked solid, part of the concrete.

"Sorry. I was just kind of, um, admiring things." She had no bluff game. The guard's folded arms confirmed as much.

Until that instant, Danica had never wished she had anything like "girlish charm," where she could turn it on, flutter her eyelashes, rub her hair and flirt her way into this guard's heart. At least, into his heart long enough for him to tell her what he knew about the night Drake's body was found.

"This is private property, miss."

"Sure, but can I just ask you something?"

The guard sighed. "If it's about recent events, I am not at liberty to comment."

"I don't even know what you mean."

"Good. I've been telling too many people already."

She logged that tidbit in her memory and scrambled to her go bag. "I, um, I have coupons. For haircuts." She pulled out the sweaty paper. It worked once before.

He looked it over.

"This is near my place," he said.

"Oh, yeah? You mean you don't live in Bel Air."

The guard's frown cracked by ten percent. She had some game after all. "Yeah. Like I can afford that. How'd you come all the way out here?"

"Google Maps."

"I mean, why are you here?"

Maybe he hadn't cracked. Maybe he was playing her. She became acutely aware of the taser hanging from his belt. The size of his arms and chest would intimidate a bear. She glanced towards the gardeners as they kicked dirt with their boots. The water broke free from a sprinkler head, squirting up like a fountain.

"I was in the neighborhood doing a cut. Film thing."

"Oh yeah?"

Game resumed: "I can't tell you the details."

"Come on."

"No, no. They swore me to secrecy. But this place caught my eye. Probably looks like a palace, huh?"

He nodded and offered no further comment. Danica took it as a great time to scoot. She gave a little wave and turned, trying not to sprint down the hill. She hadn't gotten onto the grounds, and her budding friendship with the security guard probably wouldn't get her an invite to the funeral, but at least she'd gained a little context. Seen the scene. She had possible theories on the way the attack had happened, and she even dodged security thanks to her quick thinking. Like a professional. Even the kit had been a help.

"Hold up." The security guard's loud bark popped Danica's 'like a professional' balloon. She stopped. The guard jogged to her, and the concrete winced with every heavy stride.

"Want me to take some more coupons? Pass them around? Never know, right?"

"Sure, right, yes," she said, and handed over the rest of her pile. Like a semi-pro. Like a barber stumping around fancy houses to drum up business.

Danica still got the info. She'd maintained her cover, even if that cover was actually her true identity. The renovation house at the cul-de-sac gave her a side-eye glance as she started the Accord.

CHAPTER NINE

After an unkind first portion of the 405-South, then an ill-advised attempt to take eastbound streets, Danica gave in to the inevitable and joined the 10-East toward Downtown. The Accord trembled as it approached speeds it could not handle (46+ mph). Luckily for the car, traffic made sure such speeds would not be an issue.

The car crawled off the highway at Vermont Avenue, passed the mix of fast food joints, dilapidated auto garages and house-like non-houses until it crossed into USC territory.

The world transformed. While certainly an institution of higher education, and while she would never hold the history of scandals against the current faculty or students, the campus reminded Danica of Bel Air. Like that neighborhood, the college was very much part of the city, yet made every effort to distinguish itself as otherwise. It was the Disneyland effect, where perception got managed by presenting enough positive stimuli to create miniature Vatican Cities within the larger, indistinguishable sprawl. One moment, you're in a dumpy, low-income residential area. The next you're at Harvard, surrounded by brick and elm trees.

She slowed and scanned the walkways to the side. Fall semester must have begun, judging from the fresh quality of backpacks. The students moved in packs, particularly the younger-looking ones, so scared to be away from home, clinging to others like them.

Data charges be damned, Danica pulled out her phone. "Keith Beckett's office" did not present itself in a search. Neither did a refined search for the student registration, business education department, or much else beyond the football field. Even if she couldn't locate Mr. Beckett, she could at least walk the place out and see where Drake might have eaten and goofed around. If she could find where Drake lived, she might find people he lived with. The Alberts seemed like the type of family who might have paid for their son's private, off-campus apartment, but the kid must have had friends somewhere.

Her phone struggled to hold a signal. Danica had just pictured her data bill when she A.) remembered to look at the road on which she was still driving, B.) caught movement ahead of her, C.) realized that movement came from a human person, so she D.) slammed the brakes.

The go bag flew off the seat and spilled onto the car floor. Danica's attention focused back where it should have been all along, through the windshield and to the narrow man in the crosswalk. He had wispy hair and a wispy goatee. Only his eyebrows held hair color darker than gray. And they, the eyebrows, were crunched together, looking right at Danica.

The man yelled something and shook the book in his hand at Danica's car.

"Sorry," she said.

He turned away and continued on the path across the street, onto the campus. His shirt, pants, belt and shoes were all a shade of tan. He paused at the curb to shoot another cursing look toward her.

Danica rolled down the side window. "I'm so sorry about that, sir."

He spoke with formality, as if he rehearsed enunciation every day in a mirror. "What you are doing, young lady, is illegal. In this city, state and beyond."

"I know. I'm a little lost."

"No excuse," said the narrow man. He turned away and meant it, continuing on his wispy way toward what looked like classroom buildings. He walked with a stiff kind of glide, as though he still knew how to carry himself, but had undergone some surgery on his back or knees. Maybe both.

"Could you help me, please?" An elaborate lie formed before her, where she would claim to be a Freshman who — late to attend her first year due to a tragic family illness — was already two steps behind; however, thanks to her pluck and outsider insights, she would rise above the pack if only the right grizzled old teacher would take a liking to her, take her under his wispy wing, and maybe, just maybe, learn to open his heart again.

The narrow man would have none of it. Without stopping his pace, he jabbed his left index finger to the east. "Student registration office. That way."

And that was the end of that. He disappeared into the crowd. So much for the elaborate story.

The parking lot next to the registration building had a spot open in the back. Danica pulled her go bag together again, then strapped it to her shoulder, trying to make it look more like a backpack or messenger bag, like the kids wore these days. This disguise was further nailed by Danica pulling out the notebook and carrying it against her chest. Like the kids did in her day.

For a place whose purpose was to welcome students, the student registration building appeared notably unwelcoming. Grand old buildings had always given Danica the creeps, and the security guard at the door added a special dose of 'don't bother me.' He looked like the type to ask for ID, so Danica put her phone to her ear and hoped he was also the type not to interrupt calls.

He was, but the guard inside the lobby was not. This one immediately asked, "Lost, little miss?"

"Um..." she reached for one of the free maps and immediately dropped it. Here was this tall white guy, buzz cut with mirrored sunglasses. A wannabe cop, waiting for her to screw up and she did. She didn't need his patronizing, phallocentric attitude stepping in to knight-in-shining-armor her situation. She could read a freakin' map.

On the other hand, his assumption handed Danica a role to play, and one without an elaborate backstory.

"Do you know Keith Beckett? Or where he is?"

He adjusted his enormous belt buckle, ready to feel like a good person. "Not off the top of my head." The guard checked a page of a book, then flipped it, then flipped back.

Danica shifted gears. "What about the business building?"

"Yeah, that I know." The relief in his voice was unmistakable. He grabbed her map and pointed at a spot. "We're here, yeah? Head out here, then that way to this spot. The Marshall Building. You'll do just fine."

She thanked him. He gave back the map and said, "Fight on."

Danica stepped back outside, down the stairs and onto the suggested path.

Map in hand, she followed the trail and wandered deeper into the college world. She hadn't been on a real college campus before; not unless you counted the Hawkshead Community College in Kiwanis, Illinois, which she certainly did not. Even her barber college didn't have a "campus;" it had a couple floors of an office building (lovely as they may be). USC's brick-lined everythingness emphasized the "hallowed" aspect of its halls.

The Marshall Building was stiff, even for a business school. She tried to imagine Drake the Third spending his days there, studying to be the next big whatever-rich-people-became. She couldn't do it for very long, picturing him, or anyone, spending any amount of time inside that box. Drake did not need money, so he didn't need to take classes. His motivation must have been low to attend lectures on why foreign markets did this and that. Who could feel passionate for *business*? Anyone who claimed to have a passion for business was abusing the word "passion."

A plaque next to the door listed prominent donors, separated by donation level. A USC Trojan logo sat at the top. Danica had seen that logo all over LA, thanks to the city's strange obsession with its colleges. Mostly the football teams; the Rams and Raiders had deserted them, but the schools never could, so the city clung with the vigor of a recently divorced dad to his new girlfriend. The logo on the plaque must have been an older design, as it looked much more Anglo-Saxon compared to the ones all over town, with a slender nose and gaunt cheeks.

She scanned the names and it didn't take long to find a

familiar name. The top level — the Golden Trojans — held a listing for "The Alberts Family."

The door was locked. She peered through the windows, only to confirm the lameness of the carpets. Gaining access to the building, walking around, looking for offices, meeting the right people and working her way to Keith Beckett would surely take a day or more.

She drew back and returned to the path, wound her way deeper, until she found a courtyard filled with hundreds of people. Like a festival without rides or food. Tables and tents lined a pathway and led deeper south. The tents were manned by people younger (and cooler) than she looked or was. Danica didn't know the world had produced this many game hats.

The row of tents ended at an open space ahead of a large gate. Near that gate was a small news group: two tech guys working camera and microphone, one young adult man with tan skin and a baby face, wearing a white shirt and a blue tie. A pair of glasses hung from his pocket.

Baby Face was being spoken to by another man with his back to Danica. She couldn't hear him, but whatever he said, Baby Face was not happy about it, and kept motioning to the crowd of tents. Next to the tents were a small collection of students, mostly girls, holding protest signs. Many said "YES ON 8!" and one said "MAN AND WIFE, NOT STAN AND MIKE." Danica took away points for homophobia and for crap rhymes.

"You gotta keep them back," said Baby Face.

"You're doing this on sign-up day, Roberto. You do that, this is what you get."

"They keep interrupting my shot." He emphasized 'my' in a whiny way. Baby Face needed a nap. "Aren't you the dean? Make them move."

The dean had a beard and very little patience for Baby Face Roberto. He turned away. Danica had seen that move from her step-father whenever he heard something he didn't like, wanted to get angry and hit something, but somehow pulled himself back from making that choice.

"We're alumni," said Baby Face. He raised his eyebrows a bit and tipped his chin down, like he'd called someone's bluff.

A moment later, the dean sighed, looked at his feet, then turned to the small crowd of protestors and spoke in a polite voice.

"Please stop interrupting this news crew. They have a job to do. And they apparently want to do it right here."

Most of the protestors shrugged and slunk back. One younger girl put her hands on her hips, ready to remind this man who her father was.

The dean ignored her and turned back to Baby Face, said something quick, then left.

Danica thought better of bothering the dean and watched the Baby Face News. The young reporter waved his script at his cameraman to get the show on the road, then put on his glasses. She knew they were for show. They made him look older — almost twenty-three!

Baby Face held up the shot for one more thing and jiggled an empty coffee cup. Like magic, a student ran over and replaced it with a fresh one, then disappeared back into the tent crowd.

At last, Baby Face was ready to begin. The camera light turned on and he said to it, "Drake Alberts had been a happy student here at USC. And even though his murder shook the student body, life on campus definitely and defiantly fights on."

She wandered into the row of tents, looking back to the

news crew. She should have stuck around to hear the rest. Here was a connection to her case, someone interested in the same topic as her for the first time since arriving on campus. But Baby Face wouldn't have any actual information. He didn't know enough to film in a quiet part of the campus, of which there were many. He wanted this shot because it was pretty. Because he wasn't doing "news." He was generating content for a puff piece. Danica could tell; anyone could tell.

"Signing up?" said the child working the table beside her. The sea of infants dressed like wannabe adults crushed Danica's belief in her ability to pull off the "I'm In College!" alias, while this girl's willingness to sign her up sagged her faith in the nation's youth. Danica decided she should, in fact, sign up, and she did, for some kind of drama newsletter.

"Is there a business club tent, too?"

"I..." said the young woman before trailing off. Danica left it at that.

She pushed into the crowd. The tents were poorly marked except for one: the Daily Trojan Student Newspaper. A boy with a face more acne than skin scowled at her.

"You signing up?" He had a lot of attitude for a dude wearing a plastic visor.

"Sure. Yes." She leaned closer to the kid who thought visors were acceptable to wear publicly in 2008 and said, "You work for the paper?"

"'Course," he sniffed. He looked familiar to Danica, helped by the fact that he looked like a zillion other douchey white boys.

"So you must know a lot about campus stuff."

"Yep."

"Do you know if there's a business club?"

"You can sign up for something. I think..." He scratched his head, which had to be sweaty under all that dollar-store chic. "Reese. Which tent is business club?"

Reese, too excited to stand or look away from his phone, motioned deeper into the tent line. "'Bout five or six tents down."

"Five or six tents down," said visor kid. "Near the statue. But I thought you were signing up for DT."

Her scrunched eyebrows forced visor kid to explain "DT" as "Daily Trojan."

"I am. I'm signing up for both."

"But if you're signing up for DT, you gotta mean it." Serious business.

"I do. Thanks. I'm just following up on something," she said, and pulled herself away from the visor kid's intense stare. She must have seen him at the store, or he just had a generic pimple face that seemed familiar to everyone.

The business club tent was *eight* tables down, with nary a statue in sight. Rather than ever look at the visor or Reese again to let them know that their grasp on facts needed schooling before they could become serious journalists, she let it go.

A bright blonde girl stood behind the business club table. She looked like a GOP dream come to life.

"Do you have sign ups here?" said Danica.

This creature, with straight teeth and pale skin, blinked. She processed having to actually interact with someone like Danica. "We do. It's great for students who are real real serious about this sort of thing."

"That's me," said Danica. "Real real serious."

The Reagan Youth held out the clipboard and a pen.

"Will this get me in contact with the teachers?"

"They contribute a few things here and there for sure." This girl was brilliant.

Danica read the details quickly. Regular emails would provide updates on 'the latest opportunities' in the world of economics, in the real world and in school. It also guaranteed subscribers would feel 'bullish' about the social engagements to come. Danica's fake smile held back her vomit.

It felt lazy to hope for insights to arrive to her inbox. It also felt like something Malcom Fine would do, so she signed up. Every little step closer to Drake the Third's life meant it was worthwhile.

CHAPTER TEN

6:44PM. Earl's.

Night shifts allowed for very little free-thinking time. Day shifts with Carla worked in a kind of tag-team effort, where whoever didn't have a customer would jump on the phone or work the register. The ebbs and flows got handled with varying degree of commitment. This allowed for occasional chatter, some magazine reading and thinking.

Covering Gene's night shift meant Danica inherited some of Gene's regulars, all the walk-in's, on top of phone and cash register duties. Carla once toyed with the idea of hiring another hand to work with Gene so nobody had to be in the shop alone. Yet Gene's proficiency at handling all aspects at night eliminated that need. This saved the business from paying another salary, Gene banked more tips for himself, and everything cruised along. Apparently, Gene had and did it all. If one had time to prepare, a certain person's solo night shift could be smooth and profitable.

Danica was not such a person. Every time she actually

managed to get someone to the chair, the phone would ring and pull her away. She had to answer, take a name, check the schedule, then return to try and regain her hair-cutting groove. Pondering about the Alberts case took a major backseat. Each interruption made the cuts go longer. The pace was pulverizing.

She asked an older confirmed bachelor (who had arrived with a long sigh upon seeing the shop's lack of Gene-ness) what style he wanted, looked into his imagination and let him ramble on and on about this and that for three minutes. The ramble allowed her a few precious moments to reconsider the Times article again.

The post-script rose to her attention. Something needed changing. Things always did, and the world of digital journalism surely allowed for countless changes. But this nagged her. She imagined what had been impacted. Did the reporter get the location wrong, or the time?

The bachelor in the chair screamed "Genie!" to the mirror and broke Danica's moment of ponderance. She turned to the front door just in time to see Gene himself, in the flesh, live and in person.

Normally, he wore a very basic jeans-and-T-shirt look. He always claimed Simon Cowell ripped him off, and the only flashy part of his entire person would be his vocabulary, often used to inform Danica that her shoes were dull.

Not tonight. Everyone could plainly see, tonight was not a uniform night for Gene. He had red cowboy boots with tambourine spurs. Black leather pants cradled his massive butt, and his hair contained enough pomade to choke a rockabilly tribute night. Danica had never seen so many sequins on one person, let alone a single denim jacket. He wore no shirt and stood over six feet tall. Clearly, Gene had no trouble getting another karaoke gig for this night. The woman in the waiting area let out a little gasp and dropped her copy of US Weekly.

"Don't stop me," he said. "Don't even freakin' try. I left some stuff at my station and I'm late as all the get-out gets out."

He drifted above everything, at once ignoring everyone in the room yet pointedly aware that they were looking at him. Danica imagined Gene arguing for Carla to install a spotlight over his station.

Back to her customer, and back to the sideburns work. She tried to ignore the sparkling giant digging through the kaboodle behind her and thought about Keith Beckett. The only other name mentioned in the news story. He must have had an office on campus somewhere. It might take a couple more trips, but she could find it and see if he would answer questions. The Times reporter had gotten to him, and that one Baby Face dude had gotten some kind of access to the campus. So it wasn't impossible.

The phone rang. Again. Pulled her away from her work trance and toward the reception desk. Gene stepped in her way.

"Busy?"

"Yep." Didn't even look him in the eye. With Gene, that was best. She answered the phone, booked the customer then returned to her station.

"It's usually this busy for you, right Genie?" said the bachelor in her chair.

"Busier," said Gene. "This crap ain't crap." He leaned his stomach against the sink and fixed his hair when the phone rang again.

As Danica moved away, she heard Gene and his buddy chuckle. He wasn't in a hurry to go anywhere. He was already wearing everything anyone could possibly wear. He just came in to pick on her. She thought about offering the woman in the waiting area a discounted cut if she'd answer the calls for a while so she could get Gene, Gene's buddy and Gene's spectacular spectacle out as quick as possible.

"You usually handle everything, don't you, Genie? I don't see you work with anybody."

"Nope. Strictly solo act."

"When you got a gift, you just got it."

"And when you don't," said Gene, "you just don't."

Danica's pencil lead broke. She jabbed it into the sharpener. She'd never noticed how much the pencil sharpener opening resembled Gene's eyeball. She wanted him to leave her alone so she could struggle for the next (wow) two hours in peace.

"Do you need some help, hon?" he said.

"Not a drop, sugar." She returned to her cut, perfectly capable of being incapable without his passive-aggressive BS, thank you. He had probably loved the spotlight of his solo nights, and didn't mind being frazzled as long as it meant people had to go through him. He didn't need time to think because he had nothing to think about. He didn't have the concerns she had. He wasn't working over early details of a murder case in his spare time.

The phone burst forth yet another ring. Danica let herself finish the left sideburn before heading to the desk.

When she answered, Gene's voice came through to her. "You're doing this wrong."

She dropped the phone and faced him. He must have seen the glare in her eyes because he raised his hands like she had a gun on him.

"Easy. You just gotta let the machine get the calls. Focus on your customers here and let the robots do the answering."

"We have voicemail."

"Girl, be smart. No wonder you're still single." Gene reached behind his kit and pulled out a dusty piece of equipment the size of a toaster. He handed it over. She had no idea what to do with it, a fact Gene quickly deduced. He took it back from her and carried it to the reception desk.

"Gene's Machine. Let it pick up the calls while you work, then check the messages when you're free. Which for me is the end of the night. You can turn it up so you hear the messages from your station."

"But Carla doesn't want us doing that," said Danica. "That's why she got the voicemail. She didn't want customers hearing other customer calls."

Gene stood and called to everyone in creation: "Does anyone here give a horse's hoot what they hear from other customer's phone calls?"

The other people in the salon shook their heads with various degrees of vigor.

"Anyone care if we hear your calls about hair appointments?"

Same response.

Gene bowed to Danica. He leaned over the side of the desk and plugged the machine's cables into place.

"What if it's serious?"

"A serious... hair cut? Hon, if it's serious, they'll come in. They always do. If they're not serious, then they're not worth your time. You can only do what you can do." He flipped a switch on the machine. A green light near the buttons turned on.

"You're good to go. Put it back when you're done. I'm out." And he was, and the room felt empty.

Though she hated to admit it, Gene was right: the answering machine — the Gene Machine — proved very helpful. The rest of her night went easier as she could actually concentrate on the customers in front of her, on their imagined hairstyles, on getting them done and out the door. She chugged through a family with two kids while the first phone message came in. She let it go. After doing a few single people, she got bold and turned up the volume, and to Gene's point, nobody cared and none of the calls sounded truly urgent. She finished up a couple randos and before she knew it, the night had ended.

With the doors locked, she played the messages she'd missed for background noise while she counted the drawer. There were four. The first two were from regulars who ultimately came in anyway. The next was another who said she'd call back another time. The last was forty-two seconds of dead air. The machine had allowed her attitude to shift, to prioritize work over the distractions. She wouldn't have come to it on her own. She actually owed Gene for borrowing his special something (which he referred to as his "*Gene-esequa*"). Perhaps she had misjudged him.

She checked her own phone for good measure and found a call from 8:31 — around the time that Gene had graced his brilliant idea upon her.

A woman's voice spoke with poise: "Hello. This is Mrs. Drake Alberts and this message is for Danica Luman. I'd like to speak with you about a personal matter. Call me back. Not too late, but please call and we can arrange a meeting, preferably in the near future." She left a number and said Good Evening at the end.

9:45PM. Mrs. Alberts sounded like the type of woman who would consider a call after nine o'clock to be in poor taste. She would have retired by then (Mrs. Alberts also sounded like the type of person who said 'retired'). A return call would have to wait for morning.

The register got balanced, the lights got turned off and the security alarm got set. Somehow. Danica accomplished all this in a haze. Mrs. Alberts had found her, had come up with some kind of proposition for her, and did so by locating her cell number.

How the hell did she do that?

What's more, Danica had missed the call by relying on the Gene Machine.

Danica didn't care for Gene.

CHAPTER ELEVEN

Thursday, August 28, 2008. 5:14AM. Island Estates, Apartment 213.

She rose from bed without the assistance of an alarm. Sat on the edge of the bed for another twenty minutes, hoping the pull of sleep would find her. Cigarettes used to help, she thought for the billionth time this month.

The sole positive effect of tossing and turning all night had been thinking over the hows and whys of Mrs. Alberts' phone call. Her estate surely had security cameras and motion detectors. They could have seen the weird bald woman loitering around the fence, inadvertently setting off some kind of laser detection system. But even if the security team hadn't caught her hanging around, they still would need to get her phone number (and if they were that sophisticated, they could have identified Drake's killer from the start; maybe even prevented the murder). The more likely source seemed to be the security guard. He'd taken the coupon, complete with address and phone number. If the

Albertses were noble lords who deigned to speak to their lowly staff, they could have gotten the information from him ("I say, guard person, remember that random woman you spoke to for less than two minutes? Be a lamb and tell us about her, won't you, there's a good chap").

But the call came to her cellphone. Danica hadn't written that on the coupons — why would she?

The guard had mentioned gawkers and tourists hanging around the Alberts' house, and "random gawker" happened to be a demographic into which Danica's look easily fit. Or paparazzi. Danica could pass for them as well. They were probably bothering the family in their time of mourning. But neither group left follow-up numbers.

On top of all this, no theory explained exactly why the family of Drake Alberts III wanted to talk to Danica. She had never met them before — never even heard of them until this week. Had they heard of her? Were the kooks on the bus right: did rich people really belong to some kind of cult that controlled everything?

She gave up on the bed and allowed herself the luxury of a long shower, of a solid and methodical breakfast, of a studious tooth brushing, all to fill time before 10:00AM — the universally accepted "right time to call." After picking out her clothes for the day, and more for the weekend, and folding and re-folding her T-shirts, she checked the time. She spat a swear word when the clock responded, "Only 9:02."

The Why's returned. Why her? Why last night? Why not after showing up at the fence? The chances that the Alberts had heard great things about Danica's twenty-eight hour stint as a private eye felt remote.

If she wanted to negotiate a reward for herself, she would have to play a delicate hand, having nothing to show for herself but a few hunches and a secret ability few people knew about.

The morning dragged until 9:54 when she received a phone call. Her heart jumped for a split-second as she thought Mrs. Alberts — so excited to have their talk — had called her. But it sunk again when the caller ID showed "Tommy."

Danica let it ring into the digital abyss. Maybe she would come off as so busy and so full of life without him that she just didn't hear it ring at all. She would give his voicemail the same treatment. She doubted her choice when she saw the voicemail came in at two minutes long. The Ignore Him Plan could backfire into (at best) encouragement of more calls, or (at worst) flirtation. Some time, and soon, she would actually have to talk to him again.

When 10:00AM hit, she set a timer for two minutes; better to call just off the hour than be the type of person so eager to call right on the dot. She watched the clock.

When 10:01AM hit, she turned off her timer and called.

A man's voice answered on the third ring. "Alberts residence."

"Hello. Is Mrs. Alberts home?"

"Who is speaking, please?"

"I'm Danica Luman."

"Are you assuming I know your name or anything about you?" His voice resembled a long, angry yawn.

"She left me a message yesterday. Said something about discussing a personal matter?"

"One moment please," said the voice. His words qualified as 'polite' while the tone did not. She heard footsteps, a shuffling noise, followed by nothing for a good minute. Danica couldn't decide if silence meant good news or bad news, then the footsteps returned, and so did the man's voice.

"Mrs. Alberts apologizes for not being available to come to the phone at this moment, but she and Mr. Alberts would like to see you."

"Okay... " Danica paused. Hopefully this guy would take the lead and fill in the blanks, of which there were many. She held no cards. She didn't even know what game they were playing, or if they were playing anything.

"Are you free today, miss?"

"Um... "

"The Albertses have an opening in their schedule at 2:00. I trust your schedule is not so busy to ignore this invitation."

"I think I can move some stuff around."

"Shall I commit you to 2:00?"

"Fine."

"Do you need the address?"

"Are we meeting at their place — I mean, their house?"

"Yes. At their place." The vitriol layered like cake frosting across the entire sentence.

"I'll take a number, just to be safe."

"Very well considered."

"And who is this again?"

"I am Mr. Peters," said the voice, followed by nothing more, as though those two words satisfied all further inquiries. This guy's voice pushed her buttons, and made her want to push his back. So she did.

"Mr. Peters, if you don't mind, I mean, I'm just a kid and I don't know what's all, like, proper and stuff."

The voice on the other end groaned. Grammar was his Kryptonite.

"Is this thing, the thing I'm coming to and all... is it like, you know, a formal thing?"

"It will be a tea." Period.

"OK. Cool, and why, do you know, like," Danica paused and let Mr. Peters sit with 'like' for three seconds, which doesn't sound like a lot, but you try it, "like, what'll we talk about?"

"I'm not certain, of course," said Mr. Peters. "That will be up to Mr. and Mrs. Alberts discretion."

"OK, cool. Thanks, you're so sweet," said Danica.

She looked at the clock and tried to wish a "nice" pair of jeans into her closet.

CHAPTER TWELVE

1:42PM. Bel Air.

GOALS FOR ALBERTS TEA MEETING:

1. Don't look like an idiot.
2. Get hired as their private investigator
3. Find out about possible reward (push for one)
4. Align self to receive that possible reward that you're going to push for, but not too much, but get it for solving their son's murder.
5. Get up close look at spot of yard where Drake's body was found.
6. Seriously — don't look like an idiot.

Danica re-read her list. Not her best work in a career of list-making, but it served its purpose. Goals 1 and 6 tracked with her efforts to stay professional, even if she wasn't. The Albertses were rich and likely accustomed to the very best things their rich-people money could buy; if they realized

Danica was anything less than a professional investigator capable of delivering a satisfactory outcome, they could offer a below-market-value price, or even have her arrested for fraud.

That was if, indeed, hiring her as their investigator had anything to do with why they wanted to meet her. She still didn't know.

It had to be. Danica forced optimism, difficult as it was while looking at the Accord's fuel gauge and wondering how a car could last so long being so hungry.

She set the notebook on the passenger's seat with her goals facing up. The dashboard clock read 1:47PM. Arriving early provided ample time to sit in her car and overthink things. She opened a granola bar and stared through the windshield.

Coming down the sidewalk ahead of her, the same thin man walked the same long-haired dog she'd seen the last time she visited. He wore another summer suit, this time with a saucy hat that made him look like Tom Wolfe. He tipped the hat to a house he passed, then turned the corner. Danica saw nobody at the house. She bit the granola and looked at her list again.

Alibis and stories and lies ran through her mind. Stress made her chewing faster. How could someone like Malcom Fine possibly handle so many details all at once? He likely did not handle them well, which explained his freelance work.

She decided her best chance at surviving the tea and fulfilling Goals 1 and 6 was to be honest, if not completely open. She would follow their leads and be ready to explain herself as a freelance private investigator only if they pressed her on it. Her unique skill set put her in the perfect position to look beyond the obvious paths and find the person who murdered their son.

As long as nobody asked any specific questions about her qualifications, she would come out A-OK.

Fake it until you make it.

Don't look like an idiot (See Goals 1 and 6).

She pulled up to the gate. Arriving at the estate as an expected guest yielded a much warmer response than crashing the fence. As the Accord rolled through the opening, Danica nodded at the guard and he — a different enormous man than the previous one — actually nodded back. She told him her name and he checked a clipboard. The car coughed and sputtered, and she clenched the steering wheel as though applying pressure would keep it from dribbling oil on the spotless driveway, as well as avoiding a full breakdown.

The guard told her to follow the path and park at the house. The driveway twisted up the hill without being dizzy. Small trees lined the way, each trimmed into perfect spheres. Danica stayed on the road while her gaze drifted to the southwest, to the grounds crew, still motioning to the same corner of the lawn. A white man was with them. He didn't wear a uniform and his jabbing arm motions made him look angry at the others.

The driveway opened wide at the top of the hill, and the house emerged in full force. Not that she had much experience with mansions, but from what she'd seen, most appeared to be lavish structures designed to call attention to themselves, to announce their mansion-ness. Gaudy pseudo-castles built to make the owners feel like they were some kind of lost American royalty.

The Alberts' house, however, did not. The pillars in front appeared to have a function beyond simply looking nice and intimidating. The roofline had a simplicity, gracefully bowing over the whole of the house. The windows glimmered. It made Danica imagine a less-flashy and smaller (but only barely) Louvre.

A valet in a green vest waved Danica to stop near the front steps. The hedges around the steps and long porch were trimmed into identical circles, like flat lollipops. Unlike most of their neighbors, the Alberts' place held no palm trees, keeping matters authentically California.

She stopped beside the valet, shut off her car and got out.

"Keys in it?" the valet said.

She leaned back inside and put them in the ignition. "Are now. Thanks."

The valet thanked her and got into the driver's seat.

An older man stood at the front door, at the top of the stairs. His tux, tails and bushy eyebrows put him in another time period, in another country. Somewhere like England, before the Great War. He stood proud, with lips curled at the end — a smile-like formation without exuding any friendliness.

"Good day, miss," he said, and Danica recognized the voice from the phone. Mr. Peters stepped down from the porch. Danica held out a hand to shake, then pulled it back when the butler only coughed into his own.

The Accord's engine gurgled. Danica turned back to the valet. "You gotta give it some gas first. Not all at once. No, not all at once. And turn off the AC." She apologized to Mr. Peters. "I can park it for him if you want."

"That won't be necessary." Danica shut up and Mr. Peters urged her to accompany him.

He led her toward the southern side of the house, teasing her with another glimpse at The Spot by the fence on the grass. A few gardening sun hats bobbed up and down, still arguing about that sprinkler head. They seemed eons away. If one of them screamed, she would never hear it.

Mr. Peters coughed another impatient cough. Danica had stopped walking.

"Come along," he said.

"Sorry. It's just very, um, pretty. Can we look around—"

He placed a large hand on her shoulder and gave a small yet certain push. Like he didn't want her anywhere near anything, especially not That Spot.

"Are they working on the irrigation or something?"

He said nothing. He was pretending he couldn't hear her. This guy looked like the type where it wouldn't take much to wind him up, but she had still hit on something serious. Sweat droplets haunted his forehead.

"Did you know Drake?" Danica impressed herself with her boldness.

"I did."

"His whole life?"

Mr. Peters took another four steps before he said, "Indeed."

The path led them around the edge of the house to (of all things) the back yard. Mr. Peters continued on, but Danica's feet held her back so she could take in the spectacularness of it all.

Danica thought of her mom, and how she withheld most compliments, using them strictly for very special occasions. She didn't clap at Danica's high school graduation ("Everyone graduates. It's expected. Nothing surprising."). She was a caring person, Danica's mother, in her way. Never in big, outward expressions of emotions. A classically Midwestern way to exude love without displaying it. She didn't seem surprised by anything. Danica remembered the one time her mom's breath got taken away: the Trhlin-Baker wedding.

Most weddings around their hometown took place in a church with the reception in the church basement. But Jaimie Trhlin had somehow defied convention by holding her wedding outside. In the outdoors. In nature. The Baker family owned a farm, and they decorated an old barn to act as the reception hall, with large Christmas lights stretching from the top of the barn roof, down the walls and reaching out across the yard to the farm house. A band played inside the barn, and the lights allowed for dancing and chatting to happen anywhere guests wanted.

Danica attended the wedding with her mom and when they took in the sight of all that home-grown splendor, her mom lost her breath, then used just one word: "Elegant."

She would have used the same word if she had seen the Alberts' backyard. Elegant. Classy and they knew it, and you knew it, so nobody had to talk about it. Excessive while understated. Large without making a point of it.

From the edge of the path, the grounds opened into a great expanse. The skyline cut across mountains and forest. The 405 must have been in there somewhere, but she saw none of it. Beyond the trees was only ocean and sky. The Alberts' palace lorded over all it surveyed, and it surveyed quite a lot.

Danica's feet found their stride again, and continued toward a patio with a shaded cover larger than the roof of Danica's apartment building. Lattice lined some pillars, and the perfect amount of vines drooped down, their leaves barely scraping the stone landing. The back of the large house stood proud and shimmering. Even though large glass windows blazed a reflection down on the patio, everything felt cool and comfy.

Two people sat in patio lounge chairs. The woman noticed Mr. Peters and Danica approaching. She stood. Eventually the man stood, too, on the woman's encouragement. Danica couldn't hear their conversation. The woman nodded and grinned while the man scowled in their direction. He shrugged, then started walking toward them. Hasty.

He wore a tie and a white shirt, with the sleeves rolled up; not cuffed like they were designed by some preppy twit, but rolled by hand, like he had done it, like he had some honest to goodness work to do.

His patchy goatee placed him younger than Danica, and when she made eye contact, she wished she hadn't. He gave her what would be universally known as a stink eye — just a glimmer, but indisputable — before passing by without speaking a word. He seemed familiar, but Danica could not place him. She hoped she would've remembered doing something to merit such a look.

Mr. Peters either didn't notice the interaction, or didn't care to comment.

They reached the patio and the woman standing before them had a tranquil stillness. She wore a floral-print, A-frame dress and her blond hair held a few grey highlights that somehow added respectability to her general air. Danica assumed she must have been an actress; a safe bet in Los Angeles, but this case appeared to be based on objective facts. The woman extended a gloved hand.

"Thank you for coming. I'm Evelyn Alberts, Drake's mother." They shook hands.

The whole place smelled like lavender, and as Danica stared into Mrs. Alberts' glowing, pale skin, she refocused on Goals 1 and 6. None of the other goals came to mind.

"Let's have a seat," said Mrs. Alberts. She turned to the

table setting, but stopped short, then turned back to Mr. Peters.

Without a word of instruction, Mr. Peters moved faster than Danica thought him capable of moving. He speed-walked to the lounge area, grabbed a tray and made quick work of some plates and cups. He looked to Mrs. Alberts for approval. Danica couldn't see her eyes, but she must have telegraphed something, as Mr. Peters reached down to one of the lounge chairs and pulled up something glass and squat, put it on the tray and whisked away to the house.

"Previous guests, but I've saved room. I hope you have, too."

The table area cleared of any impropriety, Mrs. Alberts floated to the lounge chair facing away from the house. Her sitting technique, the encyclopedic entry for 'ladylike.'

Danica sat in an opposite chair, facing the house. At the backdoor, she could see Mr. Peters meet a woman in a maid's outfit, who took the tray from him.

"You have a really nice house." Small talk felt like exactly that; obvious and redundant. This woman knew she had a nice house. Anyone with eyes could tell she had a nice house.

Still, Mrs. Alberts provided a gracious, "Thank you so much." She looked like an actress, but that meant nothing in Los Angeles.

Mr. Peters returned with another man in a tux, both carrying trays. They set the contents out with efficiency: plates, utensils, and the most perfect sandwiches Danica had ever seen. They set out three plates. Mrs. Alberts must have seen Danica's curious look.

"I apologize. My husband will join us soon." Once the tea had been poured by the other tuxedo, both he and Mr.

Peters returned to their post by the house. Mrs. Alberts grinned and said, "Help yourself."

Danica had once learned a valuable lesson against gorging on food during important meetings, so she restrained herself, picked up a single sandwich and placed it on her plate, just to be polite.

Politeness overwhelmed. With the weight of the house, the grounds and the situation — not to mention her tenuous, under-defined relationship with Mrs. Alberts — Danica's arms filled with sweat. Regardless of receiving an invitation, she had still invaded an intimate space. This woman had lost her son, and for all her poise, she must have been devastated.

"When my mom passed away, the funeral was one of the worst parts." The words flew out of Danica's mouth on their own. Worse, the words brought friends she couldn't hold back. "Going through everything with my step-father and deciding what to display... You gotta decide things that never needed deciding before. It's a lot to deal with."

She wiped wetness from her cheek. Either Gabby's theater studies rubbed off on her and she hadn't realized what a fine actor she could be by putting on intimate one-to-one plays for single audience members, or real tears had emerged from her eyes. She wiped again and regretted her decision to ever come to the house.

Over her tea cup, she glanced at Mrs. Alberts, expecting to see a mix of horror and dubiety.

Instead, she saw only kindness.

"My dear," said Mrs. Alberts. "How long ago was that?"

"A couple years."

"What was the cause, if I could ask?"

"Cancer."

"No good has come of that yet. It took Mr. Alberts' father as well, and far too early, I'm afraid."

"You're holding up well. I mean, you look like you're holding up. I've never seen you before so I have no comparison." Danica told herself to shut up.

"He was a good boy. And a great student, with a keen mind for business and economics," said Mrs. Alberts. It sounded like a pronouncement.

Danica wiped her cheek again, angry at herself for abusing her mom's memory. In any form, sure, but for something as tacky as to manipulate a grieving mother so she could be persuaded to pay a cash prize for information.

Mrs. Alberts continued. "He was wonderful, as I'm sure you've found in your searches."

Danica considered herself lucky that she didn't have any food in her mouth, as she would have choked on it upon hearing 'searches.' There had been no emphasis placed on the word. It was said with a casual, friendly tone, as easy as talking about the weather. Yet Mrs. Alberts had assumed something. Correctly, too.

Mrs. Alberts took a deep breath and said, "We've done some of that ourselves, of course. The deciding everything. It is taxing."

"Is there a funeral?"

"The visitation is this Sunday."

The backdoor of the house opened, followed by a slam. A man stumbled through, the first person Danica had seen come through the door without wearing a staff uniform. Instead he wore a blue button up with no collar, tight around his stomach, and jeans which — thanks to Gabby's influence — Danica recognized as designer. He was sweaty with a square jaw and walked with anger in every step, like the patio walkway owed him money.

"Lousy extortionists," he said for everyone to hear.

"Drake," said Mrs. Alberts, "we have a guest."

"Another one? Cripes, Eve."

"This is Danica Luman. This is my husband, Drake Alberts."

Mr. Alberts glanced at Danica, then shook her hand with one of his meaty ones. An act of pure obligation. He hovered over the snacks.

"Can't we just give them the copy and be done with it?"

"Honey," said Mrs. Alberts.

"Honey," said Mr. Alberts back. Disappointed in the snack spread before him, he turned to his chair and looked disappointed at that, too. Something had been taken from it. He gave up looking with a "Flff" sound and sat. He turned his green eyes on Danica and said. "OK, fine. We need your services. Happy?"

Mrs. Alberts' head lowered a bit.

This was it. The big moment. Her golden opportunity.

Danica reminded herself to stay cool and to not blow this, the best chance at lining up this gig and she couldn't believe it had come so fast and that she had cried earlier but it could all be worth it and this was going to work and how long had she been sitting there saying nothing because it would be weird to sit without responding and so Danica said, "OK." Nailed it.

"You have the book, dear," said Mrs. Alberts.

Mr. Alberts looked around the table some more. "I don't have it."

"Well, I don't either."

"You had it for whatshisname. The last one."

"And you took it," said Mrs. Alberts, "when you went to talk to the gardeners."

"I didn't take it with me to the gardeners."

"I didn't say you took it to them. You took it with you on your way. It's probably by the door."

Mr. Alberts looked at the back door, then back to his wife. "I just sat down."

Mrs. Alberts turned her head only ten degrees away from her husband, yet the embarrassment read across the hills.

He rocked back then forward, propelling himself out of his chair and onto his feet. He waddled back down the path. Losing a child would certainly put stress on a person and a marriage, but this guy looked like he had been built to explode.

"I've always had an interest in journalism," said Mrs. Alberts.

Mrs. Alberts did everything with grace, even direct conversations away from her husband's abhorrent behavior through curiously divergent topics. Danica appreciated filling the silence, even when the statement came from out of the blue.

"Me, too," said Danica. A safe answer to a statement she hadn't expected to hear.

"I thought about studying it for a time, but I was young and interested in everything. More a flight of fancy. It takes passion, doesn't it?"

"It does."

Danica leaned to pour more tea, and a sneak look at Mr. Alberts. He had his back to them, speaking to Mr. Peters. His amount of pointing was reminiscent of his performance on the southwest lawn with the gardeners. How important was this book?

Mr. Peters nodded to his boss, then walked into the house.

"I'm sure you've probably seen how the news is covering our situation," said Mrs. Alberts.

"Some. I don't really watch TV news."

"It's best you don't."

Danica grinned and looked through her tea at the back door. Mr. Peters returned and handed something to Mr. Alberts. The rich guy turned and his face showed the first signs of a smile. As he walked back to the patio, his fat-finger hands held two items. One was a black, leather-looking book, zipped around the edges. It reminded Danica of the kind of strange pleather mini-cases her step-father Andrew used to organize his car insurance.

The other item was a tumbler. Brown liquid, no ice.

Mr. Alberts sipped as he sidled back to the group. By the time he reached his seat, the tumbler was nearly empty. With a plop, he landed back in his chair — emphasizing how he heroically traversed the hundred-and-eighty foot round trip to the door and back — and set the book on his knee.

"Distracted me. The damn gardeners, Eve."

"Drake."

"I'm just saying." He took another sip for courage, and found it. "If they worked as hard as they complained, then they'd have weeks of free time. Months of free time." He made certain the tumbler was empty.

Mr. Alberts fumbled through the book, his shoulders bunched at his neck. He muttered to himself, and Danica recognized the tone in his voice. She said a prayer, hoping he would take the issue no further, that he wouldn't say the thing she knew he was capable of saying, given his position, wealth, demographic and the combination of all three. He knew only privilege and money and was frustrated dealing with groundskeepers who — as far as Danica had seen — were predominantly Latino, and who — as far as she could estimate — didn't have to deal with the problems of the super rich.

"I should call deportation," said Mr. Alberts. "I can get five more like them from Home Depot. Right off the lot. Pay 'em in siestas and tacos and call it a day."

And there it was. Danica finished her tea and noticed Mrs. Alberts appeared less adept at handling her husband's casual racism than other social situations. Her cheeks burned red.

"We are very much invested in the responsibilities of great journalism." Mrs. Alberts motioned to Mr. Alberts, who in turn handed over the leather book. "If you just do your best, that's all we can ask, for the sake of our family,"

Mrs. Alberts withdrew a folded piece of white paper and handed it to Danica. It had a bulge to it.

Inside were several hundred dollar bills.

She held back from counting it right at the table, but could see at least eight bills in her hand. Actual money. Not a mirage, but real, spendable currency. It wouldn't cover all her debts, but it would help. She could use it to buy peace of mind, free herself up to focus, then get the case solved, get her reputation out there — to more of the Alberts' rich friends — and be on her way. Her wish had come true, and without having to ask for it. It had been so easy.

So easy, in fact, that Danica knew it wasn't true. As much as she hated looking a gift horse in the mouth, this partic-ular horse had cash to throw at under-qualified non-profes-sionals.

Her confusion must have played across the yard, because even Mr. Alberts could read it.

"Eve, you're too vague." He yanked the leather book back and opened it again.

"She understands, don't you?"

Danica's head made a single nodding motion.

"I'm sure your superiors have talked to you. About our situation?" said Mrs. Alberts.

She looked from one Alberts to the other. "Sure. But just to be on the safe side, could you let me know, you know, what you expect?"

Mr. Alberts laughed with spite and took back the leather book. "Told you. You beat around the bush too long, you get crap on your shoes." His words had begun to slur a bit.

"Drake..."

"She's not getting it. They can't all be like that last kid, gettin' it right off the jump. Here we go." He found what he had been searching for: another folded piece of paper. He handed it over with a dash of bitter 'told ya' so' toward Danica.

Inside the paper were five typed lines:

"Drake was a fine student studying economics and business.

"Drake's commitment to his studies kept him from doing many hobbies.

"Drake had many friends and tried to look for the best in everyone.

"Drake had no enemies.

"Drake had no significant other."

Danica re-read the lines and looked to Mrs. Alberts. Her docile face offered no help.

"You gotta stick to it is all," said Mr. Alberts.

She folded the paper and put it in her go bag.

"And you're not keeping that," he said.

"I can't?"

"Nope."

"Can I take a picture?"

"Nope."

"I have to memorize it?"

"There's a girl."

"You will be contacted again by your superiors at the Trojan," said Mrs. Alberts. "Should the occasion arise where you need to write about recent events, these notes will be your inspiration and direction."

"Still too vague, honey," said Mr. Alberts. No sweetness dripped from his words. "It's like show bibles. Like they have in movies and TV and that stuff. I thought Lara talked to all of you. Not Lara, that's not the name. Some girl name, starts with an 'L.' Either way, Eve: didn't that girl talk to these guys?"

Mrs. Alberts said nothing, so Mr. Alberts charged ahead.

"It's like the continuity. You can't go against continuity. Is that the word? 'Continuity?' Yeah." More and more, his words sloshed around his teeth.

He turned in his chair, square to Danica. "We gotta control this whole thing. The media's totally biased and they're going crazy. Making up all sorts of talk about...."

The pause lasted only a millisecond. Yet Danica noticed, enough to be surprised by what resembled human emotion — almost guilt — coming from Mr. Alberts. It all happened within the pause, disappearing as he concluded with the word:

"...him."

Mrs. Alberts quivered as well, in her eyes, but retained her poise. A professional hostess, wife and mourner. Even the tears falling down her cheek dropped with grace.

Danica looked again at the paper, committing as much to memory as possible. She focused on the big ideas.

"Just type something similar, OK? I thought college kids were supposed to be bright."

"I am." Not a total lie; barber college had students. "So. I'll write those. Those words."

"Yes."

"In a newspaper."

"Only if you have to."

"And consider that," Mrs. Alberts pointed to the money in Danica's fist, "a support of your studies."

"Just don't blab," said Mr. Alberts. "Some idiots, even the teachers, are blabbing. We don't need that, got it? Stick to the script."

Mr. Alberts didn't say 'We done here?' but he stood like he had.

Danica rose along with him, and so, too, did a nagging question. Somehow the Albertses had confused her for a USC journalism student, and that assumption begged further research, but the real question picking at Danica's conscience came running out of her mouth:

"What about finding the killer?"

Mr. Alberts looked even less comfortable than before the booze. He sighed and glanced at his wife. "That's a matter for the police."

"Sure, but I've heard, through the news," Danica added a bit to much emphasis on the last word to sound like a natural thing for her to say, "that they are moving kinda slow."

"Everything takes time," said Mr. Alberts.

"Have you, like, considered hiring. Somebody. To. Do. It. For you?" Not the smooth pitch she had imagined, but it got the point across, even to the five-o'clock-somewhere Mr. Alberts.

"My wife and I feel it's best to handle things through the LAPD."

"That is how we want it," said Mrs. Alberts. Period. End

of discussion. She checked her watch and said "Well..." as though she had another appointment to make.

Danica's grip around the money tightened. She stuffed it into the front pocket of her jeans.

Mrs. Alberts stood to say goodbye. Her husband pulled away, back toward the house, hoping the booze fairy would make another wish come true. She let this go and held out her gloved hand to Danica. "We appreciate your help in this matter, in coming out today, and for your discretion." It seemed like the same motions she performed for the goatee-rolled-up-sleeves guy when Danica arrived. "We'll see you at the visitation. Mr. Peters will show you out."

Mr. Alberts stood at the door again. A drink cart had appeared, manned by Mr. Peters. He looked like he was standing at attention, ready for Mr. Alberts' command.

But when she said, "Mr. Peters?" the butler did not move. Danica thought he nodded his head a little, but his legs remained motionless. The more she looked at him, the more he looked distracted, watching the patriarch pour another something-and-something into his glass.

"Hey." Danica forgot her place, but it did the trick. Mr. Peters' eyes focused toward the patio and he snapped to attention. When he arrived, he had the same weird look of guilt Danica saw on Mr. Alberts' face a moment ago.

Danica's spider-sense tingled. Everything felt staged, rehearsed, but the seams still showed. "Mrs. Alberts, are you certain that... I mean, I can do what I can. But if you want things found out quickly...."

"Not necessary," said Mrs. Alberts. "We have complete faith in the police."

"Is that just what Mr. Alberts wants, or..."

She stopped. She had crossed a line, and sensed it

immediately. Mrs. Alberts' face narrowed as she said, "It's the way things are done."

Mr. Peters said, "This way," and Danica followed him on the same south-side-of-the-house path. They walked in silence.

The valet stood next to her Accord in the front driveway, a big smile on his face. "Would you like to start it yourself, miss?"

She did (only five tries!) and rolled back down the hill, through the front gates and into the neighborhood. The smell of the cash oozed through her denim pocket. Panic came over her as she imagined the unlikely yet terrifying scenario that the wind would pick up, whoosh inside her car, withdraw the money from her jeans and carry it to the ocean.

Danica pulled over and closed the windows. She counted the cash. Nine hundred dollars, all crisp and new. She folded it twice and stuffed it back in her pocket, then added an old napkin from the floor for anti-wind cushion. All for safe keeping, she told herself. She had not verbally agreed to anything, but such agreement did not seem to be required by the Albertses. She locked the doors.

Her mind flooding, Danica grabbed her notebook to get down as many thoughts as possible, to try and grab anything resembling sense. Too many to write. Where to start? The rules on the first page mocked her.

Another car — a more recent model Honda Accord — turned the corner. The driver looked younger than Danica. Another young white boy in a baseball cap. He looked at his phone as he passed her.

She recognized him from USC. That kid in the stupid plastic visor from the school newspaper table. He worked for the paper, and not in the way that Danica did.

The image of the boy in the goatee with the rolled up sleeves returned to her memory, as did the memory of where Danica first saw him: He was the boy who brought that Baby Face the news anchor a drink. The wannabe intern. He must have worked for the paper, too.

In fifteen minutes the visor-turned-cap boy drove his car to the Alberts gate and disappeared. He'd probably come out a couple hundred richer, too.

Questions mounted like a pile of ham next to a deli meat slicer. She tried to articulate any of them, to look at matters objectively. She struggled as bits of information flew around: the Alberts' faith in the LAPD, the other USC students visiting the house, their control of the tiny student-run media, of D3's image, Mr. Peters' weird attitude, getting invited to the visitation, Mrs. Alberts' protective nature of her husband, and Mr. Alberts' aggressive behavior, drinking and racism. On top of everything, she had a job at a paper she didn't apply for at a school where she didn't belong.

She wanted to write it all down and make sense of it. Instead, all she wrote was: "What the hell just happened?"

CHAPTER THIRTEEN

SUNDAY, **March 5, 1995** — The Past. Central Illinois.

Danica's hometown of Rio, Illinois, was tiny. Really tiny. And not in that "Anything smaller than Chicago" kind of tiny, like Rockford, where there were movie theaters and possibly a college. In Danica's time, Rio had only two hundred and ten residents. The single gas station provided all in-town opportunities for fuel, food and entertainment. Enlightenment was sought elsewhere, and included a fair amount of driving. With only a handful of kids in town, Rio joined a school district with surrounding towns, all of which were larger.

In high school, Danica did not grow close to anyone; she had "friends," sure, but they were more like acquaintances. People knew her birthday, but everyone knew everyone's birthday. They knew everything. She traveled by bus to school, which provided plenty of chances for added misery, and by her junior year, she'd had enough. She had no ideas for her future but to leave.

The school counselor offered a simple plan of applying to colleges, none of which accepted her. The paths taken by her Acquaintance Friends didn't cross her mind. Her father was no supplier, and her step-dad had his hands full already. The Get Out Plan required more planning.

Her mom cut hair. She saw no need to look beyond it. "Hair'll always grow," she'd say, reminding everyone of her job's secure position. Danica had years of informal instruction from her mom (on her insistence), and had observed the work for longer, absorbing knowledge through osmosis at the in-home salon. She could run clippers by fourteen and do light styling and dyes by sixteen. By her junior year — the year of the Get Out Plan — Danica had backed her way into the only thing close to a viable career path in support of her goal.

Desperate for cash and direction, she relented to her mother's passive-aggressive pressure and took a hairstyling class at Hawkshead. She worked in the salon to build credit hours, until one day, one of her Acquaintance Friends (Adrianne Gullinger) made the bold, brave decision to allow Danica to do her cut.

Since the Sweetheart Sock Hop, Danica had received a few tiny glimpses from people's minds; little flashes here and there, out of her control, and nothing as intense as with Travis Whatshisname. That was until cutting Adrianne Guillinger's hair.

Those visions came in a flood. She clenched her eyelids shut. When that made nothing better, she opened them and saw even more. The walls melted and the world filled with ice cold water, she floated below the surface and human heads and feet swam past her. Something turned the kaleidoscope and she fell into a cavern, glided like an eagle, and dropped through colored rain washing everything in thick paint.

Then, as quickly as she'd disappeared, she returned to the home salon. Her mom was holding her by the arms, shaking her and staring into her eyes and saying her name. She made some kind of excuse to Adrianne and moved Danica to the hallway between the salon and their garage.

Danica leaned against the meat refrigerator. It felt cold and unnecessary in winter clinging to March. She wanted to climb in it.

"It was nothing," she said.

"Bull. It was those visions again, wasn't it?"

It had been a year since the Sweetheart Sock Hop, and Danica had convinced herself that what happened then was just a freak accident. And that every other little mini-flash since then had just been "teenager stuff." Here, in the hall, she thought of making up a crazy excuse of getting her period and losing a tooth all at the same moment, but her mother could already see right through her.

Danica told her the truth, as best as she could recall the living horror she had seen from Adrianne's brain. She described the helplessness of being trapped inside whatever unknown hell she'd entered, and how she had been pulled from the real world and into someplace else.

Her mother listened. She reached into one of the winter coats hanging on the hooks, pulled out a pack of cigarettes, and removed two. Gave one to Danica, one for herself. She had every right to chalk it up to raising a teenager, and Danica wouldn't have blamed her. It all sounded like drivel, or rambling idiocy, or a psychotic break. Danica wished those were the case; at least they could be explained.

Danica's mom blew out clouds and thought. "So you need control."

"I need it to go away."

"I don't know if we can manage that. But I think control might be in our reach. Come here."

"Uh-uh."

"We gotta go back in there."

"Let her out the back. No charge."

"We gotta."

"But what if it happens again?"

"They can't make you do things you don't wanna do. You're in charge."

"No, I'm not."

"You will be. I have an idea. Let's go," said her mom, and they did, back into the salon.

To Adrianne's credit, she hadn't ran out or called the cops or made a big deal out of the matter. Instead, she sat and read People Magazine, looking up only when Danica and her mom returned. As Danica's mom made an excuse, blaming it on poor lunch decisions, Adrianne nodded like she understood. She might have, or she didn't think about it; she was only sixteen. What the hell did she have to care about?

"So let's try this again," said Danica's mom. She played with Adrianne's brown curls and complimented how lush it felt.

"What are we doing today?"

Adrianne began describing a style where the back of her neck stayed short and held the back hair off her neck. As she spoke, Danica's mom took her daughter's hand and directed it to Adrianne's hair.

The world disappeared and the images appeared, but not in a flood. Danica could hear Adrianne's voice echoing somewhere far away, and before her was a clear picture: it was Madonna from "Dick Tracy." She leaned across a desk, slinking around for almost no good reason other than it was just a Madonna thing to do. And her blonde locks danced all around her head, held up by movie magic.

Danica recognized the scene, but the hair looked different from the movie. It turned brown, Adrianne's color. And it seemed to grow longer in the front, with a straightness dangling from her forehead. A version of Adrianne appeared over Madonna's face; more slender, with a thinner chin, but it was her. And she had the hair.

Danica released her grip and looked at her mom.

"Think you can do it?" said her mom.

Danica nodded and got to work.

The fact that Adrianne's haircut turned out to be a failure had more to do with Danica's lack of scissors experience than with her newfound abilities to focus the visions. In the end, her mom swept in to steal a C+ from the jaws of an F, and they didn't charge the full rate for Adrianne's willingness to be a guinea pig.

Cutting-wise, it was rough.

Vision-handling-wise, it was encouraging.

Danica racked up hours through Hawkshead's program, all the while working as an assistant for (and with) her mother. They called it a "consulting position," and kept the other detail between themselves.

CHAPTER FOURTEEN

THURSDAY, August 28, 2008, 8:04PM. Earl's World of Curls and Amateur Internet Research Lab.

In addition to being difficult to pluralize, the Albertses were one of those families with lots of money but little celebrity. Danica found some internet presence, but Mr. and Mrs. Alberts had no social media outlets.

They were wealthy, and other wealthy people seemed to know them, but nobody made a big deal about it. They owned property, but who didn't in Bel Air? Their largest online footprint was the Alberts Family Foundation, a charitable arm of their business, Alberts Real Estate. Nothing had been stolen, recently or ever of note. Never been plagued by extortion. No enemies or rivals to speak of.

Confirmed by a sparse IMDb page, Mrs. Alberts had been an actress. She originally studied medicine aiming on surgery before the acting bug bit. Side roles were the biggest she ever got, leading up to a few lead-ish parts on two series that never graduated past the pilot stage. She married Mr.

Alberts and virtually disappeared into the new role. They were contributors to many organizations in Bel Air and the Los Angeles area, particularly to the LAPD.

Of the entire family, Mr. Alberts' father — Drake the First — had the most substantial existence; quite an accomplishment for a man dead nearly ten years. Drake the First helped build up Bel Air after World War II. He was a major contributor to the Bel Air Country Club, helping it expand and stay private. Pictures existed of him, all sepia toned and formal, and they came to the forefront of most Google searches, regardless of the criteria. Danica found a picture of him with the Mulholland family (one of those poses where everyone has a suit, a shovel, and a smile). The accompanying story dealt with a water project for the San Fernando Valley. Another picture showed Grandpa Alberts standing among orange groves. Some titles mentioned dignitaries, leaders of industry and the mayor of the time.

Another was on a fire engine. That one had him pointing and shouting to people, with a face he passed down to his son. The article detailed a rally around Bel Air breaking free from Los Angeles to become its own city.

Every article about D3's murder described the family in the same way: prominent. And D3's murder appeared to be the only traumatic moment the prominent family endured, at least since the death of D1.

One such article went thus: "Despite his prominent family, Drake III lived a humble student life. Splitting time between studying, on-campus living and visiting his family, he studied furiously everywhere he went, always preparing to eventually take the reins of the Alberts legacy."

Others such went like these thus:

"...with little time for hobbies, Drake lived a quiet life

studying economics, preparing to take over his prominent family's business..."

"...friends with so many, Drake's passion for his studies kept him from hobbies..."

"...heir to the prominent Alberts family fortune, Drake III lived to fulfill his business legacy, and grow the name to help build his hometown..."

It all confirmed Danica's suspicion: she knew the Albertses paid journalism students off (or at least paid off people they thought to be students), but it seemed they reached out to professional media, too and may have for years.

This exposure to the Alberts Family's history with the news left Danica with two fears:

1. They seemed powerful enough to change stories, in some kind of effort to direct the stories (presumably) in their favor.
2. She had not figured out how these changes actually benefited them beyond just fitting their own quirky self image.
3. She somehow needed to get a job at the USC newspaper in order to write a story good enough to appease them.

OK: three fears.

These discoveries were made at work while letting the Gene Machine play receptionist and neglecting a few customers here and there. After the third "Not quite that way" from a customer, she set up a Google news alert for herself and gave her mind a break. Just to concentrate on hair.

By the end of the night, she felt like she had for the last

few days: tired without being sleepy. And hungry. After closing up, she drove to Ralphs in search of cheap food.

She entered and took a hand basket, then placed the basket into a shopping cart and pushed ahead. The smallness of the hand basket allowed her to remain thrifty while the cart's wheels allowed her to be lazy.

Cereals represented economy. You could buy a lot at one time and parse it out over the course of many meals. Even dishwashing came easier with cereal. She strolled past two customers and toward the breakfast aisle, searching for Cap'n Crunch, then for the Ralph's version of Cap'n Crunch.

Her phone buzzed. A notification. "POLICE INSIST THEY HAVE SUSPECTS IN DRAKE ALBERTS MURDER CASE."

Danica's eyes glazed. She had read so much already. The pull of actually getting some new information — let alone info about a suspect — gave her some hope, only to have it dashed by the story's content. It was a story about a story, with the promise of more story to come. The police held a briefing which got reduced to "We're workin' on it." The sentiment of the article felt like more publicity from the Alberts' media wing, and her thoughts ran to the cash in her pocket. The Alberts family must have employed publicists or assistants to direct stories in their favor, even ones they didn't have to bribe. Why didn't Danica meet with them?

And was it a bribe? Danica had never been bribed before, and if this really was the first time, she had sucked at picking up on the signals. It felt more like a pay-off. Was that any different? Normally, she thought, a bribe would mean paying someone to do something they wouldn't do. Something illegal. Crooked judges got bribes from gangsters, that sort of thing. A pay off implied deviant agreement.

Her head hurt and the panic hit her again, like a bad

dream where she'd forgotten to do her homework. Did she have a due date for this article she had no business writing? Did it have to be any good, as long as it incorporated their notes? Would she have to give back the money if she failed to live up to whatever standards they had for her? Would she burn in hell for taking the money of a grieving — though very wealthy — family under false pretenses?

On the plus side, her Google alert seemed to work.

She had drifted away from the cereal and approached the pancake mixes. She looked to recalibrate herself and caught the eye of the young-ish, shlubby man at the end of the aisle. As soon as she looked at him, he ducked his head down. Like he had been looking at her.

He tried to sneak another look, then grabbed what must have been a fascinating box of raisin bran.

Danica didn't need creeps. "Hello?"

His skin was perfect, young and firm. He grimaced and said, "I've seen you before, right?"

"Maybe."

"Like at school, right?"

Her fingers twinged. He looked to be in his late teens, possibly Korean. He wore a faux-faded shirt with "CAST OF THE CENTURY" across the chest.

"Maybe." Give him rope and let him climb.

"Yeah, I thought so."

"I don't know your name."

"Benji."

"Danica."

"My parents live out here," said Benji, "so I'm just, y'know... That's why I'm all the way out here." He set the raisin bran back on the shelf. "I knew I knew you. I had those vibes, y'know? Like deja-vu vibes?"

"Yeah, me, too." A complete lie, but enough to keep this

kid interested. Since he did not look like a hair dresser, the only other "school" she could think where they might have interacted was USC.

Rats, she had barber class in the morning. She was gonna be so tired.

"I think it's in Science I."

Definitely USC. By the smell of him, likely a Freshman. Maybe in the theater, as part of this "CAST OF THE CENTURY" cast. Judging from the way he refused to hold eye contact with her for very long, Danica assumed Benji didn't have much experience talking to girls. She decided to take advantage of that.

"Did you, um, hear about this Drake Alberts guy?" she said.

Benji looked at his shoes, then to her, then beyond her, pretending to be interested in the guy at the other end of the aisle by the syrups. But his raging virginity could not hold up against Danica's moderate charms. He said, "Yeah," then laughed. Awkward.

"Scary, right?" Maybe this kid knew more about Drake, knew where he was or where he'd been the night of his death. Maybe he partied with him, or got him to buy beer, or rushed some frat or anything. Anything would be great.

The guy picking syrups must have made his choice, he'd left them alone, and Benji focused.

"Yeah, scary," he said.

"I'm probably going to the visitation," said Danica.

"For real?"

"Yeah. Seems like the right thing to do."

"Yeah," said Benji the Student. He took two steps closer and whispered, "You think Beckett will go?"

Her lips tightened, preventing "KEITH BECKETT!!!!!" from screaming out for the whole of Ralph's to hear. This guy knew Beckett — an actual lead! Danica licked her lips and tried to calm down.

Then tried again.

Then said, "I don't know."

Flustered, she couldn't get anything better out. She feigned a loss for words, hoping the kid would do the thinking for both of them.

And he did. "Yeah. That whole tribute thing? It's weird, man. I don't know. If I was him, y'know, and I'd been the last to see Drake, I wouldn't wanna draw attention like that, y'know?"

"Riiiiiiight," said Danica.

"I guess it's just a rumor, y'know? Maybe someone else saw Drake after. But it's just weird."

"You notice a lot of stuff, huh?"

His cheeks went red. Benji the Blabby Student stood a little taller and opened his big helpful mouth. "It's just... y'know, I'm not saying anything. I just wouldn't have done that, if I was in that situation."

"For sure."

Benji the Blabby Virgin Student looked up and around the aisle again, past Danica, back to the cereals he'd once found so interesting, then at Danica's face.

"I better head out," he said. "See you around." He turned and hustled toward the back of the store, faster than Danica thought necessary for a grocery store.

She turned back and caught a glimpse of the syrup-shopping guy, just leaving the syrup section. Again. For the second time in two minutes.

She hustled to the back, where Benji had just been. He was gone. Three people in an aisle a moment ago, one a chatty chatter, then suddenly she was alone again.

Danica dropped the cereal on the floor. It busted and

spilled, but she kept running to the front, to the exit. The doors were still open. People shouted, but she focused on the flap-flap sounds of sneakers hitting the pavement outside. By the time she made it through the door, she saw nobody. The parking lot stood empty except for a few cars, including her own.

Her car looked odd. It had acquired many dents and bumps over the years, and bright lights did no favors for its complexion on a normal day. But even in the dim parking light, she could see new features on the doors, running over its entire side, back and forth.

She moved closer.

Along the driver's side, several large scratches ran from headlight to tail light. She felt them. Keyed. The scars ran deep, back and forth, save for the words "KEEP AWAY" on the hood. The tires earned a few cuts as well, but the rubber had proved too tough for them.

Apparently, without hardly trying, she'd made an enemy.

CHAPTER FIFTEEN

FRIDAY, **August 29, 2008. 9:40AM. Academy Barber School, Van Nuys.**

The Academy filled its space with chairs, both barber and otherwise. Four rows, with a center row holding double-sided stations, ran the length of the building. It smelled like burned plastic.

Danica spun in a chair. Her instructor encouraged another classmate to "pull, pull, pull" as she attempted a high-top fade on a willing victim. The man in the chair dressed like a surfer, but with thick plastic glasses. He looked like he might have gotten bad haircuts his entire life. He had come to the right place.

Her news notifications had been silent all night and into the morning. Radio silence from all fronts. The more she wanted to solve the case, the fewer people she found to be concerned with it. Trust in the police was one thing, but the Alberts couple's faith verged on cultish. They appeared completely not crazy, which given the circumstances, seemed crazy.

She excused herself to go smoke, went to the parking lot and dialed Malcom Fine's office.

"Mr. Fine isn't available at the moment." Even without seeing Danica, Maggie sounded irritated at her. "I suppose you want to leave a message."

"I know he hides in there sometimes. I have to talk to him."

"Mr. Fine is not available."

"I heard you the first time, but come on...."

"He is not. Available."

"Do you have any idea when he'll become available?"

"Haven't the foggiest."

"Look, Maggie," she said, "You remember me? Young white woman with short hair and a can-do attitude?"

"I remember a young woman with short hair." Ice cold.

"I might be in over my head with this case I took on."

"'Might be?'"

"The family involved paid me to fix a newspaper article."

"Huh?"

"They think I'm a USC student. For journalism. They're paying off writers to control their story."

"And they think you're a news writer?"

"Yes."

"Why would they think that?"

"OK, I've been sneaking around and letting people believe what they want to about me..."

"...Alright..."

"Running down leads. But they don't lead anywhere. And now I'm being followed. Harassed. I'm being harassed."

"Did something happen?" The slimmest sliver of concern infiltrated Maggie's voice.

"Some kids — younger guys. I think they're actual USC students. One distracted me while the other keyed my car."

"Are you OK?" Again, a sliver.

"I'm fine. But I think I need some professional insight."

"Well, Mr. Fine doesn't usually give consultations for free."

"I realize that, but I was thinking it could be a professional courtesy thing. One PI to another."

The words sat in silence, with an echo of fakeness reverberating all around. She thought the line went dead, and the longer the silence lasted, the more Danica wished it really had. Self doubt, you won again.

Maggie finally, mercifully, cut the quiet. "You said you have a lead?"

"Something."

"What?"

"Keith Beckett."

"Who's that?"

"I think he's a teacher at USC."

"And how's he a lead?"

"The kids who keyed my car mentioned him."

"OK."

"And Beckett was quoted in the news story, talking about Drake."

"OK."

"And," this was the real kicker, the one that would convince everyone of Danica's detective prowess, "his title was edited."

"I'm sorry, what?" said Maggie, less than convinced.

"He's a professor. And the article originally printed his title. Actually, it only said 'Associate of.' But I think it used to say his full title, and then it was taken out."

"So?" Maggie said.

'So?!' thought Danica 'So, that's suspicious. So, the Alberts family pays to have stories changed to fit their needs and they might have been behind that change. So, Beckett supposedly made a tribute poster to D3 and the kid who seemed trustworthy until he helped key her car said it seemed weird.'

Maggie's 'So?' stood a bit longer before she asked, "What's this Beckett guy a professor of?"

"...Business?"

A loud semi truck rolled down the street, shaking the phone in Danica's hand. This lead didn't sound like much, especially when spoken out loud to the most cynical woman on the planet.

Danica internalized the unspoken criticism and spoke again.

"I should try to find out more about him."

"Yes," said Maggie. "Then maybe you might call us back. Mr. Fine might be available. Maybe." She hung up without saying goodbye.

The Academy Barber School instructor tapped on the window next to Danica's head. The instructor pointed at her wrist, and even though she didn't wear a watch, the message was clear.

Danica jogged back inside, made some apologies and took her assignment: a simple beard trim with a straight razor, no guard. Passing this lesson — along with the final written exam — would qualify her for full barber status.

The razor hung heavy in her fingers. Danica had trimmed beards hundreds of times in class, but today her hand felt weak.

Her instructor asked if something was wrong. She said something was, and that she needed to go to the bathroom.

Forty seconds later, in the bathroom stall, she dialed the phone again.

"USC Business department. How can I help you?"

"I'd like to speak to Professor Beckett, please."

"I'm sorry, who?"

'My biggest lead, you thick-necked, Reagan-worhsipping business jock,' she thought. 'I know he knows something, or knows where something is, or knew Drake and knows why his own job title got edited out of the Times article, and you're gonna get me in touch with him.'

"Professor Keith Beckett," she said instead.

The boy from USC Business groaned and said, "We don't have a Professor Beckett in the business department. Sure you got the name right?"

"I'm sure."

"Welp...."

Danica couldn't see this guy through the phone, but was certain he was smile-shrugging like a party guest who accidentally clogged the toilet. She hung up.

The beard trimming waited for her. Patiently, she noticed. Most people who sat for free training cuts were patient, but given the circumstances of a no-guard razor trim, she always forgave people for looking a bit jumpy. This guy wasn't jumpy. His thick beard grew auburn around his cheeks and he grinned when she returned.

That Benji kid knew Professor Beckett. Knew *of* him, or said he did. Had him for class. He knew where his office was on campus, so it must have been in a public-type place, with some access to the outside world.

She finished the trim, apologized for the cut (only one!), cleaned her hands, returned to the parking lot and, once again, dialed her phone.

"Malcom Fine's office."

"Me again, Maggie."

Maggie sighed and Danica pressed on.

"That Benji kid knows who Keith Beckett is."

"Who is Benji?"

"One of those dudes from the grocery store."

"The boy who keyed your car?"

"He was the distraction. He knows who Keith Beckett is."

"But who is Benji?"

"I just told you."

"Right, but who *is* he?"

"He's... some guy."

"You gotta describe him. And you gotta start thinking of this stuff on your own. Before you call."

"I know, I know. He's younger than me. So twenty maybe. Taller. Like 5-foot-10. Dark hair."

"Skin color? Race?"

"I think he might have been Korean."

In all the focus on Benji, Danica had forgotten her point. She said, "Beckett's not a business professor."

"OK...."

"I thought he was. But I just called the USC business school and they didn't know him."

"Uh-huh."

"Drake was a business major — and his parents sure want us all to know about his 'passion for business.' But Beckett's the one who gave a sweet quote in the news about him, all heartbroken and sad. And he wasn't even his professor?"

Maggie said nothing.

"Don't you think that's weird?"

"I suppose."

"It is," said Danica.

"If you say so."

"It is!"

"Wait. Didn't you say something about the family changing news stories?"

"Yes."

"..."

"But why would they change that? His title?"

"..."

"Is Malcom Fine available yet?"

"Not yet."

"Thanks." She hung up again. No point in even pretending. Instead of going back in, she stayed in the lot and dialed a new number.

"USC Information? This is Kelly? How can I help you?" The young woman who answered sounded *very* young, with each sentence ending in a higher register so she sounded unsure of everything.

"Hi. I'm looking for a student."

"Okay?"

"His name's Benji."

"Benji? Benji What?"

"Yeah, not sure what else to tell you. I think he's into business. I think he was Korean."

"Okay."

"I'm not trying to be terrible here. Sorry. He really was."

"Um..."

"Look. I saw this guy in Ralph's last night. We talked."

"Oh."

"Not like that. He was distracting me while his buddy keyed my car."

"Yeah?"

"Yeah."

"...Why?"

"That's what I wanna find out. By talking to him."

"I'm Korean," said the young woman.

"Great."

The young woman didn't say anything else.

"I'm not sure I—"

"You think because I'm Korean that I know all the Koreans at USC?"

"No, I... I don't know you— You're the student directory."

"Yes."

"That's why you should know. Or could know. Not the other reason. Or not just because of that..." Danica stopped. Talking wasn't working so great.

But she tried one more time, just to prove she was wrong.

"I haven't given you enough information, have I?"

"Not really."

"Sorry," said Danica and hung up. She checked the time. Fifteen more minutes of class, then an afternoon off before her late shift. She'd have to fill her car's tank.

At least, she'd have to fill it with enough gas to get to USC and back.

CHAPTER SIXTEEN

11:11AM. USC.

Danica had a little voice inside her head. Not in a weird, psychic powers kind of way, but in a normal person kind of way. The kind of voice everyone has, one that told her to do this or that, don't do something else, or what she had done was wrong.

More often than not, that's just the kind of thing the voice told Danica. That whatever she was doing was wrong. And there, sitting in her car with a ragged copy of *The Invisible Man* in her hands saved from between the back seats, the little voice cast doubt upon her choices.

'You're holding that thing too high,' it said. 'Blocking your face, so obvious.'

'Some people do it like this,' she told herself back.

'Nobody reads books in cars.'

'Lots of people do.'

'Yeah. Students,' said the little voice. 'But nobody believes you're college age.'

'That dude in Ralph's did.'

'For a hot minute. And he wasn't that bright. Plus he was helping attack your car.'

'The Albertses think I'm college age.'

'They'll figure it out. And soon.'

'Let's just keep this up,' Danica said to herself. 'We're doing OK.'

'Keep up what? You're nowhere near finding Beckett. And hanging around the theater parking lot, you're just expecting that Benji guy to wander by. Like he's gonna look exactly the same, in the same shirt or something?'

'I'd recognize him. I gotta try something.'

'Do you really think Beckett's a suspect? Really? I mean... *really* really? We're here on pure hunch.'

Nobody in or out of Danica's brain spoke for a bit. After a while — after a few more students who were not Benji strolled by — the voice returned.

'Go back to Earl's. You know how to do that. Carla and Gene are gonna be pissed if you're late.'

The worry and stress settled deeper into Danica's chest. She really had hoped to just run into Benji, or his syrup-shopping friend, track them down and learn a little more about student life. Or just punch them in their faces. She had yet to be that lucky — why would luck start now? She hated to admit it to anyone, especially to this nagging little jerk, but hunch really was all she had.

'Just turn on the car and let's get outta here.'

She took the advice, a little, setting down her book and opening her email. In it she found a couple spams and her first blast from the USC Business Club.

The Business Club newsletter — in Danica's limited exposure, which, to be fair, was extremely limited, so maybe there were times when things were different and this was a one-time status — sucked. Danica spent most of the time deciphering the jargon only to learn absolutely nothing. It mentioned a few mixers and "networking opportunities," but even those didn't sound enjoyable. It held no mention of Drake III and offered no clear paths for Danica to infiltrate their inner circle. Finding no Keith Beckett mentioned either fit the trend.

In fact, Danica decided it was a trend. The absence of Professor Beckett felt too consistent to be accidental.

'Or he's just ineffectual,' said the voice.

She ignored the voice.

It persisted.

'Don't just sit in the car.'

'OK,' she said to herself.

Danica put away her phone, pushed aside the book she hadn't read, adjusted her go-bag to "Student Position," formed a quick alibi ("My roommate changed my access code and stole my ID so now I'm lost") and walked toward the thick of campus. Either she'd bump into Benji, or find out why Beckett had been wiped clean from the school; either way, she would get some answers.

With few students around, the place was a ghost town. Their little voices probably had them going to fun places, or learning, or making out, or whatever students did. Likely making out.

'You're not gonna bump into anybody,' said her voice. 'This is like your idea where you would touch random people's heads. Actually, it's worse.'

The path forked and she took the right hand side, toward the trees. The image from the map she'd promptly lost grew fuzzy.

'And I wanna make this clear, before you get too far: the newspaper office won't let you in.'

'I'm just taking in the sights.'

'Theater will be the same story.'

'Not worried about them.'

'Then why'd you park so far away? Answer: because you thought you'd park by the theater building to meet Theater People.'

'Shut up.'

'That's what you thought.'

'We! That's what we thought. You're me.'

'Speak for yourself.'

Fall heat dripped from the trees. She heard student voices, but saw no actual bodies to go with them.

The little voice had drawn her out and left her exposed in the middle of nothing useful.

The little voice sounded more and more like her step-father.

Andrew Luman had always been a part of Danica's life. He married Danica's mother when Danica was in first grade, and formally adopted the girl a year later. She and her mother took his surname from then on. Andrew was steady, grumpy and tall. Danica couldn't remember a time when he spoke of his own family with any kind of fondness. He referred to his own parents as "Father" and "Mother," and that only came from the few occasions he ever mentioned them. He had no siblings, and she never heard him talk about any extended family.

As Danica grew into high school age, the differences between her and Mr. Luman grew more and more distinct. His type of compassion was far too conservative for her, a burgeoning feminist and established Angry Teen.

Fights erupted slowly, carrying the momentum and heat of oozing lava. She found his contradictions frustrating; he encouraged Danica to learn a trade "she could use" in cutting hair, yet refused to let her cut his own. It was a simple style — a "standard man" with short sides, a part and no product within seventy-five feet. Even early in her career, she could have done it in her sleep.

"No way," he said. Flat and to the point.

"It'll grow back," said Danica's mom. "And she'll do great, but even if... it'll grow back."

He sat in his chair, facing the TV. An edited-for-TBS version of "The Sting" on screen. Young Robert Redford walked toward his apartment, with clarinet and piano music playing him along, forlorn.

"Maybe later," said Andrew, meaning "never." Again, contradiction. He often spoke about getting her out of the house and to have her own life (he certainly didn't act like he wanted her around his house), but he wouldn't support training that would actually *help* her achieve that progression.

On screen, Redford stopped dead in his tracks. A piece of paper lay on the ground outside his door.

"What's with the paper?" said Mrs. Luman.

"You remember, Georgina. There's guys after him."

Danica's mom sat on the arm of the sofa, engrossed in On-Screen Redford's blue eyes. They looked scared as he turned and ran from the apartment and the paper on the floor. Two men burst out of Redford's apartment and chased him into the street. Just like they had every other time Andrew Luman watched the movie.

"Mom. Focus." Danica had been forced to watch Mr. Luman's movies every time he wanted to watch anything. This provided her with another point of frustration in how he rewatched movies so built upon twists that, upon the multiple viewings he had certainly put in, he could predict the entire story beat for beat.

Andrew turned to Danica, and her mom said, "Dani, please."

Danica took the cue. To leave it alone.

Her mom's look carried the little voice of Andrew with it. She slogged to her room and closed the door behind her. She knew her mom loved her, but stories were her weakness. Her mom's empathy extended to everyone and everything, including someone as emotionally stunted as Andrew.

That same year, Danica's senior year, her mom's diagnoses got progressively worse. As they did, Danica's resentment toward Andrew grew and grew. When they got the latest bit of bad news from a doctor's visit, Danica imagined him saying something like "Should'a eaten better."

Keep to yourself. Don't just go doing stuff just to do it and end up making things worse. Act with a purpose. Live right, be right.

He was full of sayings that meant nothing to tumors. Danica expected him to cut out soon, too, when it seemed clear that things would get much worse. She almost would have understood; nobody wants to be part of a downward slide. He could have ducked out, no problem.

But when the situation became terminal, Mr. Andrew Luman became a trooper, if a cold one. He stayed with her mom the entire time, keeping her company and helping her live something resembling a life. More than Danica had done. She moved out right after senior year, right before chemo, and fled two-thousand miles away.

The cancer took her mom and guilt wrecked Danica to her core. She had moved to California, lived with Tommy and couldn't pop in for the kinds of pick-me-up visits she later convinced herself would have saved her mother.

Mr. Luman gave updates by letter, without embellishment, limited to facts. Straightforward and to the point. His routines and ruts provided reliability; lame for parenting, but essential for caring for the sick. And when she died, he paid for Danica's plane ticket back.

He did not cry. Not on the phone when he called to tell her, not when Danica arrived home, not even at the funeral in the church down the road. This infuriated Danica. This woman had been her entire family and the only person who knew her secrets, and not just the supernatural one. He had taken a piece of her mom for himself, made her his own, and didn't possess the good manners to openly show the world the impact of his loss. It made him seem cavalier, like he was holding back his emotions in case his next wife would get turned off by seeing a man emote.

Standing at the front of the church, shaking hands to a town of randos, she stared at Andrew's statue face. The fury rising inside her throat. She could tell the screaming was coming, ready to explode all over him. The only thing that held back full-on war was the image of her mom interjecting. Danica and Andrew were equals to Georgina, who wanted peace above all else. She pictured her mom saying 'Dani,' one of the last times she could place her voice.

Still, the fury had to go somewhere, and it ended up going to Danica's feet. She marched down the line, passing several mourners and wrapped her arms around Andrew. The hug landed stiff and one-sided. The man didn't move, even with a grieving twenty-something tangled around his torso. The tears burned her eyes and she squeezed her lids shut. Her arms tightened around his nice flannel shirt. He smelled like Old Spice. Her fingers drifted up and met the hair on his neck.

She saw her mom — his image of her. Less clear than a memory, More of a feeling. Subjective. Idyllic.

Danica pulled her fingers back and returned to reality. Something rested on the top of her head. It was Andrew's chin. He had placed it there, holding her fuzz-top head in the crook of his neck. A head hug. It wasn't anything anyone would have mistaken with a tender embrace, but those people didn't know Andrew Luman. For Andrew Luman, this was equivalent to a touchdown dance at the Super Bowl (something he didn't approve of either).

"I'm with you," he said. She wanted to fight it off, to hug it, strangle it, make it sound nicer. The voice locked into her head that day and stayed with her. Her Little Andrew Voice.

After returning to LA, and for the next couple years, staying in touch with Andrew proved to be an uphill battle. He refused to own a smartphone, and his dinosaur of a computer self-retired. On the other hand, he helped her buy her iPhone.

They had shared so much, but the distance between them and the step-relationship and their personalities amounted to a tremendous challenge, too powerful for a once-every-three-months-maybe letter to conquer. He kept up Georgina's tradition of sending Christmas cards, almost like a tease that he might one day become a full human. They were sparse ("Happy Holidays" and a signature).

The last time they saw each other was Thanksgiving of 2006, and even then he made his perennial offer to pay for her flight back home.

"Offer always stands. Any time you want to fly, say the word."

Despite the years, Danica could still picture him: sitting

in his chair, watching some old movie he had seen a million times before and probably already owned on VHS. He looked happy. The movies had twists he could anticipate.

Leaning against a campus bench, the little voice had left her alone, stranded among the private school buildings and paved sidewalks of USC. She would be late getting to Earl's for sure. Texting excuses and apologies was lame, but it was better than nothing. Carla couldn't say she wasn't in the loop.

Stakeouts required patience, sure, but they also seemed to require financial independence. Someone hanging around doing nothing meant that someone could afford to do nothing for a good long while.

In an effort to appear productive, she jotted down some notes of what to tell Benji the Virgin or his car-keying friend if, by some strange miracle, she happened to see them. Sentences sputtered out after a few swear words, and they weren't even good ones.

Thinking back on his face and clothes, Benji seemed like the kind of dorky college kid who probably didn't set foot on campus before 4:00PM. He'd said his parents lived in the Valley, but that would be an even wilder goose chase, plus the added possibility of it being a complete lie. Another sentence scratched out, she tossed her pen in her bag.

From the expanse to her left came a body moving with a purpose. It was a he, and he hustled, walking directly toward her. He kept his eyes down while holding his forehead. No, more like tapped the side of it, as though reminding himself to do something — or to not do something — and the tapping would set the thought permanently.

It was the narrow, beige-colored man — the same one she nearly killed with her car on her first visit to campus.

As he neared her, his mumbles registered, but remained unclear.

"Excuse me," she said.

He looked back. Recognition filled his face and he stopped.

"I'm looking for the newspaper office." She'd have to find it eventually, if she ever wanted to get that article written. If she was supposed to write one at all.

He wiggled a yellow finger at her. "You're that girl. From before."

"Um..." Her fine-tuned alibi deserted her.

His face turned white. Before she could spit out any more crappy lies, he turned on his heel. Danica didn't think him capable of sprinting, but the beige man gave it his best effort, hobbling but with purpose. He even looked back behind his shoulder a couple times.

She gave him distance, but stayed with him. The theater building emerged around a corner, Mr. Beige took that turn and entered.

The thought of repelling a third man in twenty-four hours came first, followed by an impulse to follow Mr. Beige inside. Sure, she'd almost run over the guy with her car, but that was an accident, what, two days ago? That wouldn't be reason enough to run away from her; if anything, given how angry he'd been that day, and how upset he appeared to be seeing her today, he should have stayed to take a swing at her.

Mr. Beige's exit to the theater building connected to Benji's theater shirt. Not waiting for her Little Andrew Voice to explain how tenuous that connection was, Danica followed the path.

She opened the glass doors to a large room. A boy talked on his phone by the shuttered ticket area, and two other girls sat on the carpet, ignoring the books spread out in front of them. Nobody paid her any mind, and she saw no sign of the Man in Beige.

The generic design of the building was at odds with the very nature of the theater and its need for attention. It all came across as a structure built for the purpose of being built and then ignored. A few framed posters hung on one wall, and a line of doors made up the other.

All this surrounding generic-ness made the poster on one of the office doors more striking. Clearly hand-made, its yellow frame clashed against the dark brown door, to say nothing of the sparkly tinsel around its edges. The words "WE MISS YOU DRAKE" sprawled across at the top.

She moved closer. Handwritten notes covered the poster, and she felt safe assuming they'd been written with love. Their messages were all a variation on the title. Pictures covered the blank areas, and were even tucked behind the poster, clinging to the tape.

Scared she might be right, she reached out to touch it, then looked around to make sure nobody was watching. It wasn't a crime to look behind a poster, but it felt like an intrusion.

She intruded, pulled the poster back and read the name-plate on the door: "Professor Keith Beckett."

Screw that little Andrew voice for doubting her, she had been right. Beckett was a professor at USC, just not in the business end.

And Benji the Liar hadn't lied about this poster — if Beckett did actually make it, he really had gone overboard.

The kind of move someone might make to cover his tracks, to protest too much. Or — and this only came to her as a shock because it had been so long since seeing actual human emotions in play — maybe Mr. Beckett was the first person she'd seen who actually cared about Drake being killed.

Her phone found its way into her hand and grabbed a quick picture of the whole spectacle. She shook her head. Today's youth seemed so different from her time, and her time hadn't been that long ago. Perhaps business majors and theater nerds mixed better than they did when she was in school. Or perhaps the theater world, with its sensitivity and openness to all walks of life, could be just as devastated by the loss of a fellow human being, even if that human was from another part of the galaxy. They could have suffered from chronic empathy, like her, and just cared a lot.

'Or maybe it's lies,' said the little voice.

'Who is lying? And to who? These are just kids.'

She hadn't seen any other tributes like this anywhere else. Not even close. The business center was, well, all business. Bone dry, with not a tear in sight.

The words "no hobbies" re-emerged from Mr. Alberts' script.

As she stared back at the signatures and notes, three distinct possibilities instantaneously presented themselves:

1. Kids these days were very different from her time, and she was old and needed to accept it.
2. Drake must have spent a lot of time in the theater building for a business major. Or...
3. Drake had a life in the theater, and the news coverage scrubbed it out.

There seemed to be no clear motive to change the kid's history, but it felt like the most honest perspective. She couldn't think of a thing to be gained by eliminating Drake's connections to the arts, but the connections to Mr. Beckett and the theater department were the most solid thing she had found yet. Add to that the finding of Mr. Beckett's office, and this had been a pretty damn good day.

She raised the poster again, snapped a photo of the Beckett name plate, and put the poster back in place. Her legs finally came to their senses and pulled her back toward the lobby area and found a seat. Available funds be damned, she would stake it out to get a look at the guy.

The wait was short. As she sat, the door opened.

Danica froze.

Mr. Beige, narrow as always, exited the office.

He looked even more frazzled than he had on the lawn. His hair windswept, he had a duffle bag on his shoulder. He fumbled his keys, dropping them twice before successfully locking his door. He walked toward the glass exit.

Danica weighed the situation, and quickly justified hiding. She pulled up the hood of Tommy's sweatshirt and pushed her butt deeper into the seat cushion.

One of the gabbing girls waved to the Man in Beige, but he paid no mind. "Mr. Beckett?" she said.

Mr. Keith Beckett, the man in beige, mourner of Drake Alberts III, near victim to Danica's negligent driving, theater professor and expert level frazzled person, exited, stage right.

Danica checked the time. Early for classes to be finished. By the looks of things, his exit may be for a good long while. Mr. Beckett didn't strike her as the type to use duffle bags for casual purposes; only in emergencies.

He had every right to be flustered over the death of a

student. But if the rumor turned out to be true, and he really was the last person — even if he was *among* the last people — to have seen D3 alive, it might explain his constant look of panic. He could be a legitimate suspect. And he was getting away.

The little voice piped up again. Clearly Andrew's voice, only this time, for once, it offered a helpful suggestion.

Danica opened her notebook and ripped off a tiny corner of paper. She folded it, and placed it in the crack of the door to Mr. Beckett's office. If that scrawny Robert Redford ever returned, she'd know. More importantly, she'd know if he never did.

She sighed a quiet thank you to Andrew Luman, two-thousand miles to her east, then made her way to the exit. She would be late for work. She would be chewed out.

These were twists she could anticipate.

CHAPTER SEVENTEEN

Evening. Earl's.

That night's shift dragged. Mrs. Joanie Trinneer, an uber-loyal customer, requested a simple style, which did nothing to fill the hours. With only a few other customers and even fewer calls, the night moved like snails through a molasses factory.

At eight o'clock, Carla returned with wad of folders under her arm. "It's deader than dead in here." She headed to the back office to concoct more financial wizardry. Danica moved quickly past the non-existent customers and locked the front door. It might not have mattered on such a slow night, but she didn't want to push her luck and leave the place unprotected. She followed Carla to the back.

Her boss was digging through a pile of receipts on her desk. She muttered something about getting together tax forms for the third (*swear word*) time. "You gotta show you're good at renting to buy a place, but you can't afford a place if you're so good at renting!"

Danica leaned against the open doorway.

"Would Lorena let you buy this one?"

"She doesn't technically own it all. It's a mess."

The images of Beckett and the Albertses and their house and the wild theories rattled around again. Carla had a way to take rambling thoughts and put them to a fine point. Talking to her sometimes helped.

Yet Carla kept eyes fixed on her receipt heap.

"Yeah, been slow tonight," said Danica.

Carla made a noise somewhere between "Uh-huh" and "Don't care."

Danica held her position. "Gives me time to think."

"I went to look at a place," said Carla. "You can request documents on the previous owners. The last guys were cooking meth!"

Danica nodded, and moved on. "Yep, really slow. It's tough. Too much to think about."

No response this time from her manager.

"And some of it... some is really big."

A deep sigh rose and fell from Carla. She kept her eyes down and said, "You wanna tell me how your case is going?"

"You wanna know?"

"No."

"Well, it's not really a case."

"Good. 'Cause I really don't wanna know."

"Are you mad?"

"No."

"You're mad."

"Why would I be mad?"

"You seem mad."

Carla tore her eyes away from the fascinating receipts to give a withering look.

Danica tapped the doorframe with her toe. She tried to

think of a casual topic of conversation — something about work or relationships or even Gabby and her film shoot.

Nothing came to mind, and the room sank into deep silence. Carla set down the wad of paper in her hand and stood straight, pushing her chair back with her legs. She looked at the ceiling, asking higher powers to grant her peace, to bless her for the sacrifice of her time.

"Go ahead," she said.

Danica's mouth smiled, then opened to spill a bucket of information she'd been holding in for the last few days. She explained how the Alberts family thought she worked for a newspaper, and that they must be buying off stories about their son, but that she didn't understand why just yet. She told the story about her car being keyed and how those boys must be stalking her for a reason she couldn't imagine. And she explained how brilliant she'd been to not only find Keith Beckett, but to follow him to his office, and use the paper-in-the-door trick to confirm whether he ever returned.

It felt great, especially allowing herself to brag about her latest triumph.

"What about the janitors?" said Carla.

Danica's puffed-up chest receded, mostly from the confusion at Carla's question. Had Carla, a complete outsider to this investigation, noticed a detail that Danica had missed — a whole forest-for-the trees scenario — and she somehow figured out it was school janitors who killed Drake?

"No, I mean the cleaners. I bet they clean that Beckett guy's office," said Carla. "Probably gone in already today. So that paper thing..."

The idea had never crossed Danica's mind. She sunk against the door frame, trying not to look as stupid as she was. She had just completed what could have been her first successful private eye maneuver, reaching a level of private-eye-ship she hadn't reached before, only to have its validity disproven by a single question from her hairstylist boss with no interest in the case.

Carla began to babble apologies. "I mean, probably. Maybe not. You never know, you know? I mean..."

"Sure, sure. You never know."

"You could go back and still see it there."

"Right."

"It could still work. It's a good idea."

"Except I won't know when he returns. Right?"

Carla said, "...."

"I'm right back where I started."

"It could work," said Carla.

It couldn't work. Carla's intuition had it right the first time. Danica tried to come up with a way her play could prove useful. Dead end. She licked her lips and imagined quitting to work in a laundromat.

A tap on the glass brought a merciful end to the conversation. Danica found customers standing at the door. A tan family — mom, dad and two boys — stood at the door. They waved and Danica let them in.

"Hello," said the dad. "¿Habla Español?"

Yet another thing Danica couldn't do. "Any English?"

"I can," said the older boy. "We want some haircuts."

There was no other way to say this, but Earl's clientele was primarily white people. Either through habit, neighborhood demographics or just plain The Way It Is, most of their customers were caucasian and there was no way around it. Until she stared at this family of four, Danica had never fully wondered why this happened, a product of her own white-person blinders.

Danica introduced herself. Julieta, the mother, handed over a coupon. It was bent on the corners.

Danica took a guess and said, "From the Alberts house?"

"Si, Alberts," said the dad. By god, Carla was right again: canvassing worked.

"Here," said the younger boy. He handed Danica a pair of toy glasses. Black, flimsy, frames with no lenses.

The boy quickly put a similar pair on his own face, only purple. "Put 'em on," he said, obviously able to tell the woman he'd just met had no idea what to do when glasses were handed to her.

Julieta muttered something in Spanish, in a scolding tone, but the boy's smile remained.

Danica put them on. "They really work! I can see. Thank you." A glimpse in the mirror confirmed why she never wanted to wear black frames. She put the glasses in her pocket and smiled at the boy's parents.

The father's smile cracked around his cheeks. His skin was darkened by the sun, and his hands had calluses. He wore a leatherman on his belt, and it had scratches from hard use. This was a worker.

"Who's first?" said Danica.

Kids haircuts were fun. They didn't think of their hairstyles a bit, but that meant they didn't care how they came out. Danica could rely on their parents' descriptions, and enjoy the strange, non-linear images flowing through her as she worked. Despite the weirdness, these visions came with a certain binary clarity. Bad things were *bad*. Good things were *good*.

Occasionally, as in the case of young Hector, Danica got something resembling a story by way of fever dream. Hector seemed particularly fascinated with rockets, but only the launches. Not the flights, missions, landing or anything else.

Just the launches. She saw his image of himself in the cockpit, counting down the launch starting as far back as "5," then blasting off over and over again. Most of his launches were done solo, but a few managed to cram his older brother Luis Junior into the back seat (Hector's rocket had very specific seating arrangements). As in dreams, Hector's rockets were both life sized and perfectly molded to fit his smaller frame. He saw himself at his current age behaving as an adult. Or at least how he pictured adults should behave while launching into space thirty-seven times a night.

She made quick work of the boys' cuts and met everyone at the register, glancing again at the coupon. "Where are you from?"

"Pacoima," said Luis Senior.

Danica knew full well the limitations printed on the bottom, but she checked again, then glanced toward the back office. Carla was still out of earshot. Danica applied the coupon for both boys' cuts, going against the policy. This family had made a trip to get a deal, and they deserved twenty-percent off both. Besides, who knew how much abuse Luis had to deal with working for Mr. Alberts; if anybody needed a break, it was him and his.

The mother paid in cash with a small, respectable tip, said "Thanks," and they left just after nine.

Danica locked the door behind them. Relief came in officially closing the doors for the night. Tommy never understood how stressful slow work days could be. When Danica sat in the shop waiting for customers, she was not, as he said, "Doin' nothin'." She was waiting. Actively. She could read a little, clean a little, think a little, but always with the tension hovering over her that whatever she had been interested in would have to be dropped the instant someone came through the door. When the doors got locked, that tension disappeared. Done was *done*. Binary.

Carla emerged from the back office. She muttered to herself about needing to re-order shampoo and getting screwed on the last order, then said, "Who were the cuts?"

"A family. Two boys."

"They have a coupon?"

"Yes."

"Told you they work."

Danica shut up. She started to tally the drawer, and hoped Carla would press no further.

But Carla read between the lines: "What aren't you telling me?"

"You don't want to know."

"I bet, but still."

"I think they work for the Alberts family."

"Damn, girl, are you serious?"

"You asked!"

"How do you know? How'd they come here? I thought they lived in Beverly Hills or something."

"Bel Air."

"Bel Air?!"

"Well, the Alberts live there. Normal people can't afford to live there."

Carla gave a dark look with a raised eyebrow.

"Hey, you were the one who wanted us handing out coupons. So number one, you're welcome — yes, they work! They work so well that the grounds crew of a major-league rich family will make a trip from Pacoima to save some cash."

Carla leaned against the counter and folded her arms. She wiped sweat from her face.

"I'm sorry," said Danica. "I didn't mean to get you mixed

up in anything. It's not your thing. You don't have to worry about me. I'll be fine. I know you're just trying to keep me safe. I won't push any more. I can barely keep any of it straight, I actually got myself more work — more non-paying work — at a newspaper that didn't hire me. I got invited to the visitation, but it seems too risky."

Once again, saying the words out loud gave them a permanence she hadn't realized. Mrs. Alberts had said the visitation was Sunday — two days from today. One, really, considering the fact that today was almost over. Unless she stayed up late not sleeping. Which she had been. She had no suspects, no clues and no momentum.

"They were from Pacoima?" said Carla.

"Who?"

"The family just now."

Danica shrugged.

"And you're sure he works for the Albertseses... I can't say that name."

"Pretty sure. I didn't hand out coupons anywhere else."

Carla handed Danica her phone. "You left it in the office."

The alert on the screen came from the LA Times: "SUSPECT NAMED IN AL..." The headline cut off, forcing Danica to open the phone proper.

Which she did, and read, in one breath:

SUSPECT NAMED IN ALBERTS MURDER

By Lily Gradzhyan.

LAPD has named a chief suspect in the murder of Drake Alberts III, son of the prominent—

—That word again—

> —*family. Josue Dominic Rodriguez, 21, of Pacoima, California, is wanted for the crime.*
>
> *"We hope that by making this information public, we can help the manhunt go swiftly and that justice will be done just as swiftly," said Police Captain Louise Baker. "Any information that can assist in capturing the suspect will be greatly appreciated by the force and the Alberts family."*
>
> *Rodriguez worked for the Alberts family as a gardener before being fired last spring. When reached for comment, the suspect's family denied knowing his current whereabouts....*

The rest of the article described the same details Danica had already obsessed over from other news outlets.

She consulted her memories, trying to picture the gardeners from the Alberts house. None of them could have been this Josue Dominic Rodriguez, but they might have known him. It was possible.

On the other hand, from the way Drake II talked, there was a stronger chance nobody lasted long at that job, and the gap between cross-overs could be huge. In all likelihood, the staff got completely turned over every month.

The article linked to a picture of Josue, stolen from social media. He had short, dark hair, and a small Van Dyke on his chin. And a smile. She couldn't tell where the photo had been taken, but the background looked like a bar or restaurant; one of the walls was dark with specks of yellow light reflecting off blurry shapes. There were no other people in the photo. Josue was leaning on his arms, both hands at his chest, ruling out a selfie. Someone had taken the photo for him.

Her next thought felt completely stupid. She felt it, then

threw it away, remembering how she used to gag at the women she'd heard about falling in love with convicts. People like Ted Bundy would somehow charm these women *after* being convicted. And yet, looking at the photo of the wanted murder suspect, Danica's first impression was "Seems nice." She forgave herself; this Josue Rodriguez was objectively nice looking. Nobody could refute that.

"When did this come?"

"Few minutes ago," said Carla. "Weird coincidence, huh?"

"That the suspect may have worked with one of the people who was just here?" said Danica. "No, not weird at all."

She looked out the window, hoping a flat tire or some other affordable-but-time-consuming car trouble had stalled the family from leaving. The lot was empty of customer cars.

"You think they knew him?" said Carla.

"Don't know." It was possible. A remote chance was still a chance.

"Maybe they never worked there the same time, and he didn't know him at all." Carla sounded like she was trying to cheer herself up, like she hoped that the gift connection to the main suspect in a murder hadn't just brought his kids to the Earl's doorstep.

"Maybe," said Danica.

CHAPTER EIGHTEEN

SATURDAY, **August 30, 2008. 8:32AM. Bel Air.**

Weekend mornings in Bel Air felt like weekdays in Bel Air, only more moist. Sprinklers ran everywhere, forcing Irish green upon the desert world. Danica parked near a particularly lush yard, two blocks from the Alberts estate, and couldn't resist: she stepped on the grass. It felt like a pillow. Rich people had everything figured out, down to the dirt.

The stage lights, chairs and other garbage had been removed from the cul-de-sac Dream House. A fresh "For Sale—SOLD" sign leaned against its fence. Why did people even bother putting up the "For Sale" part of the sign? It hadn't been there the last time she visited. The realtors probably wanted to advertise to all the neighborhoods the measure of their success of getting that old theater garbage off the lawn.

She leaned on the fence and watched down the block. Google Maps showed no other entry point, so if any grounds keepers were to arrive (or leave), they had to pass her way.

She waited, trying to not to think about how this moment — more than most — would have been smoking appropriate.

Questioning the gardeners felt desperate. They had contact with the crime scene and with the house in general. People forget themselves around working staff and sometimes let stuff slip to waitresses and bartenders. Rich people would have thought even less of their own staff. Hector and Luis' dad could have heard fights, secrets and promises. And, yes, sure, OK, he could have known Josue Rodriguez. His image returned to her, as did the strains of empathy from the presumed niceness extracted from his photo. Nice people committed crimes sometimes. Nice people went crazy and did terrible things. The LAPD must have had a reason to name him, even after teasing it for days. Come to think of it, they must have had a reason to tease it out.

Her PI career had barely started and she would have to flirt with bounty hunting. To find a wanted man, faster than the LAPD, to get between him and a prize she didn't know existed... she hadn't trained for it.

The young man, currently being hunted by the full force of the law, had to be terrified. From all she could find, he didn't appear to be any kind of criminal mastermind. At worst, this was a poor person entangled with a much richer person's business. That made his odds of his going free decidedly low. She could confirm it in a day, at the visitation. The house would surely be decked out in appropriate and mournful ostentation. She'd have her answer and a path. She had to be patient.

The phone in her pocket begged her to contact Freddie. He could share details that were beyond his authorization to share, putting him in an awkward position, but — due to their close personal relationship — he would take the chance, just for her.

She kept the phone in its place. Calling Freddie for any kind of legal help carried too heavy of an ethical dilemma; asking questions about an active manhunt would probably be illegal and even dangerous. She would be taking advantage of their friendship, or their Whatever It Was At This Point. Freddie was a nice person. He was a cop and a customer. He was the most reliable man in her life, and to reach out to him like that would put any future they could have together — not that she was thinking of that, at all, it was just an example — at risk.

For want of anything else to think about, she drifted to Keith Beckett, all tension and light-brown clothing. An under-listed drama teacher with a tribute poster to a dead student on his door. A nervous man with nothing to worry about. His jitters while he wasn't named as a suspect seemed suspect.

Minutes pulled themselves together into an hour, then found some friends to form another. Danica walked the block a bit to stretch her legs and avoid being caught loitering. The only notable appearance was that snooty Tom Wolfe dude again, this time driving a car from somewhere near the Dream House.

By 10:00AM Danica wondered if she'd picked the gardener's day off. With no gardeners to interview about a former co-worker of theirs, the day headed for Bust Town.

At that thought, the front gate to the Alberts estate swung open. A cream BMW cruised through the gate and headed south, toward her corner. As it drew near, she could tell its driver was Mr. Drake Alberts II, angry as ever, holding his wheel in a tight ten-and-two.

Panic grabbed Danica as she realized how exposed she was. Mr. Alberts would certainly see and likely recognize her. They had met only the one time, and Mr. Alberts didn't seem the type to remember anyone worth less than two million dollars. But Danica was a nearly-bald woman in a hoodie standing alone on a corner in Bel Air, the only pedestrian for blocks. She stood out in a normal crowd, let alone in no crowd at all.

She stood back, trying her hardest to blend in with the tree next to her, and stuffed her hands in her pockets. Her fingers found something flimsy: the toy glasses from Hector. She put them on without thinking, her hands assessing the desperate situation.

Carla had once mentioned that glasses were the kind of thing that threw people off, that people made assumptions about glasses wearers like her. She and Danica had debated this so called "Clark Kent Syndrome," with Danica in a firm camp of "No Way."

Even though she now wore glasses for a disguise, she waited for Mr. Alberts to honk or yell or show some kind of acknowledgment of her. She would have to tell him why she was there, and returning a kid's toy glasses that she was presently wearing felt as weak as the frames themselves.

The car pulled to the stop sign, paused just shy of a full stop, and drove away. No honking. No acknowledgment. Nothing.

Clark Kent was a genius.

The opportunity before her demanded quick consideration. She had come to Bel Air to meet with the gardeners, to get first-hand info. Tailing Mr. Alberts would be a detour and would set back her bounty-hunting before it even started. Then again, if she tailed him and found out more about the father of the victim, it might add to her very-thin case. Her research had uncovered nothing close to a scandal in the family's history, so following Mr. Alberts might be her best shot at finding a skeleton in a closet.

The thought stuck. She paused her bounty hunting career and watched the car. She allowed him to turn the corner before jumping in her Accord.

The Honda caught the BMW at the entrance to the 405-South. He drove the highway like he lived his life: furious and drunk.

Traffic afforded her time for meditation on how clean cut the Alberts family had appeared. For generations, no less than spotless. By virtue of being wealthy, surely they had cheated on their income taxes or forced some poor person to do their bidding, but she hadn't found a whiff of such atrocities online. Either their history really was clean, or their bribing game truly was tops. How long had they done it — years and years? And bribes to college students seemed like small potatoes, something that could easily get excused away ("Supporting education," they told her at tea). Bribes to large media outlets, spanning generations, carried serious ambition.

They made good time, reaching Downtown LA in less than a day. He swerved into a parking garage under a large auditorium. The minimum parking payment kept Danica at bay, and she opted for an available meter. As allowed by the quarters she could find, one hour and forty-five minutes would have to be enough time to accomplish some detective work without getting ticketed.

After jogging back to the parking garage entrance, Danica found herself at the main entrance to the Deaton Auditorium, a building made of glass and steel, grey and imposing. An air of hustle hung over the block, captured by the uniformed police talking on the steps. As she looked around she saw more cops here than she'd seen at police headquarters. The other men and women around, all wearing ties and shirts tucked into jeans, fooled nobody;

they were cops, too. But none of them stopped her as she walked through the door.

The lobby was just as impressive and oppressive as the exterior. Catering crew members rushed here and there, adjusting tables and settings and various this and that, all in what looked like a collective effort to fancy up the joint. One of them, a Black woman in a black tie, demonstrated to a younger white man the proper way to fold a napkin.

Beyond the napkin class lay the auditorium itself. Shouting came from its open doors. One of the catering staff exited the auditorium, passing a friend on his way. The one coming out shook his head; Danica had seen that move before — the "I wouldn't go in there, man" look.

The voice booming from inside, though muffled, carried its booze-soaked anger with crystal clarity. Danica wound her way inside, and once she did, Mr. Alberts' swearing hit her with full volume.

"Like I'm hiring illiterates or something?"

Mr. Alberts' voice came through the speakers, though he didn't need help. From his position on stage and given his natural capabilities, he could have screamed the house down all on his own.

The recipient of Mr. Alberts' rage was leaned against the wall to his right. It looked like a long table, tipped on its side with a brown curtain covering it, as though a fancy homeless person had infiltrated the Deaton to build his lean-to.

It was a grand space. Streamers and bunting hung around top of the ceiling, and the walls held many trappings of a fancy banquet. Danica gave a quick glance to the table next to the door, with its name tags for the guests. She recognized some names right away: some from the mayor's office, including the mayor himself. Some she recalled from Tommy's fantasy sports league (actual players, not Tommy's friends). The rest sounded cartoonishly wealthy. "Mr. and Mrs. C. Bentley." "Mr. R. Thomas Spire." "Dr. Douglass Corwall." Even the paper looked top shelf.

"Behind you," said a voice.

Danica moved to the side of the aisle, allowing two caterers to pass. They carried another long, covered object. She couldn't imagine the sight of another of these things would help Mr. Alberts' mood.

The caterers stopped and leaned the object against the wall, next to the other object. Its curtain dropped.

It was a framed oil painting. Danica immediately recognized the images of the Alberts family. A grumpy-faced Drake the First stood over his family. His wife stood next to him, and on the other side sat their son, Drake the Second, flanked by Mrs. Alberts. She had her arm around a young boy whose face held traces of the family's grouchy resemblance. Drake the Third. Couldn't have been more than ten.

Even from a distance, the framing of the figures drew Danica's attention. The painting arranged a line of the three Drakes, with Drake the First at the peak in the upper right corner, sloping down through D2 all the way to D3. From what Danica had seen of old rich people in movies, the king usually got positioned in the center of these kinds of things, with clear lines connecting everyone else to him. Yet this arrangement put the middle Drake — Drake the Second, Mr. Alberts — in the center, in the middle of the sliding line. Having the patriarch off center could have been an artistic choice by the painter, but Danica doubted Drake the First appreciated such expressive deviations. Even Grandma Alberts' arm had been cut off at the edge.

Danica slid out her phone and grabbed a quick picture of the painting, while Mr. Alberts continued his on-stage rant. He was laying in to the poor stage manager who had been foolish enough to get within his eyesight.

"I don't know what I have to do to get you people to listen, for chrissakes."

The stage manager nodded with vigor, his headset microphone flopping around.

"Just get it out of here. I'm clear, aren't I?"

"Yes, Mr. Alberts."

"Yes?"

"Yes, sir, Mr. Alberts." The stage manager picked up his headset from the stage. He turned away, whispered an order into the microphone and ran off stage.

Mr. Alberts must have been referring to the other object under the curtain. While catering staff attempted to hang the massive, off-center-but-that's-art oil painting tribute to the family, Danica could tell that the other object was roughly the same size. Another painting.

No. Not the same size exactly. The one under the curtain looked more square than rectangular, like it had more to it.

She looked around the aisle. She had been careful to stay out of the way and not draw attention to herself. If she could maintain her cover, she might get a glimpse at whatever the other painting was.

"DL?"

Cover: blown.

This voice came from a dark figure ahead of her, with the stage lights behind him. He moved closer, and into focus; a plain-clothes officer, badge hanging on his belt. His dark skin accented his bright smile. It seemed especially bright at seeing her, looking right at her, as bright as when he came into Earl's.

"Hey, Freddie."

Damning the whole button-down-shirt-tucked-into-jeans look she'd seen on the other cops outside felt premature. Somehow, Freddie Ford made it look good.

Professional, not "good" good. He looked good in a professional way.

"You got eye problems now?"

Freddie was immune to Clark Kent Syndrome. Danica pulled off the toy frames she'd forgotten about.

"You don't have to try this hard. You can register to vote in your own neighborhood."

He had the unique ability to remember their last conversation, and pick up like they hadn't been apart for weeks. Last time he came for a cut, they had discussed Prop 8, and Danica finally let it slip that she'd never registered to vote in California. She argued that since it was a blue state already, her vote might as well stay linked to Illinois, which Freddie rightly pointed out was blue already, too.

"I'll do it. I promise."

"You better." He stood next to her, facing the stage. "How'd you find me?"

"I wasn't looking for you." A giggle found its way into her words. Danica hadn't giggled in two decades.

"Then what brings you by?"

"You know me. I like to be around the center of things."

"Then you've come to the right spot. As you can see," he made a dramatic wave, "this is the epicenter."

"Fundraiser?"

"Yep. It's a big annual thing. The donors and organizers, all make a big deal about it. Don't get me wrong, the force appreciates the kindness. I just don't know why we need the whole show. How much money gets spent to raise money?" He stood next to her. He smelled nice.

On stage, Mr. Alberts read into a microphone, dropped his notes, swore, and kicked the podium.

"He one of those big donors?" said Danica.

"One of the biggest. That's Mr. Alberts."

"Big donor makes big waves, and big drama."

Freddie watched his words carefully. "We appreciate all the support. Of everyone." Like he needed to convince himself. "But, yeah, his family's always been a big supporter. He's been really laying into the staff though," said Freddie. "Got everyone on eggshells."

"Is he like this because, you know... his son?"

Freddie took another careful moment. His breath smelled like Trident. "You heard about that? I would say yes, but he's always kinda like that. Any time I've seen him, anyway. He brought his props, his staff, his own mayor, and dude's still not happy."

Danica took stock. The painting must have been the props, the staff seemed to be the caterers buzzing around him, but... "Hold on. His own mayor?"

Freddie nodded toward the audience seats. A scant group of people sat in the front couple rows, none of whom looked noteworthy.

"Am I supposed to know what that means?"

"Right there."

"I don't see him." Danica put on her toy glasses. She drew a restrained laugh from Freddie Ford, a kid trying to not crack up in church.

He put his hand on her shoulder and turned her a few degrees to the right. She inhaled at his touch. Not a gasp. Not excitement. Just breathing.

"Second row, against the wall," he said. To her ear. His breath brushing her neck.

A man sat alone. He wore his white hat while indoors, and a suit. The side of his face looked indistinct, yet familiar. He was too Anglo to be Antonio Villaraigosa.

"That's not the mayor, Freddie."

"Mayor of Bel Air, yeah, he is."

She squinted again. Maybe she really did need glasses. She'd have to take Freddie's word on it as she couldn't have picked this guy out of a line up of two mayors. Yet the more she stared at the man's white hat, the more familiar he became.

That was because she had seen him before, on her way to visiting the Alberts estate. The thin man with the white hair, the Tom Wolfe look. She'd seen him near the Dream House. She was sure of it. She had all but met the guy — or would have if he had looked her way or considered her worthy of noticing. A leader of the community, and all she had done was nod at his long-haired dog.

Thoughts warped and coagulated, mixing with the hundreds of old news stories she'd glanced at regarding the Alberts community service. She recalled the ones about Drake the First yelling (naturally) about their town removing itself from the confines of Los Angeles.

She said, "Bel Air doesn't have a mayor."

"It's what we call him."

"Who? The cops?"

"Yeah, you know how it is. He's some big shot, or thinks he is. Always up in our business. Comes to every board meeting, every town hall. Noses into every spot he ain't needed. 'The voice of his neighbors' what he says."

"He know the Albertses-sez... the Alberts family?"

"Pfft! You kidding? I think they carpooled."

Danica kept her knowledge of Mr. Alberts' driving habits to herself.

Freddie squinted her way. "What brings you around here?"

"Are you interrogating me?"

"I think it's a legit question." He looked at her with a playfulness in his eyes, but when she failed to answer immediately the rest of his face went Full Cop.

"I'm exploring," she said. Not wrong, nor wholly accurate.

"'Exploring?' And you explored your way into a room full of cops."

"There was a chance I might see someone I know."

"And you did. How long were you looking?"

"I got lucky — this was my first try. Oh! Did you refer me to somebody?"

"I did."

"That James guy, right?"

"He come in already?"

"Yep. Thank you."

"You're welcome." Freddie leaned back on his heels. "You're not here because of Alberts, are you? And all... all that?"

"No." She said it quickly, and hoped it wasn't so quick that he doubted her. "Are you?"

"I'm here for the event."

"Lots of cops around for a rehearsal." A tiny pause, then right into: "Do you think Josue did it?"

"Now who's interrogating?"

"I'm just wondering. Do you think he's the killer?"

"I haven't seen the case. Just what I got in the news."

"But what do you think?"

"I got no reason to doubt the decisions of the force," he said.

"You don't think it all seems a little fast? The teased out news stories, the promise of a suspect, then the naming of the suspect. It feels like a movie trailer. The teaser for the teaser for the trailer of the movie. At this rate, they'll have him in custody by prime time."

"I'm not working the case," he said.

"Neither am I."

"That's what you said." His cop senses had been tripped again. If he found out, he'd turn her in, shut the whole thing down.

A different noise came from the stage. An official-looking woman waved in their direction. Danica had never seen Captain Louise Baker in person, but recognized her from her news appearances. She stood next to Mr. Alberts, but clearly did not stand *with* him. She wore stress like a smile and her shoulders looked tight.

"Ford, we need you up here."

"See you sometime, DL," said Freddie, and jogged toward his commanding officer.

Danica gave one more look around and checked on the Mayor's white hat in the second row. He sat like a lump, bad posture barely keeping that hat up. Then Mr. Alberts said, "Need you up here, too, Ronald," and the man transformed.

He stood and buttoned his jacket, giving the slightest shiver when it fastened. After that, he moved with presence. The former lump now ascended the stairs. A strut without the cockiness, carrying casual confidence in his hip pocket.

Spanish swearing came from the lobby, the only thing that could tear her attention from the one-man show at the front. She thought of shouting a goodbye to Freddie, but he had already moved too far away.

The catering crews continued their hustle, and one nearly clobbered Danica with a table. She spun and saw them — the two men who had hung the oil painting emerged, this time carrying the other one, curtain intact. They paused in the middle of the hall to wipe the sweat from their noses and speak in a blur of rolled R's. They seemed younger than Danica.

They picked up the painting again and carried it the span of the lobby. She followed. The white noise of the air conditioning and staff chatter died down as they made it to the service entrance.

A large garage door hung open, and a moving truck idled outside, with a few wooden chairs resting inside its carriage.

The two movers stopped. The truck driver had on his argument face, and gave them some business. He looked older, boss age by comparison. The movers left the curtained painting leaned against the open doorway, then went to get their talking to.

Danica slid her toy glasses into position, assumed their power, and moved quickly. She stopped at the corner of the painting, near the curtain's drag, then bent down to tie her already-tied laces. A few words of their conversation registered, courtesy of her B- work in Señor Hershel's Spanish 101 class. Words like "Now," "it," "the man," "boss," and "work."

She slid her phone into camera position, and placed it on the floor next to her foot, aimed at the curtain. Her toe rested on the edge of the curtain.

She gave her laces another pointless re-tie as the movers re-grabbed the painting. They lifted and the curtain dropped. Danica snapped pictures and stood, careful to hide her phone after a few shots.

It was, indeed, a painting, as she had guessed. Of the Alberts family, and in a very similar position, with all three Drakes in a line. Yet this one had Drake the First in the traditional center of his patriarchy.

And to the far side stood the other key difference: another woman. About the same age as Mrs. Alberts.

The movers offered more commentary, and though she couldn't be sure, Danica thought its tone sounded similar to "Screw that rich guy and his stupid curtain." They loaded the painting into the truck and shut the door.

Twenty minutes remained on her meter by the time Danica reached the Accord. Rather than waste the time she paid for, she examined her photo work. The shots of the painting with the +1 woman came out blurry, but the general idea still came across, especially when compared to her other (just as blurry) shots of the -1 woman painting.

She zoomed in on the picture, not to the painting, but to a figure in the aisle. It was Freddie Ford, looking right at her. He must have seen her take the picture. He was smiling.

It was a nice smile.

CHAPTER NINETEEN

LUNCHTIME. Downtown LA.

The whole thing happened because of hotdogs. One hotdog, with the works.

After a relatively successful if rambling reconnaissance mission, Danica left the Deaton Auditorium in a westerly fashion. She thought about the woman in the painting, how she'd been removed from the other one, and about the contradictions around the Alberts family. These contradictions included, but not limited to being rich enough to commission a large oil painting of themselves, while also being cheap enough to cut out the woman from the painting rather than commission another one without her.

Thoughts flowed to Mr. Alberts himself and the kind of business he must do, and how in the few interactions she'd had and the research she'd done, she didn't see where the income came from. They just seemed to *have* money, around them, at all times. And when they needed more, it came from *someplace*.

After all this cruising and thinking, Danica found herself in a corner of Los Angeles she had not seen before. Her map thought she was in "Historic" South Central, with the major highways still more west, so she pressed on.

Hunger arrived at last. Like a miracle, a row of shops and hotdog joints emerged. She chose the one offering free parking.

The only person in the place was the guy working both the grill and register. He didn't look happy to see her, but he also didn't look like the type to be happy with anything. He asked if he could help her, and Danica — knowing her wallet's situation — ordered the cheapest thing on the menu. It came with fries and a drink, and offered grilled onions, chopped tomatoes, and various works.

The hotdog came quickly. Danica loaded it up and, rather than bother the guy any more with a potential mess in one of his two booths, she opted to eat in her car.

She sat ready to eat when another car pulled into the lot. A Mustang. Recent model. A billow of smoke oozed around it, some actually from the engine, but most of it from the occupants inside.

The three occupants stumbled out, all boys, carrying on a joke that must have been hilarious a moment ago. They shoved each other in various directions, proving their incredible heterosexuality beyond a shadow of a doubt.

The tallest boy went a step further by kicking the "No On 8 Is No to Hate" poster in the flowerbed. One boy forgot to close his door, and they all forgot to roll up the windows.

The last boy to enter the shop was the kid from Ralph's. Not Benji the Blabby-Probably-Korean-Definitely-Virgin kid.

His friend. The one who keyed her car. Right there. Right in front of her. Clear as day and high as a kite.

She must have wound her way close to USC's campus. A quick glance at her map confirmed it.

A stupid idea formulated. It had some risk, but also some just rewards. She settled her mind and got to it.

Ten minutes later, the three boys found their way out of the hotdog place (one could only imagine how the owner loved seeing them; unless this was a normal college hangout, in which case his grumpy distaste for young people felt even more understandable), and stopped when they saw Danica sitting on the hood of their Mustang.

"I know you, right?" Benji's Car Keying friend played it cool, a little extra simmering beneath his words.

"Yeah. We met at Ralph's."

"Oh, yeah!" This was incredibly funny to the other boys.

Danica pressed. "Were any of them there, too?"

"Where?"

"At Ralph's, the night you keyed my car."

This was funny, too, but not quite as uproariously funny as the previous 'Oh, yeah.'

Car Keying Kid straightened up. "Yeah, yeah, that was you."

"Right. Why did you do it?"

"Huh?"

"Keyed my car while that Benji kid distracted me."

"Wasn't me."

"Was it one of this numb-nuts crew."

A member of the numb-nuts crew heard this, comprehended it, and slowly took offense. He wound up his face and delivered a crushing, "Not cool, lady."

The match-up at hand became very aware to everyone. Three young men against one woman. She considered a run to her car, but it meant betting her life on a first-time engine start. Her boots were heavy; they hurt when they fell on her toe, so a precise kick could do some serious damage.

Weighing it all out, Danica was left with only one option. Her only advantage.

Sobriety.

"Hey," she said. "We met in Ralph's, right?"

"Wha?" said Car Key Kid.

"Yeah," said Danica. "We talked about our class."

He blinked his eyes, losing more focus every time.

"We met in Ralph's," she said again.

"Yeah, I remember. Yeah."

"That's what you said." She looked at the other two boys. "He said that already!"

They laughed. She joined them, almost convincing herself into a contact high.

"What were you doing there?" she said.

"Getting food, man."

"Just like here!"

Another huge laugh.

"You're friends with Benji. What's your name?"

"Logan," said Car Key Kid.

"You sometimes wear a visor, Logan?"

"Oh, man! She's psychic!" said Logan, more right than any of them knew.

"Yeah, I totally am. You guys got sent there by somebody, right?"

"Sent where?"

"Ralph's."

"I just said that!"

"Yes. Did you all get something for writing stories for the Alberts family?"

They laughed again as calls of "Dude!" filled the parking

lot. One of them stammered about what he called the "gypsy machine" in the beginning of the movie "Big" (the title eluded him, too; it would have probably frustrated him more had he realized none of his friends were listening).

"OK, you all got something from the Albertses. Like extra weed money, right?" She paused for more laughter, then said, "Did you think I was cutting in on it? 'Cause I would never do that, you know?"

"That's all Lil'G, man," said Logan.

"Oh, totally," said Danica, and joined them in a round of saying "Lil'G" over and over.

She got off the hood of the Mustang. "You can tell Lil'G—"

"We don't see Lil'G," said Logan. He stood close and mustard dripped off his breath. "And Lil'G says you better stop horning in. Get it?" Even though his voice squeaked, he looked ready to kill her.

Danica put up her hands. "Got it. All good. You don't have to worry about me." She slid past Logan the Tough-Guy Car-Keying Kid and made it to her Accord. With sick irony, it started on the first try.

She pulled away, eating the rest of her naked hotdog, sans-works.

The whole drive back to the Valley, she shook. Those boys would have jumped her. If they hadn't been so high, they might have managed it.

A weird pang of guilt came over her. Those boys were dumb. They were just soldiers following orders. She'd have to find Lil'G, whoever the hell that was, and figure out whatever he was doing. But those boys were just idiots. She almost felt bad for scraping off the onions into their glove compartment.

They'd find them, eventually. When the onions wanted to announce themselves in a couple weeks of sun-baked heat, they'd let Logan know where they were. Nice and loud.

CHAPTER TWENTY

Sunday, August 31, 2009. 7:55AM. Island Estates, Apartment 213.

Gabby's absence had left many holes in her life; companionship, rent money, a feeling of security in numbers. One gap Danica had not considered until recently — until she stood staring into her sad closet — was that of fashion consultation. Her wayward roommate had always offered tips on dressing, mostly unrequested. But the woman had a working knowledge of not only recent trends in how to dress, but of which trends worked for Danica's particular style.

Without Gabby, Danica's closet had become a wasteland of useless cloth.

Desperate for some semblance of control, Danica got the notion to call Malcom Fine, to try for more free advice she probably wouldn't get. She wanted an opinion on recent events, on the woman missing from the painting, on the

Mayor of Bel Air, and on the strange intimidation tactics of college boys.

But most of all, she wanted his opinion on gate crashing the Alberts visitation. Mrs. Alberts had been very polite and welcoming to her, the one time they'd met. She thought Danica was a student. She would probably be okay seeing her hanging around the house again. Even though she'd been invited, she still didn't belong.

He wouldn't take her call. He didn't have to — she knew what he'd say.

She needed to go and she needed to belong. To appear that she belonged.

She texted Gabby, "Help."

A mere four minutes passed. Then Gabby wrote, "What up?"

"I need clothing help."

"4 realz? [Three heart emojis]. Ive prayed fr this day. Whats the occasion?"

"Visitation."

"..." sat on screen for a fat minute, followed by, "Oh no"

"Nobody you know."

"Whew! I mean I'm sorry. Was scared."

"np"

"When?"

"Today."

"That's soon."

"I know.

"Start with black. Send pics."

"u know what clothes I got already."

"yes I do. Go to a store and send me pics"

"Wait. I have to shop?"

Gabby wrote, "Do u think anything u own is funeral appropriate?"

Danica looked at her closet again and considered the upcoming event. A houseful of Drake III's friends and family, all of whom would be dressed tight and right. And while she felt a little proud for knowing enough to realize that a visitation at the Alberts estate would not be a "nice jeans" kind of event, she also knew Gabby was right.

Malcom would probably just go. Crash it, that's what he'd do. Probably what he'd tell her, so she would, and she needed the right clothes to do it.

She texted back: "What store?"

The Westfield Fashion Square Mall in Sherman Oaks was a kind of hell. Horrible parking. Overrun with teens. Obnoxious moving posters. Danica usually avoided the entire block on principle. This day, for the good of a higher cause, of getting into the Alberts visitation without making too many ripples, Danica gave herself over to Gabby's intuition and willfully set foot in the mall. The morning crowd would be small, with the stench of rampant commerce at its early stages. And the air was cool outside, so parking in the sun wouldn't be unbearable. But that didn't mean it still wasn't hell.

She took pictures in Lord & Taylor, a store she didn't know existed let alone dreamed of entering prior to this moment. Such suffering would all be worthwhile once she got to the visitation, got through the line and actually interacted with D3's mind.

Danica dragged an armful of clothes to the dressing rooms to take some discreet selfies. While Gabby weighed the options of a dark blue sleeveless thing, Danica scrolled through more Alberts Family news. Stories arrived supporting Freddie's notion about Mr. Alberts' generosity toward the cops; she found story after story on the family donating countless sums to police charities, retirement funds, gala events, balls and black tie affairs with commissioners and captains. One picture from last Christmas had the family with a crew of smiling (all white) cops in front of a huge pine tree. The listing placed it at the Alberts' house. At first she considered the listing a typo, since the size of the tree and room resembled a museum more than a dwelling for humans. Then she remembered that — at least from the outside — their house actually did look a lot like a museum.

The LA Times had coverage of Drake the First shaking hands around the cop circuit, with some featuring pictures of all three Drakes. The youngest about five years old and barely seeing over the giant novelty check he held with his grandfather.

The Alberts family walked the walk when it came to supporting the police. Probably why Mr. Alberts felt so comfortable screaming at the captain on the Deaton stage. Danica's Midwestern conscience reminded her that the man had gone through extraordinary circumstances; she had only seen him during his grieving period. She knew first hand the lows one can sink in times of loss. The bad feelings and bad behavior didn't just vanish.

Then again, Mr. Alberts was a rich white guy who had been part of a family who had paid up good to the cops. Entitlement ran through his blood. He could certainly make an argument for his "ownership" of everything around him, including the police.

She snapped a picture of a pantsuit and sent it to Gabby, mostly as a joke. Mostly. Plus it would buy more scrolling-through-news time.

Each story contained at least one Drake Alberts and no less than three police officers or officials. Most photos involved handshakes or giant checks. The variants came in the additions: Mrs. Alberts and Grandma appeared and disappeared without pattern. D3 appeared consistently through his grade-school years, becoming more sporadic during late high school, then rebounding big time in 2004, early college.

The deeper she dug, the more it seemed possible that the Alberts family simply enjoyed having cops in their photos. Like it was a family hobby. One photo with a dead-link news story had the family (D2, D3 and Mrs. Alberts) flocked by blue boys in front of a large house. It wasn't even the Alberts' house, or anything half as remarkable, though it carried a general air of affluence in its dark shingles, long porch, and large front door.

Standing in front of that door was a woman. Danica might not have thought much about this before, probably would have considered her a plain-clothes maid. But since seeing the oil paintings, she recognized the face — the woman cut out of the family. Even here, this woman had been cut apart from the family unit, separated by a line of a police. Her smile looked forced.

Danica re-viewed the other photos, just in case she had missed the cut-out woman. She had not. In this mini gallery, this woman was a ghost, appearing once, only to disappear again.

The only thing that could replace such a ghost-mystery woman was the emergence of the other mystery person. Danica's first confirmed sighting of the Mayor of Bel Air in the news came from a May 2003 article. The guy had effectively wormed his way into the family photo album by the summer, and as time went on, his proximity to the center of the photos improved. There he was, in 2004, standing between Mr. and Mrs. Alberts, flanked by cops. Mr. Alberts looked as grumpy as he ever had.

Danica slipped into a black skirt. While she sent the picture, she thought again of Keith Beckett, drama professor, dead-end lead, and over-all skittish weirdo. She thought of D3, and wondered how he ended up on the wrong end of someone. How did it possibly happen? His family aligned itself with every arm of the police force; they were practically deputized. They surely had enemies, somewhere.

Mr. Beckett's knowledge of Drake's true college life may have offered insights into a private world that the family wanted to keep private. He could offer information into Drake's schedule and classroom behavior. Friends, enemies, weak spots. Such information wouldn't necessarily make Beckett a suspect, but then again, neither did being someone's former gardener. Had the police harassed Beckett and that's why he acted so squirrelly? And with the naming of the suspect, shouldn't he have gotten a little less shaken up? Was this guy hopped up on coffee or worse? Why had he been quoted in a newspaper, but had the theater connection erased?

Doubts, second and third guesses rang out. What says a man can't be jittery? The first time she saw him, she'd almost hit him with a car. And every time he'd seen him, Beckett had been living in a fresh post-murder-of-a-dear-student frame of mind. Hustling away from one's office was common, she assumed. Especially if one had appointments, which one often did.

Still. He was freaked out about her being there. Just being.

Gabby sent her approval on the skirt, then gave directions to the shoe department. While Danica sent a picture of some sensible flats, she considered Josue. The gardeners must have had it awful working for a monster. The possibility of losing one's cool after getting screamed at by a racist (while almost definitely using racist slurs) could have set someone off to do terrible things.

She had no reason to dismiss the decisions of the police, just like Freddie said. They were trained professionals and she was markedly not. They had been working the case longer than she had with access to experts and tools she couldn't even spell. They had even taken the time (she supposed) before announcing their suspect's name for a good reason, the most likely, sensible and cool-headed of which being that they wanted to ensure they were correct.

Not because they were paid to do so by the Alberts family, or that the Alberts family had instilled a sense of entitlement into the roots of the police force based on their monetary support over the last six decades. Not that.

Not at all.

The cops knew what they were doing. They obviously liked the Alberts family, but of course they did. They're supposed to help them.

Then again... lots of people hate their work, their jobs, their careers and employers, and they didn't do anything about it but whine. If you disliked your boss — however horrible he was — killing his son seemed like an odd way to go about "showing him."

Gabby liked the shoes and talked Danica down from the scary price tag. She insisted they would last a long while, and were good to stand in at work, should Danica incur a severe head injury and begin thinking wearing shoes like those to work was a good idea. The shoes were a business investment. She accepted it and moved on.

Danica relocated her car to the underground parking, in a corner. Then she climbed into the backseat and put on her new mourning clothes. She hoped the wrinkles would disappear soon.

CHAPTER TWENTY-ONE

Sʊɴᴅᴀʏ, **August 31, 2008. 11:50AM. Bel Air.**

LA funerals had bright sun and sunglasses and felt weird. The sun put everything into question. Danica wondered how much of her opinion had to do with her knowing LA's weather situation compared to the movies she'd seen — movies made *in* Los Angeles — where the funerals were universally drenched in rain.

On top of that, this particular Sunday was hot. It had been hot for weeks, but it never felt more gross than when wearing a skirt. She was already self-conscious about showing her calves; now she had to worry about being sweaty.

Somehow, someway, with all that bright sun and hot heat, the Alberts estate appeared appropriately dour, down to the ties worn by the security guards. She queued behind a silver Lexus and waited her turn. She thought of her plan.

She had a plan.

It was simple, like all good plans (or so she told herself to believe). Not like her other recent plans. This one could work.

The plan was:
- Get in.
- Get through the line.
- Get the vision.
- Get out.

"Get reward" had initially appeared at the bottom, but were crossed out after being deemed too tacky. The success of the plan depended on getting past the first guard who may or may not check for invitations and RSVP's. The conversation the Lexus driver was having didn't fill her with more confidence.

Toward the dead-end stood her dream house. Its for-sale sign had disappeared. Maybe next dream.

The Lexus pulled away and her turn came. Her ankles already felt sweaty. She recognized the guard from the tea meeting, but she still gave her name. He recognized her, too. With a measured smile, he directed her up the drive.

Step one had been accomplished. She checked off "Get in."

The same smiling valet directed her to pull to the right, toward the north side of the house and away from the main entrance. She followed his directions to find another valet, a woman with a flag, ushering her to a stop facing the wall.

The grounds overlooking the mountains and expansive gardens looked as green as ever, despite the row of cars building up one by one. She parked next to the silver Lexus she'd followed. Before she opened her door, she checked her mirror and stopped as a second, on-coming silver Lexus pulled into the spot on her other side.

With so many guests already on hand, she had a decent chance of blending in to the herd (another key component to the crashing of gates). She scanned her plan one more time before getting out. The driver of the second car lingered, as did the woman in the passenger seat. Both looked at their phones, and didn't notice Danica or much of anything around them. They seemed familiar, like she had seen them in movies or tabloids. One could barely notice the driver's nose job.

Danica walked the long journey to the front of the house, admiring the work the grounds crew had done for this sorrowful day. The lollipop bushes were damp with irrigation or treatment. Only one bush stood out, with a cowlick branch pointing up from its backside, a defiant middle finger from Mother Nature. Other than that one, all the other middle fingers had been trimmed.

A crowd of people milled around on the driveway, chatting like they knew each other because they probably did. A group of eight looked like contemporaries to Mr. and Mrs. Alberts, down to the anger of the husbands and the overall got-it-togetherness of the wives. Another group was much younger, with full heads of hair and perfect phone accessories. The boys wore ill-fitting suits. The girls wore shawls and scowls. They had all the trappings of college students, which made them likely friends of Drake's.

Danica made a casual turn away from these young people, toward a collection of confirmed adults near the porch steps. Her fragile "friend of Drake" cover story could shatter with one nasty look from actual friends.

As the group of mourners grew, Danica recognized more and more attendees. Local luminaries, including one loud-voiced movie producer who appeared on several DVD special features. She didn't see any Oscar winners, but there were more than a few nominees, complete with singers and musicians of great stature.

Among them all, looking eager to please and ready to say hello, walked the Mayor of Bel Air. He wore another smart suit with a sensible silver watch, and he shook hands while placing his left on the receiver's forearm.

He shook hands with a large Black man with a wide squat neck. They mentioned football, and how the Mayor thought this man's legacy at USC had reached "such heights." He offered a "Fight On" as he continued on his path. When he passed by Danica and gave her a little nod, she felt kind of honored.

Beyond the group's perimeter — beyond an NBA legend and a former model — were two other men. They also wore suits, but appeared as sweaty as Danica felt. One snapped pictures with an expensive-looking camera while the other took notes. They weren't paparazzi; the guards wouldn't have let them make it up the street. These were reporters, probably with credentials and references and strict instructions. The one writing notes looked to be in his sixties, a white man pushing into retirement with a nice donation from his loyal Bel Air readership.

Danica heard a young-sounding voice. "Any idea when we might start?"

"Not yet, miss." This voice was Mr. Peters, and it came from right behind her. Danica had been pushed to the front of the house, and his breath practically knocked her over. Mr. Peters didn't strike Danica as the type to forget a face he despised (even though he probably despised everyone). If he picked her out, he might have reason to question her attendance. She kept her back to him as she drifted back into the crowd, to blend in and preserve her plan. Get in, get the vision, get out.

"I've seen you, right?" said one of the college-age-looking

boys. It took Danica a moment to realize he was talking to her. She acted like she didn't hear him.

"Yeah," said one of the girls. "I think so. Hey."

Danica turned to face them, wishing she'd kept those flimsy fake glasses "Sorry?"

"You go to SC?"

Danica's response leaped out of her mouth. She couldn't hold it back — her defenses took over and released the first thing that seemed to fit, even if she had no way to back it up.

She said, "I'm in art."

The college-age girl nodded, like this made complete sense. Her eyes focused a bit too long on Danica's shaved head.

Another girl tore her eyes from her phone long enough to cast a glower on the situation. She, it seemed, did not buy it. "Art? With who?"

Danica held back an "Um" and turned to face this inquisitor head on. If these were Drake's friends, and if they knew why she had come and what she was trying to do, they'd protect her.

Right?

That's what kids were supposed to do: protect kids, and want justice for their friends.

They didn't get hung up on specifics as to why someone was hanging around them at a visitation so she could blend in with the crowd, passing off as someone who had every right to be there. They didn't care about that stuff.

...Right?

"Who you got for art?" The inquisitor wouldn't let up. She put her phone in her tiny purse, prepared to go all day.

All young eyes turned to Danica. They studied her shaved head and Danica's confidence dropped into her sweaty, overpriced shoes. She felt like a child, but unfortunately not enough to fool the actual child-like people questioning her. She was in high school again, the first day she showed up with short hair. She told herself she didn't care what anybody said or thought, which was exactly the type of thing someone who *does* care tells herself. They could smell her adulthood. They knew she was a person who paid bills (mostly) and held down a job (sort of). She told herself not to cry. Adults don't cry. Children cry.

She let it out. The tears fell and Danica cried. She held her face. The emotions welled up and burst from her.

It was a grand performance. Children do cry, so she behaved as children did. And the college kids responded as children do when someone's upset: they crumbled. The boys made passing remarks of concern while the girls rubbed Danica's shoulders and offered help. The Inquisition Girl even offered a tissue from her tiny purse, which somehow had room for more than an iPhone.

"I just need some air," said Danica. The children all agreed and recommended she walk it off. So she did. The tears stopped as she reached the edge of the crowd. Hopefully she wouldn't see the kids during or after the visitation.

Her drifting walk carried her to the southern end of the house, along the path to the back yard. Near the scene of the crime.

The lawn cascaded over small mounds toward the fence and street. And from the side fence came sounds of activity. Shears. Her brain faltered at the sound she heard all day in her professional life. Definite snipping. Metal slid against metal, repeating over and over. She moved closer toward what sounded like an outdoor barber shop.

Another sound emerged, that of a branch cracking. While clipping hedges made more sense, Danica would have assumed the grounds crew had this day off. For a myriad of reasons.

Yet the sound continued. She stepped off the path and onto the grass, which was even softer than James Van Owen's visions had led her to believe. If the grounds crew had not been given the day off, this could be the opportunity to start a conversation, get some info on Josue.

The lollipop-top bushes continued along the side of the fence. And there, facing one of the bushes, stood Mrs. Alberts. She wore pearls, gloves and heels with the kind of black dress Gabby had been trying to get Danica to find. She held lawn shears — the kind you need two hands to use. With them, she was trimming the bushes. She took a few cautious-but-definitive snips, then inspected her work, before moving to the next bush. At this next bush, she brushed the top leaves before pulling one leaf off, then moved to the next bush.

Curiosity opened Danica's mouth, but her discretion closed it again. She knew how funerals, mourning and sadness in general could mess with a person. Listing out the weird things she'd done when her mom passed away — weird things that made complete sense at the time of doing them — would fill an encyclopedia. In times of confusion spurred by desperation, the mind grabs for anything to make sense. Even when things don't make sense, the mind justifies so that it can *feel* like things make sense.

Mrs. Alberts had lost her son, so she had to trim the bushes. That's all there was to it.

Danica withdrew, back toward the front entrance. She looked back to see a maid appear from the rear of the house. The maid said something, and Mrs. Alberts cut her off. "I realize that, and I'll be there soon. If I didn't have to do everything myself...."

Danica returned to the herd. A few minutes passed then the crowd rumbled, and they moved toward the house. Danica fell in line behind a man with very broad shoulders. They slowly ascended the steps and entered the house.

Upon taking in the luxury of the foyer, Danica resisted the urge to spin like a Rom-Com heroine in Times Square. Its breathtaking-yet-understated beauty was expected, falling in line with the rest of the house. Sure, the entrance room was huge, and of course it had a tall, curved staircase that rose to upstairs luxury, but it all seemed to fit, even with the floral tributes lining the banisters.

The curved foyer walls had doors in all directions. Guided by velvet ropes, the reception line arced to the left, toward an open doorway.

They moved through the foyer quicker than Danica thought possible, until she actually got through the doorway, at which point all progress ceased. The reception line snaked around to fill what could be called a kind of family room; leather couches had been pushed to the walls to make room for attendees. Only the paintings above the fireplace gave the slightest indication that a family had ever occupied this room, and all of those were sepia-toned tributes to Di.

The line progressed, and as it did, Danica's eyes adjusted to the low lights of this "family" room. She could tell the line actually continued through a wall to a break-out room. That room had brighter lights and — judging by the glimpses she could muster over the enormous man's enormous shoulders — many more flowers. Reading these signals, she made a guess as to the contents of this other room, and after another bend of the line, her suspicions were confirmed: she saw the lid of the open coffin.

Her back tensed. She had three bends of the line to go

before Drake III's body. A quick assessment and Danica calculated that if everyone took thirty seconds to pay their respects, she would have her answers in less than forty minutes.

The whole thing felt like waiting in line for a celebrity's autograph at a trade show. As she tried to relax, the tension displaced itself through the rest of her body.

Ahead of her, the large man leaned down to one of his (shorter) entourage, giving Danica a glimpse toward the fireplace. Standing on the hearth were Mr. and Mrs. Alberts. Just them. An assistant with a headset stood to Mr. Alberts' side, but off to the side. Nobody near the couple resembled anything close to a family member.

At her mom's visitation, the family was well represented, at least in numbers. They were technically extended family, but it counted for something. Her mom's brother, his wife, their kids, Andrew's sister, her kids, their father, cousins, cousins of cousins. It drew everyone in and completely overwhelmed Danica. And she had felt pretty overwhelmed for a good long while.

She had been MIA for much of the cancer downslide. Danica told herself that she believed her mom was so strong before the illness that seeing her in a weakened state would be too difficult to process. That was a lie; she was simply terrified. Her mom had been her closest family and friend. Losing her meant she was truly and completely alone. A full adult with no safety net, floating through the world solo. Confronting her mom's illness meant acknowledging that her last free meals had come to an end. From then on, she would be on her own.

Before the funeral, the funeral director had given them very easy and obvious directions. Things along the lines of "Stand there and greet the guests," and "You can shake their hand or hug them or both or neither."

Danica tuned out, him and everything. Pretended to be interested in the new handicap-accessible elevator installed in the back of the church sanctuary. She let the old funeral director man drone on as she moved closer to the pretend-fascinating instructions about closing the door before pressing up or down. If any gates were ajar, the elevator would not work. A safety feature. The lift would move very slowly, another safety feature. She stayed there, in the back, staring at the instructions, hiding in plain sight.

"Danica." Andrew's voice was flat. She told herself that he was nice and caring, and tried to remind herself of all he was going through, too. It didn't help, and she frowned at him.

"Now would be a good time to talk to her."

He said, 'her.' Not 'your mom' or 'Georgina' or anything human. Kept things professional and ice cold.

"I already have."

"Oh. OK. I didn't see you."

"I did it. Earlier." She hadn't, but he didn't need to know that.

"Oh," he said. "I didn't see you." Like he had been in charge of her all the time, and in charge of every single moment with the coffin. Had he installed motion-detection cameras to make sure he saw every in and out around his dead wife's body?

He continued. "You need anything? They have food over there." So helpful and considerate, it had to be completely fake. Probably how he tricked her mom into marrying him in the first place. Lure 'em in, get 'em on the line, pull 'em in the boat and lock 'em in the kitchen. If they make money, that's gravy. More for him.

"Food. Genius." The sarcasm came out clear. She didn't care. She pressed the button and rode the handicapped elevator. It went slow and she kept her eyes at the wall, away from him.

The kitchen in the basement bustled with chattering church ladies. The chatter lulled when they realized Danica had entered the room, and everything went thick with pity and pouty lips. All from people Danica either didn't know or wanted to forget. She stole a cracker and headed back to the elevator before any of them could pat her on the freakin' shoulder. She sat in the elevator without pressing the button, and waited for the visitation to begin.

The funeral director staged the family near the pulpit, after the coffin, and put Danica between Andrew and her mom's brother, Uncle David. By that point, her proximity to Andrew didn't bother her. She didn't care about him. Let him feel the ice.

Through the course of the next couple hours, she shook the hand of every person within a fifty-mile radius of home. Uncle David offered poor details on her mom's relations. "This guy coming up is a cousin. I think. I'm going with cousin... This one's been to our house a few times. You were there, too, pretty sure... Here is a familiar face right here, who will hopefully introduce herself."

Some people lingered over the casket, and it made Danica's skin crawl. She tried to keep her eyes away, but the offense had been made. They didn't know her mom. They were nothing people. They showed up for a free buffet and a glance at the sad girl who cut her hair off. They didn't really care. They hadn't lost anything. Tourists.

Despite all this, Danica stuck it out. She did her duty,

shook the hands, kept her eyes low, then bugged out as soon as the last old lady waddled past her. She didn't shoot another word to Andrew. He might have said "Want a ride?" but she didn't stop to check. The doors closed behind her.

She made it home in record time. Her stuff had stayed packed from her trip. Tommy stayed back in LA, which made leaving easier. She could stay in a motel near the airport, stay there before her flight, get to the plane early.

Rather than drag her bag on the rollers, Danica carried it so as not to leave a trace of herself anywhere. When she made it to the kitchen, she smelled a weird staleness in the air, and against her best attempts at being a focused, angry, bitter young person, she allowed an investigation.

The smell came from the salon. She hadn't been in there for a while, and from the look of the dust on the sink and the shampoo bottles, neither had anyone else. Nobody would confuse Danica's mom for a neatnik (a trait they shared), but this kind of disorder would have driven her crazy. "That's your business," she'd tell anyone listening as she cleaned up between cuts. "It's the business of business. Stay ahead, stay ahead."

Danica stood in the doorway for five minutes, or maybe an hour, watching dust rise and rest. The vacancy in the salon seized her. It had to be accepted, and wouldn't take "no" for an answer.

Tears wanted their way up and out. Forget them. She wouldn't do it. Too late. No way. Fighting tears back required action. She dropped her bag on the floor and grabbed the duster. By the time she left... well, it wasn't spotless, but it was damn near close. And she knew she had done some good, something her mom would have actually valued.

Years later, standing in line at Drake Alberts III's visitation, looking at the lonely couple by the fireplace, Danica realized two absolute facts at the same time.

First: attempts to make sense of something during a time of grief are, apparently, very common.

Second: family — however lackluster it may be — counts for something. And that standing at her mother's visitation with some semblance of family, even closed-off Andrew and unhelpful Uncle David, greeting people who came for whatever reasons they had, helped confirm her mother's life. She had been something to them and for her. The vacancy had to be accepted, and those in attendance — by attending — made the vacancy a cold reality.

CHAPTER TWENTY-TWO

The Alberts Estate. **Living Room and Break-Out Room.**

Staying calm got harder and harder. The line turned again and Drake's casket came into full view.

Danica's breath turned rapid. Only two people stood between her and answers. Even at this close proximity, doubts rose again, and she looked toward the Albertses. They would notice Danica touching their son's head, and Mr. Alberts might recognize her from the Deaton, or from hanging around on the corner, or just remember how much he hates people in general, and find an excuse to fly off the handle and get her kicked out. Especially if he saw her touching his son's head.

Didn't matter. She wasn't doing anything morbid. She belonged here, whether they knew it or not.

The large man with large shoulders approached the casket. Danica rubbed her palms on her dress, then pressed her fingertips together. A kind of priming movement, though she'd never thought to do it in the past. She reminded herself to keep calm no matter what she saw.

The large man with large shoulders stepped aside, and her turn at the casket finally came.

Whoever got hired for embalming did great work. The makeup seemed natural, with no signs of bruising like she'd seen in the visions. Drake's hands rested on his stomach, folded to receive appropriate goodbyes. Danica placed her right hand on his, to retain the air of appropriateness, and hopefully distract any onlookers from her left hand feeling through his hair.

His skin felt like a cold belt. Giving a little twist, she saw blue ink on his wrist. A tattoo of the USC Trojan.

A tingle ran through her legs. She inhaled quickly.

What if she saw Josue? If she saw Josue, then she could rest easy and let the police handle things. She would also have to re-examine her personal biases against the cops. Maybe.

What if she saw Keith Beckett, the one person she'd encountered who seemed deeply upset by Drake's death (up to seeing Mrs. Alberts freaking out over uncut bushes, that is)? If she saw Beckett, she could still reach out to the cops, or to the USC higher-ups, or possibly mention a tip to Freddie, or even James Van Owen. That guy needed all the help he could get.

What if she saw someone she hadn't met? She would still have a face to go on.

What if she saw someone's face she had met, but hadn't suspected, like Mr. Peters? She'd probably have to follow some kind of path to embezzlement from the family funds, or some other route way over her head. Still, that might be cathartic; she might actually feel good about ruining that guy's life.

What if... she looked at the family. They shook hands with some gray-haired woman with a cane, and they strained to smile in a genuine way. Mr. Alberts nodded a hello, then rolled his eyes. If she saw his face, her heart might tear in half.

Her left hand reached out and touched Drake's hair. She closed her eyes to welcome the visions, the answers.

None came.

CHAPTER TWENTY-THREE

The Alberts Estate. **Break-Out Room. 12:54PM.**

She opened her eyes. Adjusted her grip and closed her eyes again. Maybe she hadn't gotten a good feel.

Still. Nothing.

CHAPTER TWENTY-FOUR

The Alberts Estate. Break-Out Room. 12:54 and 42 seconds.

Absolute nothingness.

CHAPTER TWENTY-FIVE

Danica's eyes opened and stayed that way. She must have stepped away from the casket and into the back half of the line, but she couldn't remember. Her feet moved on their own, full auto-pilot. She looked at Mr. and Mrs. Alberts, standing before the grand, cold fireplace, flowers lining the mantle and framing their heads.

'Run away,' she told herself. 'Run straight out the house, down the path, down the street, bum a ride on a bus and never come back to this state.' She had placed everything on this one big gamble, and nothing hit at all. Less than nothing; it didn't even land on the table.

A voice said, "Thank you for coming," and Danica snapped to nearly-full attention. Mrs. Alberts had her hand out, and Danica shook it. "Drake, this is one of Drake's friends."

Danica looked away from them, back to the casket, then away again. That was too much. She looked at the man to the side of Mr. Alberts. He had an earpiece and a scanning look in his eyes. Some kind of assistant or bodyguard. This was a guy with focus and a mission. That must feel nice.

"We've met before, right?" said Mr. Alberts. He shook her hand. Calluses jabbed at her knuckles.

"We had her for tea the other day," Mrs. Alberts said. "A journalism student."

"I feel like it was somewhere else."

"I feel that way about everyone here today," said Mrs. Alberts. "Everything is a blur. I can't keep a thing straight."

Mr. Alberts released his grip. Danica nodded, maybe said something, then followed the line back to the foyer. It was over. Her somnambulant form drifted across the shining floor, barely registering Mr. Peters' shouts from the top of the stairs. Yelling at some maid, who speed walked away.

On the other side of the foyer was another grand room. Like a dining room without the giant table. The grieving community congregated about the grand room, and wait-resses carried trays with cocktails and snacks. A finger sand-wich found its way into Danica's hand. She did not eat it. She took a seat on a window seat and leaned against the glass.

How had she seen nothing at all? And not "nothing" like some kind of emptiness, like your soul dropping out of life and falling evermore into the vast abyss of limbo and beyond. No, she saw Nothing, capital "N." Same as anybody else would see if they touched Drake's hair. Same as she saw when she touched an apple.

She had made good contact to the scalp. She had given it plenty of time to register, though time had never been an obstacle in the past. Being real with herself, she hadn't really expected to have it be so super easy. She wasn't honestly expecting to see the killer's face, home address, and mother's maiden name. But she had expected to see *something*.

No Josue, no Beckett, no faded memories or life flashing before her eyes. Nothing. Nothing happened.

Another waitress with drinks found Danica, and the drink found her lips. She could still drop the entire enterprise, the sleuthing and detecting and tailing and everything associated. Her only losses had been free time and chair hours. The possibility of a reward was a long shot to distract her from passing her barber exams, like a garbage man playing a lottery ticket. A dream. Cutting her losses would not be that bad. She could consider the matter a vacation from her regular life and normal problems. Like a flight being rescheduled, and she had to cut her vacation short, come back to real life and let it go.

She'd give the money back, too. The Albertses probably didn't even notice — they didn't mention it a minute ago. But it felt like the right thing to do, since she had even less reason (or knowhow) to publish news articles.

She finished the drink. It helped a little. The second drink helped a little more.

The crowd grew bigger and louder. A distasteful level of cheerfulness permeated the conversations. They didn't care about any of this. They didn't have to. None of these people cared about Keith Beckett and his nervous demeanor, or his weird disappearing career in the theater department. They didn't think about whether Josue had connections with the current groundskeepers, if that's how he built his grudge against D3, or if he even had a grudge in the first place. They could pass as concerned for the grieving family in as much as they had all paid respects, but the speed at which they moved along with their lives voided the transaction.

They seemed just as concerned with the shrimp hors d'oeuvres. The tourists had all accepted that terrible things happen sometimes, and that this one happened to a young man from a very rich family, where no money was requested for ransom or information, because sometimes these things just happened. It just occurred, and everyone went along with the process. They might have cared about the victim, but they didn't care how he became one. Maybe they were right.

She thanked the next waiter for her third drink. He walked back to the doorway, and Danica's eyes found Mr. Peters. He was just stepping down from the stairs, and his gaze burned across the room. He looked at her, studied her. Judged her. He understood full well that she did not belong there. Maybe he was right, too. Drink Number Three blurred him away.

Through the bottom of her glass she saw a dark smudge enter the room, and it moved like it was headed right for her. Danica focused her three-drink vision as best she could as Mrs. Alberts whisked by, talking to a security-guard-looking dude accompanying her. The courage of alcohol brought Danica to her feet. She interrupted them.

"I'm sorry. Again. There was nothing."

"I... thank you," said Mrs. Alberts.

"I want to help."

"There's really nothing more for you to do, dear."

"Danica. Luman. We spoke earlier. Earlier this week and tonight — today. I'm sorry. And I saw you earlier."

"At the visitation?"

"Ma'am?" said the security-guard-looking dude, but Mrs. Alberts asked him to wait.

"You saw me? Where?" she said.

"I get it," said Danica. "There's nothing you can do, so

you just do something. You trimmed the bushes. I saw it. I saw you."

"Oh. I understand."

"And they're lovely bushes." This was going really well. Mrs. Alberts would never be able to tell that Danica had downed three drinks. She was really pulling this off. "The bushes. I only saw one that wasn't..." Danica kissed her fingers "...perfecto."

Mrs. Alberts nodded. "And where was that?"

"Back a ways. That way, I think. I'm a little turned around. It's by where we parked. Anyways, I wanna help, but I can't, but... y'know. I can't."

"Sure, sweetie. Thank you." Mrs. Alberts put her hand on Danica's shoulder, then excused herself and hustled out of the room.

Secure in her total nailed-it moment of casual cool and sophistication, Danica slumped into another chair. The drink that spilled on the floor might have come from her slumping, or it might have been there before. She couldn't tell.

Perhaps she had become a little drunk. She took a picture of herself to be sure, then took a few more of the lovely room and foyer and stairs. After ten or twelve more confirmation pictures, and a few of the really great lamp next to her chair, the truth set in. She didn't need to look at herself to know how drunk she was.

Her eyes drifted from the fascinating lamp to find a man on the other side of the room. He waved. He looked like a swarthy troll in a tight suit. Meaty hands held crackers and cheese without a plate, and the man looked even more sweaty than the first time Danica had met him. She told her legs to stand up, told herself to sober up, as Malcom Fine lurched her way.

"Whoa there," he said. "Don't gotta stand on my account, even when you can stand."

"I can stand." She did so, barely.

He nodded. "So. You're here."

"I am."

"You don't seem happy to see me," he said. His breath reeked of tuna.

"Just surprised." She couldn't hold back. "I called you."

"I know, I know. I meant to call you back."

"I wanted more advice."

"It seems like you took your own. Mostly worked out, too, I think."

"Yeah, I'm here. In the house. Whoopee." She sucked on her lip and stared at him. "Why are you here?"

"Come on. Can't miss a big event like this?"

"Oh, sure. Free food. Like groceries for you."

"No. Well, sure, but that's not all. Events like these bring in everybody from everywhere. Sometimes someone I'm looking for."

"You're working?"

"I'm always working," he said, and finished his cheese in one bite. "Did you get anything?"

"Like what?"

"Clues? Info? Dirt? Anything on that case you are supposed to be working?"

"Some." Lying felt good, especially to this guy. He probably knew she'd gotten nothing and came over to rub it in her face.

"Anything good?"

The lying caved. "Not really. All I saw was the body."

"Were you expecting a stage show?"

"I was expecting more than I got."

He finished his crackers and dusted his fingers on his suit jacket. "Come on, Valley Girl. You didn't get nothing."

"I got jack squat. Actually, less. Less than having jack squat's what I got."

"You got in the house. Think about that — that's huge!"

"So did you."

"Yeah, but I'm a professional. You, clearly, are not, and you got in. You're standing on Ground Zero. 'In' Ground Zero? Which is it, 'In' or 'On?'"

She pressed forward. "But I don't have anything."

"Yet," said Malcom Fine. "You don't have anything *yet*. You're inside the house. In the crowd. You can see the family in a vulnerable position. That's a great place to be."

"If you say so."

"I do say so. Look: the family been doing anything weird?"

She held back the juicy detail of Mrs. Alberts' sudden compulsion to garden. "They're sadder."

"People get real honest when they're sad."

She squinted. "You just decided to come here? 'Cause you're a professional?"

"Yes," he said. "Some of my clients know the family."

A suspicious look ran across her face, one even Mr. Fine couldn't ignore.

"Well, friends of my clients." He changed the subject. "You're inside. You got nothing for now, but you're in, so... look around for any, you know, odd-ball stuff."

By any standard, the entire room was filled with odd-ball stuff. The incongruity of watching a future hall-of-fame point guard chatting up a reality show host while a man with a very large mustache stared between them jarred her.

Then she remembered Mr. Peters. He had always been tense, so his current expression of "more tense" seemed to be only an escalation of his character. But the way he snapped at that maid upstairs seemed excessive, even for someone with a resting angry face such as him.

And there was the whole to-do at the Deaton with two oil paintings.

"Maybe," she said. "There's this painting that the old man got all pissed off about."

"A painting?"

"Yeah, it's got some extra family person in it."

"I bet there's stuff upstairs"

"Upstairs? You think I should?"

"Yes — Hell yes. This painting you're talking about could be up there, or some kind of clue, or something. The bedrooms are probably up there."

Probably Drake's bedroom.

"What if the rooms are locked?"

Malcom Fine shrugged. "What if?"

"I don't have a key."

Malcom Fine shrugged again.

"You want me to bust down the doors? I'm gonna get caught."

"So you get caught. You got somewhere better to be? Did you have some kind of haircutting emergency you'll miss if you get caught? You were just griping about going home empty handed, then I come up with a great idea and you don't wanna do it. 'Cause you *might* get caught."

Mr. Peters strolled into view again. He scanned the whole of the room. Making his presence well known to all, he planted himself at the foot of the stairs, and the tall woman stepped away.

"I'd have to get by him though. And nothing gets by him."

"Him who?"

"That main butler guy. Peters. And I don't know if anything gets by him."

"I'm gonna do you a favor," said Malcom. "Another one, that is. See that lady by the stairs?"

He pointed at the tall woman, her faded black dress the only thing appropriate for a visitation. Mousy-brown hair hung in a disheveled wedge, either by design or neglect. She looked like she'd been crying by way of sobbing. She wore a rain coat despite the lack of rain and the fact that it was blazing hot outside. An absolute train wreck.

"She seems like trouble, right?" he said. "I'm gonna engage her. Should make a little scene in case any lookie-loo's are around like your boy there. Then you bolt, fast as you can." He looked at her, and she could sense the assessing going on. "Can you walk?"

Danica set her empty glass on the floor with defiance. "When I get up there, then what?"

"Then whatever. Look for that painting you're talking about." He dusted off his tie. "This business, you gotta be ready to take every opportunity you get. Especially the golden ones I'm giving you. For free."

Danica nodded.

"Good luck," he said, then turned and walked to the foyer. He reached the tall woman and started talking. Whatever he said made this flustered-looking woman even more upset. Danica could relate; Malcom probably had that effect on most people. The tall woman flung her arms, spilling some bottled water. Malcom put his hand on her arm and she whipped it off with a "whoop" sound before beginning to cry again.

Right on cue, Mr. Peters approached the couple, leaving his post at the stairs. The three exchanged words. Whatever got said, everyone appeared offended: the tall woman at

Malcom, Malcom at Mr. Peters, Mr. Peters at all the spectacle.

Malcom pointed and the woman shouted, and when Mr. Peters motioned to the door, they refused the invitation. Danica heard the woman say something about "at my house" and "freakin' butler there," to which Mr. Peters raised his arms, as if to corral them toward the exit.

Danica saw her opening. In a fit of fleeting sobriety, she moved quickly, hitting the foot of the stairs at full speed, taking two at a time, and reaching the second floor in under nine seconds, all without slowing down or throwing up. She cleared the upper wall and pressed against it, hiding herself from view. Her speed surprised her, as did her guts.

She chanced a glance back toward the foyer floor. Mr. Peters, the tall woman and Malcom were gone, and the milling crowd seemed as indifferent as ever. Hanging above the front door, facing her and the stairs, was a large oil painting of the truncated Alberts family, like the one brought to the Deaton. The eyes of the eldest Drake Alberts stared through her.

As if reminding her of her new mission.

Things grew dark a few steps into the hallway. Doors lined each side; some singles, a few doubles. Covering the entire house would take a month.

She tried the first door and found a bathroom. The next ones were bedrooms, guest rooms at that. Not the kind used by residents of the house, and certainly nothing worth hiding from anybody. The next bathroom felt slightly more used (the toilet paper wasn't set to that new-roll standard like at a hotel), and she turned the corner, leaving behind the sunlight from the foyer for good.

The first door after the corner hung half open. The room was larger than any of the prior guest rooms, with a simple, made bed in the far corner. Posters on the wall, all in the "Fight On" vein of USC support, and completed models of jets sat on a small, tidy desk. The dresser drawer had socks and shirts.

If she had come to this room first, or if she had somehow stumbled in without Malcom Fine's prompting, Danica might not have given it a second thought. She might have accepted it as Drake's Room. Yet staring at the framed posters and the desk with no mess, and even the folded clothes in the dresser, the words "even nothing is something" rang through her. Sure, D3 had more servants than toes, and he likely didn't know which wing of the house held the washing machines, but the vibe of the room felt alien. More like a museum or tribute to a person than a room ever inhabited by a human, let alone a human who lived in the house with regularity. And certainly not — however stereo-typical the thought — the room of a college-age boy.

Surely the cops had been through the place looking for clues, and the house staff had probably cleaned it twice a week. Maybe to make it nice for visitors to look at and pay tribute. But the question of "Why?" stuck itself to the room. Why would anyone bother folding his clothes so neatly? Why put the laundry bag back in the closet?

As fascinating as a room with "nothing wrong" could be, she didn't need more distractions. She snapped three quick pictures and closed the door behind her without a sound. A few more doors and bathrooms down, she came upon double doors, wide enough to fit a couch with ease. The knobs did not turn, but the door pulled open, like the latches didn't latch.

Danica stopped and yanked her hand back. Something had scratched her palm. She touched it again, gingerly, and found scratches around both door knobs. There were more on the wood, near the bottom and top edges. Somebody had tried to break in, or perhaps even managed the task.

The door opened as if by a breeze. The office inside was not fancy and hardly befitting the rest of the estate. Metal file cabinets and a metal desk and lots of cardboard accounting boxes. Trying to keep her work thorough, Danica snapped a couple pictures of the room and the scratched knobs.

The floor creaked from behind her. Somebody was coming, a fact confirmed by Mr. Peters' voice saying, "She went this way."

She ran deeper into the house. She tried another door, finding it locked. Another voice said something. Her head ached, her stomach lurched. Danica ignored them both and charged ahead. There had to be another way out.

Or maybe there wasn't. She had no guarantees, and her tipsy mind went from paranoia to full panic.

She opened the next door she came to and ducked inside a larger room.

Between keeping her breath low and listening for the footsteps to pass her up, she glanced at the room. Clearly the master bedroom, with windows looking toward the side yard. A four-poster, king-size bed sat in the middle, facing what must have been an antique vanity. Everything on the vanity, the bedside tables and dressers — from the jewelry to the hairbrushes to the books — sat in place, as if they occupied the only spaces they were meant to occupy. That necklace belonged *there*. That book belonged *there*. Different than the D3 room, where things appeared staged. Not unnatural, just precise.

In the hall, the footsteps charged by. She closed her eyes, imagining the remaining hall ahead of them, listening for the footstep sounds to dwindle.

The steps continued, lower in volume. Danica accepted it as the best, most-golden opportunity she would get and — taking Malcom's advice again — seized it. She charged out the room and down the hall, back toward the stairs.

Someone behind her shouted. She might have understood their words if her pounding heart hadn't been deafening. The stairs appeared ahead of her. She took them three at a time, blasted past some mourners, through the front door and off the porch without looking back.

Her path took her toward her car, but she thought better of it and ducked behind the bushes. Her car would be a dead giveaway. She would have to wait for someone else to leave.

Mr. Peters and a maid came out onto the porch. Danica ducked down, barely making out their voices. The sounds of heels on cement ran past her, then died down.

The lollipop bushes smelled fresh, like they'd been trimmed. She looked for the cowlick branch near her car, the one she saw when she arrived. It wasn't there.

The maid returned to the front a few minutes later, and reported to Mr. Peters that she had "lost her."

It did not improve his mood.

"Inside then," he said. "And do not share this information."

Danica crept out of the bushes, only tearing her new dress once. She slunk into her car and took a deep breath. If she backed out in neutral, she could start the engine and it would be a relatively straight shot to the exit.

Through her windshield she saw an empty spot in the row of lollipops. As though someone had dug a bush up rather than tend to its insubordination.

——————

CHAPTER TWENTY-SIX

——————

Same day, **just later. Van Nuys Library, Parking Lot.**

"A museum?" Malcom Fine sounded like he was chewing, which Danica took as Standard Malcom. "That's pretty weird."

"Super weird." Her parking spot at the library put her near the front. Their wifi signal was especially kind. She put on the speakerphone.

"And they locked up their junky office?"

"Yeah."

"You're sure?"

The doubt in his voice slowed her momentum. "I guess it's just kind of weird, but maybe it's dumb."

"No, no. You might be onto something. Weird is good, even just a little."

"Maybe."

"Are you still drunk?"

"No." She didn't think so. Mostly sober, but she didn't want to tell him that.

"You just gotta keep thinking," he said. "That's a big part of the job. Just thinking. Sometimes it's the whole job. It's like meditating or writing or any of that crap. Doesn't look like much, and sometimes it isn't, but it is, y'know?"

His version of logic made her feel more drunk. "Did you see anyone there who seemed out of place?"

"What do you mean?" he said.

"Just thinking: Mr. Peters seemed upset when you had your scene with that woman."

"You're welcome."

"And that office. Someone tried to break in. There must have been other people sneaking around."

"Like you."

"And like you."

"No, I didn't notice anyone especially out of place. Though this is LA. Everyone's a little out of place."

"Technically Bel Air."

"What?"

"The Albertses technically live in Bel Air."

"Which is *technically* in LA."

She groaned and regrouped. "I saw some pro-athletes, reality stars, the Mayor of Bel Air."

"...Huh?"

"He's this guy they call the Mayor."

"Who calls him that?"

"They. The Albertses, I think. I heard a cop say it."

"You talked to the cops about this?"

"No. Just gathering information."

Malcom chewed his food nice and close to the receiver.

"He's a friend."

Malcom chewed some more.

"I didn't tell him anything."

An email notification buzzed against her ear. "RESULTS

— ACADEMY BARBER SCHOOL HAS POS...". Final scores from were in. She swiped it away for later.

After a bit more chewing, Malcom at last said, "Bel Air doesn't have a mayor."

"What?"

"You said they call guy 'The Mayor.' Bel Air doesn't have a mayor."

"I know. It's just something the cops say."

"Why?"

"It's just kinda how the dude behaves. You probably saw him. He walks around glad-handing, all haughty and with a fake smile. Like a mayor. It's a nickname."

"What's his real name?"

"Don't know."

"You should find out," he said. "That's weird right? Guy with a weird nickname. There's something there. Some story, somewhere."

"I will."

"See? You didn't come away with nothing."

"Yeah, I got an assignment."

"Still. You got something. Take the assignment. Go get something else, and let me know."

"OK."

He shoved something else into his mouth, then made an excuse about meeting a client.

"Thanks, by the way."

He said, "No problem. Professional courtesy."

Danica plugged her phone into her charger and leaned back. The parking lot at the Van Nuys library was, by library standards, hoppin'. Busy parents formed a line of cars at the drop box, carefully shoving large board books into the slot, slowing everyone down and thus negating the convenience of the drop box.

Staring at the clean library wall, Danica considered her victory snatched from the jaws of defeat. Contemplation came easy, as she thought of grabbing tight to this momentum, charging inside the library and doing some real, hardcore, *book* research. She'd open up a pile of dusty tomes and carefully turn the yellowed pages so they didn't rip. She'd find the head librarian and ask for access to "the archives," and the librarian — perceiving Danica's inherent expertise — would unlock a special door to allow the sleuth to pour over old newspapers on microfiche, access old stories about old people with connections to the Alberts family, to Bel Air, to Los Angeles power brokers, and to Drake the Third. And if anybody asked her why, she could give a cryptic answer of "It's important," and it would be enough.

Her phone buzzed again, about the email notification, and it brought her back to reality. She wouldn't charge into anything, not without a good reason. All she had were the scatological graspings of random events, the encouragement of a dirt-bag mentor and the remnant hangover from funeral wine. Might as well just accept the facts. The school scores were in. She passed, she just knew it. She would be in that job, secure and forever.

Her thumb dangled over the screen when a flash of blue steel blazed across the street. A blue station wagon sat at the intersection, turn signal on. As the driver fumbled a paper, the light turned green. She didn't move, earning a honk from the car behind. The honk frazzled the driver even more.

Danica squinted through the sunlight, finally getting a good look at the driver's face.

It had to be a coincidence. Nothing more. A freak thing and no big deal. She should just chalk it up to chaos of the city and let it go. Get back to work, get certified, earn more money, fall in line and live a standard life. That driver? She was just trying to live her life, too. She deserved to be left to it. It was probably nothing. No big deal, just a coincidence…

That the driver of the blue station wagon was the tall, frazzled woman from the visitation. The one Malcom Fine had used as a distraction.

No big thing. Just something that happened sometimes, seeing the same unique woman twice on the same day, separated by half the city. Should be left alone.

The frazzled woman actually saw the next green light and made a turn.

Danica consider this "Just one of those things" for another split second before she hit the gas. A block later, she caught up to the blue wagon.

At the next red, she got a good look at the plates. Oregon, standard issue, no vanity message or symbols. The car could have been a rental, but the faded "I'd Rather Be Acting" bumper sticker said it was owned and had seen some miles. This woman made quite a journey just to make a scene at a rich guy's house.

The wagon made a few more turns, headed north, and Danica kept up. The collection of car lots and liquor stores felt like the same ones she'd seen for all her life in LA. The two cars crawled along together, with Danica being careful to leave a buffer car between them.

The woman was clearly lost, or at least muddled in her directions; twice she pulled off Sherman Way only to get back on again. The car between them slammed on its brakes when the blue wagon made a sudden turn left, cutting off a few on-comers to pull into a business park. Danica drove by the park, rubbernecking as she did: the blue station wagon had parked in front of Malcom Fine's office.

Danica drew her own chorus of horn-based criticism as

she made a quick u-turn, then parked at a meter just shy of the parking lot entrance. She parked and stared at the coincidence in the blue car.

The flustered woman stood up from her car, then jumped back in when she realized she'd left it in gear, stopping it before making permanent foundational damage to the building. She gave a passing attempt at straightening her hair, then entered the PI's office. Her hand was wrapped in gauze; Danica couldn't remember if it had been so at the house. The memories of the visitation swirled into a mess.

A moment later, the office door opened and the flustered woman stormed out, slamming the door against the wall. She paced the sidewalk and gnawed on the gauze. Then she walked to her car, opened the door and sat in the drivers seat, door left open.

Danica got ready to follow, but the Oregon wagon didn't start. The frizzy hair in the front seat trembled, leaned forward to the steering wheel, bouncing a little. The shoulders joined in.

Once again, ignoring the woman and leaving her to her business seemed like the rational option. Danica could have stayed in her car and watched the whole thing unravel, or even just drive home and leave well enough alone. Engaging with this woman at such an obvious low felt borderline cruel and over-the-line exploitative, and Danica considered herself to be better than both those things.

She got out of the Honda and approached the building. 'Just passing by,' she lied to herself. 'A common pedestrian, walking to work or the store or something. Just passing by.'

As she just passed by, she caught a quick glimpse into the station wagon. The woman was certainly crying.

'Just passing by. Looking for an office in this office park.' The lies carried Danica to the walk leading through the parking lot, past the empty offices, toward RESULTS and the woman in the wagon.

The woman's frizzy head rested on her hands, and her hands rested on the wheel. She lifted her head to gasp for air and filled the parking lot with a long moan.

Her eyes locked on Danica, who, to her own surprise, had stopped walking. Some pedestrian.

The woman's gaze looked through her, pleading for anything close to compassion.

"Can I help you?" said Danica.

This startled the woman. She spoke through gritted teeth. "Who are you?"

"I'm just... I saw you and you looked like you needed something."

What little of the woman's tough exterior crumbled into a look of desperation. "Do you know Mr. Fine?"

"Um...." Danica looked behind her, then tried to act like she hadn't looked directly at the office door. "Not sure who you mean."

"Then no, you cannot help me. Nobody can." While Danica couldn't refute this statement, the woman had spoken in such a grand and dramatic fashion that it came off rehearsed. Put on.

"I meant do you need water or tissues or something?"

"I saw you." The woman sniveled and sat up. "You were there, at the house today."

"You mean the visitation?"

The woman had light blue eyes, framed with red irritation. Her thin lips bent into a weak smile. "You knew Drakey."

Now, in what limited exposure Danica had enjoyed with the Alberts family, they had not given the impression that their son — or anyone in their family — would ever —

under any circumstance — ever — be called "Drakey." It was too chummy, and a little lazy just to add "Y" to the end of a such a regal name. Yet this woman spoke the name with absolute comfort and confidence, and it seemed natural, like she'd done it her whole life. Or at least for Drake's whole life.

"You did, too, huh?" said Danica.

She wiped her nose with her gauze.

"Someone's got to do something." She started sobbing again. "Someone has to care. Nobody cares. Nobody wants to find out what really happened to my nephew."

The woman's panache tripped Danica's sensors, and she questioned her sincerity. She could have been lying. She was very dramatic, putting every word she spoke at an elevated level of pseudo-sincerity. She could have been exaggerating, and only been an "auntie." Danica had a couple aunties growing up; women who lived in the area, who were friends with the family and helped out every now and then. Caring adults with no blood-relation. Aunties would cry over losing a child they knew.

They probably wouldn't cry as much as this woman. They probably wouldn't drive hundreds of miles from Oregon to attend a visitation. They probably wouldn't enlist a private investigator to solve a crime that didn't concern their own family. Not unless they really cared. Really, really, really cared.

Or, unless, they really, really, really were the aunt of Drake Alberts III. A direct relative who somehow had come to believe that the case had not been solved. The woman's round face and nose settled and her place in the family came clear. She was family, and judging on the round face and natural scowl, came from Drake's father's side.

Danica grabbed a tissue from her pocket and handed it over. "I'm Danica."

"Thank you. Samantha." She — Samantha — blew her nose and wiped her eyes. Her crying did not cease, just came in smaller amounts. "I'll be OK."

Danica took the hint, dropping back into her Helpful Pedestrian Role. She walked into the parking lot in the same direction as her original fictional course. After taking the long way out of the parking lot, she made her way back to her car and (after only three tries) started it and pulled onto Sherman Way.

Someone else had the same hunch as her, that the case had not been solved properly. Sure, that "someone else" was a complete wreck, and clearly unstable, but it was something. And she had a name: Samantha. Possibly Samantha Alberts.

Malcom knew this woman. Possibly before the visitation. Their encounter had made a scene, but if he knew Samantha (Possibly) Alberts ahead of time, he would have known how easy making a scene with her would be.

And if he knew that, then they knew each other before the event. And the likelihood that this distraught woman from the Pacific Northwest had the wherewithal to contact a random, sleaze ball "survivor" who would do anything it took to...

Malcom Fine had poached the case. He wasn't dumb; he took the information Danica handed to him, smelled blood (and money) in the water, and sniffed out a client for himself. He was at the visitation working her case, right under her nose.

Two could dance that number. She did another u-turn and headed back to the office park. Convincing Samantha to trust her wouldn't be too difficult, especially with the anger motivating Danica beyond propriety. She would demonstrate how much she cared about D3, that she was on the case, and that she could truly help. Samantha would have to believe her, and give her a golden opportunity to throw Malcom's "golden opportunity" speech in his fat face.

When Danica got to the parking lot, Aunt Samantha, the blue wagon and the golden opportunity were gone.

She hung around the office park for an hour, in hopes of seeing someone come back, but reality soon set in. Even if they did come back, what could she expect to get from them? They had their team, their side, and she was on the other end. They weren't going to share anything.

<hr>

CHAPTER TWENTY-SEVEN

<hr>

Same afternoon. **San Fernando Valley Streets.**

An angry drive around the neighborhood felt necessary. Her Honda had been trained to search out the cheapest-looking gas station. It passed a couple Mobil's, a Shell and even an ARCO on its way to We Got It, a place that preferred cash and sold cheap cigarettes.

When they were a couple, Tommy bought cigarettes from We Got It all the time. He acted like he had a special relationship with the guy who worked there (she wanted to say Amir). Like this guy gave two craps about the opinion of some hipster white boy. Didn't matter. The place was still open and still selling. She'd pre-pay, and if she had change to spare, would ruin her streak of good behavior.

Danica cut off a black Audi to get in the turn lane. After she turned the corner, she glanced in the mirror. The black Audi was there. In a few blocks, she made another turn onto Woodman, and the Audi followed.

So what? People drove cars on streets. Free country. She

wasn't special for going all this way to some little cheap gas station. Anyone else would do the same.

The Audi matched her turn onto Roscoe.

A red light stopped her and she kept her eyes on the mirror, trying to catch a glimpse of Logan or Benji. This stalker move smelled like their style. Logan was probably so high he forgot to pass the message to Benji; or forgot she'd talked to him. They probably thought it was still last week. Their car got an upgrade though.

The sign for We Got It appeared, and Danica pulled next to a pump. She watched the Audi roll through the turn, then pull into a No Parking section.

Danica got out. If they were to have it out, she thought, best to do it in plain sight.

"Hey, Benji! Listen, man, we talked this over. I'm not doing the newspaper."

The black Audi made no motion. Its windows were opaque.

A man in a pickup truck at the light held up his hands like he didn't understand what she said, in this conversation that wasn't his. Danica waved him off and pointed at the Audi.

"I said I'm not doing the stupid newspaper! And if you're looking for, um, what the family gave me... uh...." She was getting too wordy about money for a shouted street conversation.

The light turned green. The pickup pulled forward, along with the other west-bound folk. The Audi did not join them.

"I see you! I'm calling your teachers. I don't have anything to do with your stupid paper!"

The Audi held its position. It drew honks for blocking the right turn lane, but it did not seem to care.

Danica's stomach churned and her legs went tight. The Audi had her in the wide open. She got the strange sensation that she should not go home, that she should draw Benji away from her home, on some wild goose chase.

Then she got the even stranger sensation that it might not be Benji in that car at all.

She walked backwards, keeping her eyes on the street. At the cashier window a man grunted a welcome.

"You okay there?" he said.

Danica ignored him, maintaining her stare.

The Audi revved its engine. When the light turned yellow, it blasted through the intersection just as the light turned red.

That wasn't Benji. It wasn't college students, or student journalists. They didn't say anything or do anything. They were just following her.

"Miss?" said the cashier.

She turned to face him and saw his name tag. His name really *was* Amir.

"Ten on pump three, please."

"Sure, sure," said Amir. "Anything else, miss?"

She looked at the cigarettes above Amir, then said, "No. Thanks."

Amir let Danica loiter around for another two hours, as long as she stayed in the back and occasionally bought a Mountain Dew.

Maybe she was paranoid, and working and thinking so much about suspicious, unprovable things had driven her to see connections where none existed. But that car did follow her. It had sat on the corner for a while. Even though she couldn't see the driver, she could tell he was staring at her.

It didn't have to be paranoia. It could've been legit. She had already made enemies with the Daily Trojan, a feat accomplished by accident. It seemed possible that she could have inadvertently pissed off lots of people. She settled on this "best case" as she arrived at work.

Carla had a sizable amount of scolding and chewing out built up, so by the time Danica entered the shop, they didn't waste any time. Carla blew up, letting loose a barrage of no-customers-around chastising this side of a drill sergeant. When she finally ran out of breath, Carla went to the office to "finish up," slamming the door behind. Danica thought it best to leave her to it. Just another disappointment for the day.

For masochistic fun, she tallied up the other missteps. She hadn't gotten any visions from Drake III, she let Aunt Samantha slip away, and — upon closer, sober inspection — her pictures from the Alberts Estate were blurry. Not that she expected to get anything from a dark shot of junky office, but the lack of focus added insult to injury. The bright side called to her about getting to snoop around the bedrooms, and while that was true, the fact that she'd been manipulated into doing the snooping by Malcom annoyed her. He must have wanted her out of the way.

She wrapped up a customer (Diane, one of her semi-regulars who wore too much mascara) then looked at her photos again. The wine must have been even more potent than she realized. She sent the photo into the trash, and the previous photo replaced it. The lamp wasn't even as fancy as she remembered. How many had she taken? She selected the pictures from the day and trashed, them, too. The Deaton Auditorium photo popped into the forefront. Another fuzzy shot, taken stone sober, of the family portrait that had enraged Mr. Alberts beyond his usual level.

A walk-in walked in, as they do. Danica greeted the gentleman without looking away from the phone. She drew him to her station, listening to him describe his style, all while looking at that fuzzy painting picture.

Though blurred, the eyes of the extra woman stared back at her. Young and vacant. The painter had invented a smile on her face where it didn't belong.

Her customer made a polite cough. He had a mustache, a flip phone and grey temples, and was too nice to yell at her for her neglect. "Do you need a moment, miss?" he said with gracious passive-aggression.

Danica zoomed in on the picture, blurring it all the more. But it helped.

"It's her," she said.

"Who?" said the customer.

"Samantha Alberts."

"Who?" he said again.

Without pausing, Danica showed the photo to him.

"Right there. See that woman? I met her."

"Is this an iPhone?" he said. "I've heard about them."

She ignored his awe at modern smartphone advancements and snatched back her phone. Her fingers opened up the trash, pulling the drunk shots from the Alberts Estate and stopped when she saw the one from her Lamp Series.'

The picture was just as blurry as her memory of the event, but she remembered this part right: the photo of the lamp had captured Samantha in the background, in her faded black dress, gauze, and looking nearly straight into the camera.

"Can I ask you something?" Danica said, returning her phone to the gentleman's face before he could answer. "You see this woman?"

"Behind that lovely lamp?"

"Yeah, her."

"Kinda blurry."

"Right, but you can make out some of her, right? Wedgy hair. Round face. Now..." Danica swiped back to the painting — the one that had angered Mr. Alberts — and pointed at the extra woman on the side. "What do you think?"

The customer pursed his mouth. "They look similar."

"It's her."

"May I see?" He took the phone and adjusted his eyes around his wire glasses. "Can you... how do you zoom in on these things?"

Danica zoomed in for him and handed the phone back.

"I suppose you're right, miss. Those little curly cues there, along the side of her face. Does the other one have those?"

"Yep," she said. She swiped back to the Deaton portrait."It's her, isn't it?"

"Could be."

"It is."

"Sure."

What did this guy know? He just stepped in off the street. He didn't know Samantha's personality, her dramatic tendencies — PS, totally on point for her family — and he didn't know how important her part was to all of this.

Neither did Danica. But she did know that Samantha was alive and a part of the Alberts family. She got clipped out, but she was alive.

And Danica let her slip away.

"You mind if I ask," said the gentleman, "What's all that mean?"

She had no answer. Not yet. She turned the gentleman to face the mirror and touched his hair. "Sorry about that. What are we doing tonight?"

CHAPTER TWENTY-EIGHT

LATE SUNDAY NIGHT. Too late. Technically Monday Morning. Island Estates, Apartment 213.

That night, sleep came to Danica no easier than it did in the nights prior. It dodged around the ceiling, drooping down in the dim bedroom light to tease her, playing like it would finally settle, only to dash away again, scared away by another thought floating around.

Danica closed her eyes and listened. The alley traffic sounded heavy. Headlights cast shadows through her dusty blinds. Some birds on the other side chirped angry sounds at each other. Birds making noise so late at night sounded unnatural.

Again, sleep got scared away by the lingering thoughts of the day, the week, and how they didn't make sense with each other.

"Someone has to find out what really happened." Samantha's words ran over and over. The validation of having someone out there who agreed with Danica's hypothesis paled in comparison against the uneasy sensation of being right about something terrible. The case was messed up. The Mr. Alberts' faith in the police to drag their feet was messed up. Something was off.

Danica rolled on her side. Her pillow felt warm.

Samantha had probably been close with D3. She must have kept up with his life, and the news surrounding the end of it devastated her. She must have heard about Josue Rodriguez, too. It was no secret, getting broadcast like lightning across farmland. If Samantha thought someone had to find out what "really" happened, then she did not believe the story about Josue to be true.

She must've had a reason. Possibly a suspect of her own in mind. And she would have certainly shared that information with her hired PI. Whoever she suspected, Malcom knew about it by now. Probably knew about it at the visitation. Samantha Alberts didn't seem like the patient kind, and after the visitation, crying in her car, that patience had come to an end.

People didn't grow more impatient when a suspect they believe to be guilty is named. They grow impatient when they believe the actual guilty party was getting away.

A search for "Samantha Alberts" pulled up only early-in-life results, with the young aunt-to-be joining in the family tradition of shaking hands and smiling with cops. She dropped out of the picture (and the pictures) around 1986. Disappeared. Clipped. A passing mention of "travel" came in a September 1986 article about Samantha helping to fight poverty, and that was the end. She could have changed her name, but Danica found no breadcrumbs on that.

Samantha knew something. She probably knew many things, where to find them, who to ask, where to look and more insights into Drake's life and why he was killed. Samantha knew, and Danica had lost her.

Malcom must have known where she went, where she lived and much more. At least he knew her full, current name. They must have spoken and gone somewhere together, or she got angry and left. He knew her, knew how to get in touch with her and he'd keep all of it to himself. He'd keep up the ruse of mentoring Danica. 'Professional courtesy,' like he did at the visitation, acting like he didn't know Samantha. But he did. He knew her. It was his business to know.

Which meant Maggie knew her, too.

Crazy schemes rolled through Danica's imagination, one after another, all with a basic premise of tricking Maggie into getting a haircut, leading her to think about Samantha, and then drawing the contact information from her brain. None of them would work, and Danica's psychic ability — the thing that made her truly special — rested, even though her brain could not. What use was a magic ability if you couldn't actually use it?

Sleep retreated into the ceiling. No use fighting tonight.

CHAPTER TWENTY-NINE

Monday, September 1, 2008. 8:03AM. Parking Lot Outside Malcom Fine's office.

Maggie Howard-MacCloud arrived to open the office, alone. The few minutes she was late herself was beside the point. Malcom was not at his work, as Danica had hoped, just as she'd hoped that the office would still get opened by his diligent, put-upon assistant.

When Maggie saw Danica get out of her car, she rolled her eyes.

"I'm not even gonna ask if you have an appointment. He's not here."

"I actually just wanted to check on something," said Danica, catching the door from closing on her face. "There was a woman here yesterday. Set on seeing Malcom. Did she?"

"We get lots of people coming in and out." Maggie rinsed out the coffee pot.

Danica described Samantha in a breezy fashion while she sidled up to the side of Maggie's desk. Her hopes of seeing a note jotted down on a loose scrap of paper sank. The desk was the neatest thing in the office by a long shot. Maggie's computer was locked (and probably password protected), and the two piles of paper were tidy and cornered on opposite sides.

"I just had to help her," said Danica.

"You're a humanitarian," said Maggie, keeping her back to Danica.

Danica leaned against the wall near the coffee maker. "She was in a bad state. I saw her earlier, at a visitation. Just beside herself. Said some crazy stuff. You must have heard her. Did she say anything to you?"

"Not much." She wasn't cracking.

"If she had, you'd agree with me. If she'd said anything."

Maggie filled the coffee filter without turning away. Time for Danica's Plan B.

"So if she.. I think her name's Samantha. If Samantha — Hold it. Don't move."

"What?" said Maggie.

"Do. Not. Move."

Maggie reacted to the sudden serious tone and froze.

Danica said, low, "I think I see a bee."

"A bee? In here?!"

"In your hair."

Maggie flung her hands, but Danica caught them.

"Don't. It'll sting you."

"Get it out get it out get it out!"

Danica held Maggie's collar with one hand and swung through her hair with the other. "Wait." She swatted again, and looked around the floor. She let go of Maggie.

"Did you get it? Where is it? Did you get it?"

Danica bent down and picked up a scrap of paper. "I think it was just this."

"You serious?" If it had been possible to sound more irritated than when she opened the door, Maggie did it. Her glare melted the paint.

"Sorry. Gotta go." Danica left with a quickness.

Typically, Danica's psychic abilities got their clearest connections when she touched the center of the scalp. She assumed this had something to do with proximity to certain neurons within the brain, but had put no serious scientific study to it. When she wanted a good look, she targeted the center. It was reliable. Every now and then, though, she got a tingle from the other spots around the head, including the section down the neck, just above the collar.

Just where she had touched Maggie Howard-MacCloud.

Visibility in this non-traditional position increased through making suggestions, leading the visualizer to load the images into their consciousness.

Just as Danica did by mentioning Samantha, describing her and keeping the Samantha Idea in the forefront of their conversation.

Sometimes those off-mid-head visions came through murky, even with suggestions helping them along.

Yet somehow, with Maggie Howard-MacCloud, the images came through in brilliant Technicolor. Danica saw Samantha storm into the office, yell for Mr. Fine, get told he wasn't there, then take offense at his absence. With her hand on the door, she stopped to leave her name and insist that Mr. Fine contact her ASAP since she was leaving town that night.

Maggie wrote it down: "Samantha Willows."

· · ·

Danica found a quiet-ish neighborhood with space to conduct her Google searches in peace.

By all public accounts, and by any definition of the term, Samantha Willows-Alberts was the black sheep of the family. Aside from attending USC, marrying early (in 1988 to Mr. Blake Willows) and occasionally showing up for public events, her history cut a divergent path from the standard "business and business" Albert business, veering toward the artistic, the risky and the failing end of life.

In college, she studied art history and theater, throwing herself into plays and other live performances. The titles she worked on were ponderous and excruciating ("The Way of Things," "A Distance Too Far, My Love Told Me Before," "Wishing Well and the Boy"). Apparently, Samantha was one of those people who wanted to make theater that tried hard to "grab people."

Out of college, Samantha's story ran toward philanthropy and closer to the Alberts Family Way of Things, though her toe found an occasional artistic affair in which to dip. After her husband's passing in 1999, she re-ignited her love of theater and made a serious attempt to grab people in Bel Air. Samantha bought property to turn into a local theater. It collapsed in less than a year, perhaps due to the theater's radical public views about the rich establishment, or maybe straight-up misman-agement. Or both. They mounted only one production, then folded. After that she sold the place and moved, either out of shame or seeking opportunity, or a little bit of both.

The address of Samantha's Helmet of Zeus Theater had a familiarity to it. Danica adjusted her search and found a map. It was approximated, not a hundred percent, but the location of Samantha's former theater was at the end of a cul-de-sac in Bel Air.

Close to the Alberts Estate.

Probably with a nice long porch and recently sold.

She made notes, little beyond wild theories and conjecture, but it felt like progress to write something down. Danica let her imagination scribble, allowing assumption to take hold.

Danica wrote how Samantha was a drama queen, by trade and in person. Dramatic people did not give up spotlights cold turkey, even if they ran out of money and left town. The money she got for selling the Dream House could have set her up for something else someplace else.

Gabby used to talk about little theater companies sprinkled in remote places, summer stock types and seasonal city-supported programs held close by their communities. Maybe Samantha found one and holed up. Northern California, closer to Oregon and far from Hollywood, surrounded by protected forests. A way to hide from So-Cal, but still draw attention to herself. Yet Danica found no evidence of Samantha trying anything, using her name. As uncharacteristic as it sounded of a one-woman show like Samantha Alberts-Willows, she wanted to disappear, and she did it.

Danica looked at her notes. Researched guesses; attempts to build a timeline and a biography of Samantha, of someone with tenuous connections to everything and connections to nothing.

Everything except for Drake the Third. Nobody had reported on how much she loved her nephew, but Danica got that straight from the horse's mouth. And that drama horse doubted the current process. The horse thought Josue was innocent.

If Danica could reach the horse, she could gain key

information. Maybe get ideas of how to find Josue. She might know exactly where he was.

They could find him, together, and get the truth.

CHAPTER THIRTY

POLICE GUN DOWN SUSPECT IN ALBERTS MURDER

By Lily Gradzhyan.

Panorama City, CA — In a dramatic scene last night, the LAPD surrounded an apartment building on Van Owen and Coldwater Canyon with their primary goal of apprehending Josue Dominc Rodriguez alive. For the chief suspect in the murder of Drake Alberts III, this was not to be.

"We announced our presence and intentions, following standard procedure, when the suspect opened fire," said Police Captain Baker. "LAPD returned fire and pursued the suspect through the backyard, where bullets finally took the suspect's life."

Drake Alberts II, father of Drake III, spoke to the press after the shooting, his first such contact with the press since losing his son. "My wife and I are proud, as always, of the police force for their tireless work in delivering justice. I know they were strained, with Los Angeles being so large and with crime every-where. We want to help with that. We appreciate their efforts with this matter."

Rodriguez had been on the run for a week since the murder took place, hiding with friends and relatives around the San Fernando Valley. He was 21 years old.

Danica re-read the article, in case her emotions had jumped to some stupid conclusions.

They had not. She'd read it all correctly. Josue was dead, and her heart plunged through the floor.

Danica barely made it up the stairs to Apartment 213. She might have closed the door behind her, or might not have.

Given recent events in Danica's life, Carla would appreciate a phone call. Something to let her know Danica was OK and doing just fine, thank you. She made it almost forty-two seconds into the call before unloading her information about Samantha, both the actual observations and the ones she'd cobbled together.

It felt good to say them out loud, hearing for herself how ludicrous-yet-relatable they really were.

During what could be politely referred to as a ramble, the other end of her phone stayed silent. Danica had expected her boss to interrupt, with either a contrarian view point or a cutting "That's a waste of time" aside.

Danica awaited Carla's rebuke, and braced herself for the full fury to hit her with a figurative punch in the mouth.

It didn't come. What did come, from Carla, was more shocking. "So Samantha is like a sister or something?"

"Yes. Related to Drake the Second. First born it turns out."

"And she pulled herself off the grid."

"Maybe. Or she was taken off." Danica reminded Carla about the two oil paintings, but stopped short of emailing her a copy.

She paused to allow her manager a chance to fight back. When no such offering came, and to keep the conversation moving, Danica continued. "I bet that happens, you know? With rich people. Somebody steps out of line, grandma doesn't like what you wore to Christmas and, boom, you're out of the will."

"And you saw her."

"Yeah. Met her even. And she looked like a black sheep. Of any family, but certainly of this one."

Another pause for polite back-and-forth, the invitation remained ignored.

"This woman might know where all the skeletons are buried," said Danica. "I don't know if she's a suspect exactly, but she's definitely a person of interest. She's an interesting person, let's put it that way."

"But a suspect?" said Carla.

"I don't know."

"Don't discount it. Put her on the list. You do have a list going, right?"

"Um... yeah."

"Well...?"

Danica picked up her notepad and wrote the names, ignoring the fact that she should have made this list earlier. "I got Josue Rodriguez — gotta put him on there, right? Mr. Peters, the butler. He's hiding something. Maybe from Mr.

Alberts or for him, but still. I got Mr. Alberts, too, as gross as it sounds. And the Mayor of Bel Air—"

"Bel Air doesn't have a mayor."

"It's just his nickname."

"What's his real name?"

"Don't know yet."

"Add this Samantha person."

Danica did.

"And what about Beckett?"

"What about him?"

"Don't you got him on your list?"

Danica gave no answer.

"I think you should consider the guy," Carla said. "Being so close with Drake and all."

"You 'think'? As in 'You've been thinking about it?' That sounds like something you'd say if you were interested in this case."

"It makes sense. Just put him on."

She did. The list, while short, still ran too long. Only Josue had anything close to credibility behind the accusation, and the rest relied more on faith than anything else.

The re-inclusion of Beckett gave the list a bizarre bend. Danica had spent the last couple days trying to forget about that dead end, allowing for the fact that weird people sometimes do weird things and that's just the way it is.

Only the sound of Carla's fan came across the line, for at least ten seconds, until the manager finally spoke: "Nor-Cal's really far."

"What do you mean?"

"You said that this aunt lived in Oregon. Or Northern California. It's far."

Danica agreed, then said, "I think I could cross Beckett off."

"Wait. Why?"

"He's just some skittish weirdo who got freaked out. There's some story there, but not the one I'm looking for."

"He's gone."

"Right, exactly."

"No, I mean he's gone," said Carla. "He never came back to his office."

Danica adjusted the phone to her other ear. "You were off work yesterday, weren't you?"

"Yes."

"What'd you end up doing?"

"...Stuff."

"You go anywhere?"

"...Yes."

"Where?"

"...The city."

"Where in the city?"

Carla let out a long cough, then said, "...USC."

"The theater arts building?"

"Okay, fine! I went to check on your paper thing. The thing in the door. You said this guy seemed like a good suspect. He had access to the Drake kid, all out in the open — I had a high school teacher who was a real creep and we all thought he did stuff with this one girl, Naomi Washington. Then Naomi disappeared and we thought he'd killed her."

"Jeez, Carla..."

"He didn't; she just moved to Oklahoma or someplace without telling us, but still, it didn't mean the teacher wasn't creepy. When you said this Beckett guy was close to Drake, it reminded me of that. So I went and looked at Keith Beckett's office."

"To make sure it had been cleaned?"

"Your paper was still stuck there. Still in the door frame."

Danica couldn't tell if Carla was proud, envious or terrified. "The Sting" had good ideas after all!

Sort of. "That doesn't mean much. It was the weekend."

"He works on weekends," said Carla. "Some kids told me. Beckett's in there all the time, stays late, on weekends especially. 'Til now. He took sabbatical."

"As of when?"

"As of Friday, the last day you saw him. He called in an "emergency scenario," like he pulled some seniority move, and — poof — dude's gone."

Danica rubbed her forehead. "I'm sorry, but I need the whole story. How did you get all this information? From students?"

"Some. And the registrar's office. Don't you think that's all a bit weird, even for such a weird guy? He's been there his whole career, every day for thirty some years, now all of a sudden he wants to start a vacation? At the beginning of the school year?"

"They know where he went?"

"Nope. Not. A. Clue.'"

"Hold it. Don't go anywhere." She put the phone down and flipped back in her notes, found the latest scratchings about Samantha. 'Attended USC. 1983-1987.'

She picked up the phone again. "Beckett's been at USC for thirty years. I think... never mind."

"OK," said Carla.

"Beckett's been at USC for thirty years."

"You just said that."

"He started in the seventies. 1978, I think."

"Okay."

"Samantha Alberto attended USC in 1983. And she studied theater."

It clicked. "Damn, this chick knows everybody."

They knew each other — Samantha and Beckett. Which tied them in a knot with Drake. Given the intimate knowledge she could have had about both men, Samantha may have suspected Beckett the whole time. It didn't change the fact that they had all disappeared, leaving no good way to lure them out.

Not without good bait.

Carla broke the accidental silence. "Glad we cracked this."

"Far from it," said Danica, "but this helped." She needed a lure. Something to get Samantha's attention. To tell her she was on her side, or after her, she still didn't know.

In the meantime, she had a connection, and clung to it like a desperate prospector finding a golden glimmer in the river. Another half-baked plan took form. She had an email to write. She'd need some Samantha bait, or some Beckett bait, but she also needed to find the hook.

"Thanks for this, Carla."

"Any time?"

"Really? Because—"

"Oh, no."

"I don't think it's dangerous, but since you're so clearly good at this type of stuff—"

"Just tell me already?"

"I wondered. There's a house that recently sold. That stuff is all on record somewhere, right?"

"Yep. How I found out about the meth-head salon."

"You can get the name of the owner and all that?"

Carla sighed. "What's the address?"

Danica gave her the address of the Dream House on the Bel Air cul-de-sac. Carla promised to run it by her realtor.

"That's it?" said Carla.

"That's it. And I'll probably be a little late again."

"I'm getting way too used to it."

True. Danica owed her manager more than she could afford. She'd make it up to her somehow, with more than some expensive-feeling coffee.

A question arose and Danica couldn't help herself:

"How did you get the registrar to tell you so much? That place was locked up tight."

"...I dunno."

Danica smelled the lie. "Just tell me."

The confidence in Carla's voice dropped. "I said I was a parent of a current student."

Danica yanked the phone from her face to keep her laughter at bay. Even from the distance, Carla heard, and the groans and shouts vibrated through Danica's hand.

"I'm so sorry," said Danica. "Thank you so much. You've done great work."

"Pfft. They didn't even question it either. Probably thought I was old enough to be a grandma. The turds."

CHAPTER THIRTY-ONE

MONDAY, **September 1, 11:39AM. Magnolia and Buena Vista, Burbank.**

A waif of a woman sat outside Bean and Pie coffee shop, tapping her foot against the leg of the table and trying not to look at her phone. Refusing society's requirements of waiting to eat before all the guests had appeared, the waif sipped her tea and nibbled her butter croissant. She had places to go.

Danica didn't want the waif to see her car; she looked like someone who watched her diet, probably focusing on getting to TV one day, and would likely judge someone by the car they drove. Danica walked from the corner, having parked her Accord in front of a different pricey coffee shop. Burbank was sick with the places, with more money to throw at coffee and tea toppings than any sane person would think possible.

She passed two young men drinking chocolate milk

under game hats at a little table, and headed straight for the table of the waif.

"Ms. Gradzhyan?" Danica said.

The waif pushed back her flat, black hair and looked up. Her smile arrived rehearsed. She stood quickly and held out her hand. "Lily."

Danica took the seat across from her and watched her open a MacBook Pro. Notes were to be taken.

"Let's just jump into it," said Lily. "You're interested in the internship program."

"Very," said Danica. "Fight on."

"Fight on indeed. I'm always happy to help someone from the alma mater. Are you a current student?"

"Not any more. Joined the work force."

"As?"

"Barber. Well, hair stylist."

"OK." Lily made some notes as a frown pushed her eyebrows together.

"I know it sounds a little weird, but it gives me access to more information than you might think." Danica leaned closer. "And from what I've heard about the internship, that's what counts."

"Definitely. Now, you didn't write for Daily Trojan. Do you have any samples?"

"Does it matter?"

"Not entirely, if the information you're talking about is good, we can probably work something out."

"For college credit?"

"Sure."

"Or something else?"

Lily blinked, then said "Sure" again.

"Actually, I've already got some good stuff on a pretty big story. Is that how this works?"

"It can."

"I know you've got other interns — people like me, running around getting info on various stories. It makes sense. Gives you more legs. You're only one person. So we run around town and try to drum up stories. Then, we give them to you."

"I don't know if I'd put it quite like that—"

"And when one of us gets a whale — one of those big stories connected to deep pockets — that's when the program really picks up. That's what I'm most interested in. How much money are we talking about?"

Lily stopped typing. "It all depends."

"Of course," said Danica. "Some people care more about this stuff than others. I think the trick is to find the ones who really care about it, and get to them fast. People who care a lot about their appearance in the newspapers and magazines and all that stuff. People with image consultants and fat wallets. Do you meet with them ahead of the story, or do they just hand you what to write?"

Lily's head tilted to the side and her hair moved in a blade, stuck together.

Danica continued: "I think it's mostly the second way. The rich people connect with you and your interns, and you type up what they give you, everyone getting a little cash here and there."

"Seems like you've got it all down."

"I do. And when you can send in a flood of interns to get paid, there's tons of money going everywhere, right?"

Two perfectly-painted lips parted, then said, "Not tons."

"Do you live in Burbank, Lily?"

The question threw her a bit. "What does that matter?"

"It's nice. Not Beverly Hills or Bel Air, but it's isn't Van Nuys either. You're drinking primo tea at a primo place, with the latest computer and your nails look great. You own a house, despite the fact that you've only been writing professionally for three years."

"Okay."

"So the money adds up, if you're organized."

Lily closed her computer and moved to stand. "I think that's enough."

"Some of your boys shook me down a while back."

Lily did not stand up. "I didn't tell... I... What is this?"

"Nothing. I haven't talked to cops or anything, but I thought you should know that when you hire idiots, they can turn out to be greedy idiots. They thought I was horning in on their cut, whatever scraps you toss their way, so they keyed my car and tried to scare me off of writing an article."

"I thought you were a barber."

"I am. There's no article to write. Like I said: idiots."

Lily studied Danica's face for a moment. "So you want them to stop?"

"I wanna talk about the murder of Drake Alberts III."

"Holy Christmas..."

"Specifically about your article from August 26. 'Son of Drake Alberts Found Stabbed to Death.' You edited something out after it was first published online."

Lily had high cheekbones, and they reached her eyes when she smiled. "That was a bait."

"Pretend I don't know what that means."

"You write the story with details that you know someone won't like. Someone involved. These aren't lies. They're just... details. To draw a reaction. Sometimes nobody says anything. Most times, actually. But every now and then, someone reacts. And you'd be surprised how into the details some people get. Height, weight, hair color, hair style all that kind of stuff can really matter."

"So you put the wrong details in the right place, hoping someone will get upset."

"Sort of, yeah. They take the bait and reach out. This is where social media is very important." She talked like a saleswoman, making her pitch for her plan's effectiveness like she was up for a promotion. "If they're smart, they contact you directly, and you set up the terms, remove this and that for a price, and it's done. No harm, no foul. Nobody thinks twice about the whole 'has since been edited' line at the bottom."

"Your editor just thinks it's typos?"

Lily nodded. "It's the internet. Junk gets printed all the time."

"But they're not all typos," said Danica. "And not with this article."

"It could've been. I honestly don't remember."

"It wasn't. It was about Keith Beckett being a drama professor."

She shrugged. "If you say so."

"Remember who made you take it off?"

Lily sucked on her teeth, then said, "It happens so fast and I can't promise my notes are up to date."

"How much did you get?"

"More than normal, I think."

"But not a lot. Not enough to remember."

"No," said Lily.

"So you wrote the story as directed by the Alberts family, used mostly their wording and template, but added some extra facts here and there. And one fact was about Mr. Beckett. Then you got contacted to remove 'drama teacher' from the story."

"Congrats. You're a genius."

Danica stood and dug into her pocket. She pulled the

nine-hundred from her pocket and peeled off four bills. "I would like to buy your services."

"Say what now?"

"Simple job, so this should cover things, right?"

"I'll need details. Name of the article, links if you have them."

"It's your recent work. The one about Josue being shot and killed."

"What am I removing?"

"You're adding. I want you to add that Josue Rodriguez was five-foot-six and, let's say, a hundred-and-ninety pounds. And that he had dreams to become an actor."

Lily waited for Danica to go on and when she didn't, she said, "That's it?"

"That's it."

"Can I ask why?" Like she suddenly cared about why people throw money at the ethics of journalism.

"Just make the changes, OK? You could probably do it from here. It's Burbank. This place has wifi."

"Actually, the whole city should have it for free by 2016."

"Make the changes, please."

Danica stood over Lily's shoulder and watched her log on to her LA Times employee account. The addition took less than thirty seconds.

"Good," said Danica, then she dropped the remaining bills onto the table. "Now. When you get contacted to change it, I want you to tell me who contacts you, and where they contacted you from."

Lily spit a little laugh. "They don't usually tell me their life's story."

"Get someone to look it up for you. Like how your boys found me by using my email address."

Danica had pointed this last part toward the chocolate

milk boys at the nearby table. Sure enough, they turned on cue. Benji and Logan looked at her from under the brims of their hats, finally aware that the conversation involved them.

"You two are millennials. You know about IP addresses and that stuff. When your boss asks you to look this up, do it." Danica turned to Lily. "Got it?"

Lily nodded. "You know, you might not be right for this program."

"Probably not."

"You paid for information you already have. You know where the Alberts family lives."

"I do," said Danica. "But I don't think the Alberts family will contact you. They already paid you for the first article — why would they do it again?"

Danica looked at the butter croissant. A twinkling of toughness rose within her, and she considered taking Lily's food on her way out, as a kind of obnoxious power move.

Then she thought better of it. She still needed Lily's help, so she stepped away, adding, "And tell these two jackasses to stay away from me," and left it at that.

CHAPTER THIRTY-TWO

4:56PM. Island Estates, Apartment 213, aka 'Headquarters.'

Keith Beckett must have been a smart person. At least he didn't qualify as text-book stupid. He taught at a prestigious university, traveled and met important people. Anyone who survived that long in the world of Los Angeles and the world of professional academics wouldn't be so stupid to stick around after murdering someone.

Danica leaned into her couch and refreshed her phone's Safari page. The wifi came through crisp but delivered no new results.

She considered the distinct and all-too-probable possibility that an email might never come, that Lily would just bank the money and ignore her, and that she would have to resort to other means of extracting information, however half-baked those might be. A quick map showed she could make it to the county morgue in good time, but offered no suitable means of entry.

The story facts lined up in her mind, easier and easier with each minute, but fell apart just as easily. While the Alberts family and the LAPD had formulated a narrative suitable for public consumption, they hadn't worked out the details of Mr. Beckett. Tossing him into the mix added weird links to Drake's life. A secret life. The teacher had gotten close to the kid. Maybe too close, whatever that entailed. Did Drake discover things about Mr. Beckett that needed covering up? Beckett could have had a fit, lashed out and made a terrible mistake.

And the fact that he knew Samantha... that gnawed at Danica. A failed theater business wouldn't help anyone's temper, and it could have fostered into a Snape-hates-Harry-Potter-because-he-reminds-him-of-his-family type of thing.

Danica rolled on her side and made up her mind that Beckett had disappeared for one or both of the following reasons:

1. Josue got pinned as the killer and Beckett — aware of the opportunity to escape — split.

Or...

2. Beckett went looking for Samantha to tie up any loose ends by killing the only other person who seemed to care about his connection with Drake. The frazzled, freaked-out person who was convinced the cops had gotten it wrong. Samantha must have had a good reason to feel so strongly.

Number 2 could have been it.
Danica checked her messages and found it in the same

stasis as the news article. The updates about Josue's height and weight remained in tact.

If the story got re-edited, she'd have to be ready to move quickly. She checked the story again, saw no change, and went back to her stress planning. Maybe she could straighten up the apartment, but why start now?

Her phone dinged, her heart leapt, but she settled again when she saw it was a text from Carla. It read:

"R. Austin. Current owner. And just cuz you would ask, owner before him was B.C. Peters."

As in Mr. Peters, the grumpiest butler on the planet? How much did butlers earn to afford a house in Bel Air? Or did he flip it? If he had flipped it, did he waste his money on even fancier tuxedos?

Danica texted back a thank you and continued her mull. She grabbed a duffle bag and went to her room. A change of socks, underwear and a fresh T-shirt, just in case. In case the change did happen, and in case her hunch was right. She took the same duffle bag to the kitchen, made two PB&J's (stretching out the remaining drops of the J), wrapped them in a Ziplock and added them in among the spare clothes.

What if she'd guessed wrong? What if this all led nowhere? Even going to the morgue would be meaningless. It would save her the trouble of calling in a favor she didn't want to call in, but still....

The doubts dug in. If she'd guessed wrong — if nobody made a fuss about the changes to the story or anything, and her wrongness became fully confirmed — it might not be so bad. She could just... give up entirely. If nobody cared, she didn't have to.

Then again, if she had guessed right — if someone did contact Lily Gradzhyan to change the story...

This thought drew her to the phone contacts. Carla had

put His number in there. 'As a joke,' she said. 'Mostly.' Danica had considered calling Him, in the past, but brushed off those times as passing things. Eliminate the option and it's not an option at all. She would not call Him.

But if someone had changed Lily's story, and it provided her a destination, and if that destination proved fruitful, then she'd have to call Him. Freddie.

She opened her front door and wandered to the apartment's communal balcony, overlooking the street. The cars below looked sweaty as they crawled along. A couple of cars pulled out of spots across the street, quickly swiped up by a couple others. They had places to go, with their own concerns.

Her fingers returned to Habit Mode and refreshed the inbox. Still nothing.

It was fine. It was good, actually. It was good nothing had happened. Perhaps the cops did their job right and Josue was the actual culprit. Maybe the reason nothing happened to the story was because nobody cared because nobody *should have* cared. It was good. Probably good. She wandered back into 213.

The day wasted into evening, and Danica became more antsy. Hoping for nothing was restless work, and she wore a path from her apartment to the communal balcony. The streetlights outside Island Estates Headquarters and Crappy Apartments hummed, and the moths swarmed in and out of their beams, hoping to get whatever they needed from the artificial sunshine. Hazy light pollution and smog gave a dark green mixture to the sky's natural navy blue. All the while, the cars on the street kept to their own business.

The encounter with Samantha looped through Danica's head as she made a loop from her apartment to the balcony. Samantha didn't look the part of an "Alberts." She was her own person. She lived far away and seemed to stay out of people's hair. Seemed to, until she set foot in their home, then everyone flipped out. She claimed to be close to Drake III, and implied that she knew more about everything than the experts let on. Possibly secrets. Samantha lived a day's journey away. Driving there would require not only a serious commitment, but luck and a good reason.

Danica refreshed again and a reason appeared.

The subject line of Lily Gradzhyan's email read only: "Changed."

Inside: "Don't know how you knew. Got contacted at about 5:00. Check it out."

She included a link, and the words, "It came from someone named Willows. Couldn't pay cash or see me in person. Used PayPal. For a bribe? So dumb."

Lily finished with: "Nerds cracked the IP. Source came from Leggett, CA."

Danica confirmed the story. Sure enough, Josue's description had been scrubbed. Out of the protective nature of an auntie.

Then she checked a map, and nearly barfed at the drive ahead of her. She closed her phone, and a pang of dread rolled across her chest; things might have been simpler if she'd been wrong, but she had no time to worry about being right. She grabbed her keys, locked her door and took the stairs to the front exit.

Then stopped.

The cars dragged along Oxnard Street like a sluggish river, with a few pulled over on the banks. And across the street, near the liquor store, sat a black Audi.

The black Audi.

Danica pulled back to the mailboxes by the doorway.

She poked out a bit to get another look, upset she couldn't remember whether it had been there earlier in the day.

The street light glared the windshield, obscuring any confirmation of the faces within. The driver's side window was down. Danica's was not a neighborhood where cars — particularly nice, recently-washed ones — sat unoccupied with the windows down. It was also not a party neighborhood, so traffic and parking near the liquor store should be low, especially for a Monday.

So either someone didn't care about partying hard on a weekday, or they were sitting in their car and waiting. Across the street from Danica's apartment.

She pulled back against the wall. The only access to the parking area came from the alley, and the only way to the alley was from the front sidewalk. To reach her car, she would have to cross in front of the Audi.

Doable, but totally exposed. Once she exited the mailbox area, she would have no cover for the length of the building, and even after reaching her car, the alley had limited options. She'd already turned off her lights upstairs, so she couldn't go back.

They must have noticed, if "they" existed and were watching her building closely, which, at this point, pressed against the mailbox wall, Danica had to assume they did and were.

Above the din of engines and lights, she heard clear and decisive footsteps on the sidewalk. She placed her keys between her fingers like claws.

The footsteps reached the doorway. If this was an attack, she would be ready. She took a deep breath, set her key-fist in the launch position and spun.

The young man's surprised face stopped time. He was a little older than Danica. His hair was short and pulled back, and he wore a gold chain over the neck of his designer T-shirt.

"Tommy?" Danica lowered her key-claw.

He grinned. "Hey, girl."

She clenched her keyless hand and punched him in the chest. She was not, it turned out, ready for anything.

CHAPTER THIRTY-THREE

The Past. Early 2000's. Illinois and Los Angeles.

Danica had always considered herself to be an independent thinker, and school had never sat well with that self-image. Tommy Swanson made the same claim, and with that came the problem of inventing contradictions for every situation.

Independent Thinkers are never fully satisfied. They're not supposed to be. Even when they think they might be OK with things, their "free" brain must search for new reasons why first impressions could be wrong. Cynicism sets in, judgment arises, and finding faults in everything becomes habit. If some form of success gets achieved, it was because the Independent Thinker did something wrong. They cheated, or stole, or sold out or performed some other unforgivable sin. Being unsuccessful garners nobility, and being successful marked evil. It's cyclical insanity. Basically what killed Kurt Cobain.

Independent Thinkers distance themselves from the status quo to avoid that horrible moment of picking a side.

This distance can include poor life choices, such as drinking, drugs, and dating a boy who is clearly a flake but seems nice, ignoring the advice offered by one's parents and dropping out of college sophomore year.

Danica first saw Tommy working at a Bloomington, Illinois record store, one of the last in existence. He was oddly proud of this job, both during his time there, and especially after quitting, and *especially* especially after the store shut down permanently. He certainly made that "unsuccessful = noble" rationalization for himself. Despite being part of the work force and gladly accepting paychecks, Tommy acted above it all. He was aware of his self-declared superiority, and spoke about how it was part of his straight white male privilege, as if acknowledgment made reaping the benefits OK.

He was an actor, and he was cute. He was loud and sounded smart, but a little dumb, too. Confident, or seemed to be. He complimented her boots and they exchanged numbers. He visited her the next week and they went out. A short time later, they moved in together.

Danica threw herself into life with Tommy, with its mix of bohemian living and monogamy. Tommy got the notion that Hollywood held great promise for his career. He asked his parents for money to move, and Danica — desperate for space between her and her mother's failing health — went with him. She would later recognize this as cowardice and the biggest regret of her life.

Tommy found a nice apartment that soon proved to be too nice to afford. They quickly downshifted and found Island Estates. Whatever punk-art lifestyle they wanted to live, showing that they were struggling was a struggle given the Hollywood sheen. It's hard to look like times are tough while wearing flip-flops.

Danica got work cutting hair at Earl's. She had arrived with her stylists certification, and made plans to become a barber. This hadn't been their original plan, but someone had to earn something, and the honor fell to her. She cut hair, he auditioned. She cut hair, he got headshots. She cut more hair, and he went to networking opportunities (aka parties). Intellectually, Danica understood these to all be necessary steps. Part of Tommy's "job" was to go places where people with jobs also went. It just didn't seem like work when it was so fun. Jobs weren't fun. Jobs were jobs. This became a discussion point between them, with increasing frustration and volume and passive-aggressive barbs.

He'd say, "You don't have to go if you don't want to."

She'd say, "I know."

"But I'm going."

"You made that clear."

"And you're punishing me for going."

"You're just doing it 'cause you're supposed to. I thought you were a free thinker."

"I thought YOU were!"

She'd say, "This is not my fault," and he'd say, "Danica," in four syllables, followed with a sigh loaded in false guilt.

They would continue in this manner, then break down, make up, make out, and Tommy would go to the party anyway. Every weekend for five months until it bled into the weekdays. The making up part was good, with the power to wipe out all the bad feelings and fool her into thinking everything would improve. But he would leave for the party with a kind of enthusiasm that she felt was inappropriate and she would dissolve into a pile of resentment. She began to question Tommy's loyalty, and wondered if she should find out for certain.

However, Danica had kept a rule about looking into the minds of loved ones. The rule was: don't do it. Besides the invasion of privacy, she might see things she wished she hadn't. This represented the righteous way of looking at matters.

On the other hand, the real world way of looking at matters was that she wanted to see if he was cheating, and that she was going to look.

"Let me cut your hair," she said one morning over Cheerios. She cited budgetary reasons.

Tommy protested. He said if anything got messed up ("Not that it would, it's just...") then they'd fight about it, even though they were already kind of fighting. The haircut didn't happen, and she decided to conduct her experiment at night.

She had never tried to view someone's visions while they were sleeping. They could have been a weird, non-linear mess. On top of that, she would have no way to guide his concentration; Tommy barely listened to her when awake. Without vocal directions to nudge and focus his thoughts on parties and people and girls, she would be at the mercy of his subconscious.

One night, she took that chance.

Danica stayed awake in bed and waited for Tommy to return from that night's networking event. After he came to bed and she heard his deep-sleep snores, she rolled over to face him. His short hair felt soft as she reached to his scalp.

She closed her eyes and did, in fact, see a mish-mash of directionless images. His parents, a strange plot about planting trees on the street, and a weird focus on automobile license plates.

Danica pulled her hand back, satisfied for the night, and went to sleep herself.

The experiment continued the next night, and the night after that. Every night, they would go to sleep at different times, and Danica would attach herself to see Tommy's swirls of strangeness. She saw stories that made sense only to Tommy (if they made sense to anyone), but no girls. No recurring characters.

On the first night, the lack of girls came as a relief. As she continued, though, she considered her results and noticed a trend: Tommy did not dream about girls, but he didn't dream about her either.

A 1950's cliché ran up her back, upset that her man wasn't literally dreaming about her. Danica had tried to be available and open, and encouraging to Tommy's choices. She thought she had. Yet he didn't seem to think about her.

Panic gave her an option, and that night, when he came to bed, she climbed on top of him, giving him a sudden, welcome ambush.

They chatted for a little while after, he got water for both of them, then fell asleep. She touched his head.

Again, she did not see herself.

Her obsession grew. The chaos factor, she reasoned, meant that she should see herself eventually. Given enough time, her image would surely cross his mind. She gave it more time, tried again and again, but never saw herself. This was worse than infidelity. She meant nothing to him.

After two months of the experiment, Danica's sleeping problems began in earnest. Her lack of sleep certainly didn't help her mood, fueling the fight on the morning of September 29, 2006. She made up some excuse to fight, and he took the bait.

She stormed off for work to cut hair for a day. Carla asked her what was wrong. She said nothing. Carla got the hint and left her alone.

She should have never reached into Tommy's dreams, should have obeyed her own rule. Maybe she should have tried being more understanding, even though he shared some blame for their situation. They were all but alone in the city — Danica had done much less networking. Their standoffish intellectualism and free-thinking snobbery had ensured that all they had was each other.

After her shift, Danica returned to Island Estates, ready to fight for their relationship, not against it. She would swallow her pride, admit some guilt and grudges, and was prepared to admit to reading his dreams. Which meant she'd have to come clean about her special skill, too. It was gonna be a doozy.

She opened the door, ready for a fight, but not ready for what she saw: the apartment was nearly empty, with most of Tommy's stuff gone. No note, just random vacancy about the place. He wasn't as impulsive as he wanted to seem, so he must have thought for a while about ditching her. He knew when she worked, how long it would take her to come home, and how to avoid her. He'd developed a plan, gave himself a window and timed it just right to make a clean getaway. In his haste, he left a few things behind, including the sweatshirt.

Tommy had avoided their last fight. He wanted to leave, but didn't have the balls to tell Danica. And she had been denied a chance to respond.

Until the night of the black Audi.

CHAPTER THIRTY-FOUR

MONDAY, **September 1, 2008 again. 6:02PM. With Tommy.**
Again.

He rolled on the entryway tile, holding his chest. Danica could have blamed the punch on her current stressful stalker situation, but the truth was Tommy would've been punched no matter what else was going on.

"What the hell?" he said.

Danica held up a shushing finger and glanced at the car. The driver's side window had rolled up.

"That's not your car over there, is it?" She hoped Tommy had gotten his life so together to afford a nice car, then decided to park it in the old neighborhood for the day.

Tommy got to his knees, short of breath. "My stomach hurts."

"You're fine. Answer the question."

He said it wasn't. "Took Mom's van. Look, girl, are we OK?"

She could feel the words coming — the old way of

speaking to him. Resentment and anger arrived and settled in their traditional, comfy spots, ready to end this relationship once and for all. "What are you even doing here?"

He rubbed his shoulder. "I live around here."

"Since when?"

"Couple months."

"How many is a couple?"

"One month."

"You stalking me?"

"That's a pretty narrow way of thinking, Danica—" Oh, sweet mother, here he goes.

"So you just happen to be walking by our old place, which happens to be by your new place, and you wandered over here after weeks of 'accidentally' calling me and not leaving messages?"

Tommy managed his way to his feet and leaned against the mailboxes. "OK, I can see how it looks weird. I've been in town a little while, but I don't know nothing about where you are or what you're up to or anything. Nothing."

"Well, I've been here."

"Alone?"

"None of your business." Danica checked the street again.

Tommy leaned closer, and lowered his voice. "You in trouble, girl?"

He almost pulled it off; he almost sounded sincerely concerned, even with that stupid 'girl' at the end. Danica nearly gave him another punch for it. She wanted to crack him in the nose and tell him off. To scream, "I don't need your crap and you can drop dead!" or something even more cruel. Really tear into him and make him feel terrible for existing, but mostly for having the gall to just show up unannounced and uninvited and expect her to be available to him.

Instead of all that, she said, "Actually, how interested are you in making things up to me?"

He beamed. "Totally."

"Really? I said 'make it up to me,' not 'make out with me.'"

His smile dimmed a smidge, then returned in full. "Anything." Then another dimming. "Hold on, girl. What would I have to do?"

She ignored that 'girl,' too, and continued. "Listen carefully."

"Is that my sweatshirt?"

"Are you listening?"

"Yes, jeez."

She handed her car keys to Tommy. "Go to my car and drive it past that black car. The one by the liquor store."

"Where?"

"Stay back! That one, right there. Drive by him with the windows up. Lean way back so nobody can see you. If he follows you, then drive for a while until you get to the Ralph's or something."

"Then I can roll the windows down? 'Cause I get hot in cars."

Her eyes fought to roll at Tommy's odd choice of priorities. "Sure. Just, if he follows you and you get to Ralph's, try to make sure he sees you then."

Tommy folded his arms and entered a state of (for him) deep thought. His man-brain churned, searching for a better, more testosterony plan. He thought for a good three seconds, and when no plans with attacks and karate kicks came to mind, he shifted to simply questioning her own idea. "So, I gotta make sure he doesn't see me, and then make sure he does?"

"Exactly. Just like that."

"OK. I get to Ralph's, then what?"

"Then go home."

"That's it?"

"That's it."

"This is kinda—"

"That's what you gotta do. You wanna make it up to me for the dumping and ditching, this will almost do it."

"Almost?"

She nodded.

He said, "What if he doesn't follow me. What then?"

"Then you can just come back here."

Tommy thought it over again, then took the keys from her hand. "Your car still in the usual spot?"

She said it was, then, "Hold on. I need your keys."

Asking to use Tommy's things had been one of their most dependable fight catalysts. If this exchange had taken place years earlier when they were still together, he would have given a list of reasons why it was a bad idea. He'd make up some crap about insurance coverage, or his mom's rules, or something about it needing 'a special kind of handling' that she supposedly couldn't provide or even learn.

Danica watched as a List of Excuses flashed across Tommy's considering face. A twinge of regret came over her; she hadn't considered her audience. He might, as their history showed, put up a fight.

He opened his mouth, ready to let the argument run wild.

Then he closed it and did the first smart thing he'd done in years: he gave her his keys.

"I'll bring it back later," said Danica.

"I figured. When?"

"Tomorrow. Probably."

"And this — all this — will make us even?"

"No," she said. "But it'll help."

He looked down the sidewalk, and rubbed his hands together. He'd never looked younger, a boy scared of something he didn't understand.

Danica picked up her duffle bag and looked him in the eyes.

"Tommy," she said, "thanks for dropping by."

He gave a little salute, then stepped onto the sidewalk without looking back. He made it to the alley and turned in, disappearing from her sight. The black Audi remained still.

She gripped the straps of her duffle bag as a minute passed, and then another. A familiar mechanical whine popped up from the direction of the alley, then another. Finally the roar of her Accord told the block that it had finally started.

It rolled out of the alley, turned left without signaling and cruised down the street in plain view of everyone who cared to look.

Tommy could have leaned back a little more, but Danica still appreciated the effort. He made it to the red light when the black Audi turned on its headlights.

Danica pressed herself against the mailboxes and watched the car roll past her. It pulled up behind Tommy and the Accord, and when Tommy made the next turn, so did the Audi. After all these years, Tommy had proven useful.

With the street clear, Danica ran down the sidewalk, pressing the button on the key fob, looking for a sign of life. The lights of a minivan flashed at her. It started right up, but needed gas if it was gonna make it to Leggett.

CHAPTER THIRTY-FIVE

TUESDAY, **September 2, 2008. 12:01AM. Northbound.**

Tommy's mom's vehicle handled the road well, with pretty good mileage for a minivan. Danica wasn't a superstitious person, but years of driving her Accord had developed her sense of Automotive Momentum. When a car got on a roll, she didn't like to interrupt it. Tommy's mom's minivan had a good roll going, so she rolled with it. She allowed a gas-and-snack break at Bakersfield, eating trail mix and checking the oil as best she knew how (she confirmed the existence of oil). Given that the engine had not yet burst into flames, she decided to press further.

Hours later, she crossed into "Nor Cal," the land of trees and wine and camping, and other things Danica knew little about. The McCain-Palin signs got thicker, as did the "Yes On 8" posters. Another break came in Los Banos.

The mountain trails slowed her down, and the road construction near Jackson State Forest shortened her temper. She steered west. The PCH would have to do. The evening sky loomed darker above to the ocean, with no city lights around. Danica wished she could hear the waves, but her speed wiped those sounds away.

Her phone's battery power ticked away, and Mrs. Tommy's Mom didn't provide a charger. Danica spent a call to cover her shift, as her chances of making it back on time got smaller and smaller with each mile.

Night bled into morning. The map said she had fifty-three minutes remaining on her drive until the address she had received via angry nerds. All the while, facts ran through her head. Just keeping everything straight, like a professional. A professional might think that the theater connection between Beckett and Samantha and Drake III was tenuous at best. A professional might also consider a second "correction" of the Times article on that suspect to be a grasp at straws.

Still, straws could be something. Straws in the form of people who knew D3 could provide another sliver of information. Perhaps actual facts, something Danica desperately needed.

The highway downshifted into a road as it lead to Leggett. Danica had grown up around these kinds of little towns, where pockets of people somehow lived and (presumably) didn't go nuts from the isolation and lack of quality movie theaters.

The thoughts raced once more. Beckett and Samantha had some sort of past connection. Beckett lived in Los Angeles. Samantha, too, at one time. And she had her own suspect for the murder of D3.

Samantha might have suspected Beckett.

And Beckett could have realized this. And in his realization, could have rushed away — as he did! — to Leggett to deal with Samantha. If he found her. He had to know where she was. Or at least had a general idea. If Danica could figure it out, anyone could have.

She drove past the "Welcome to Leggett" sign toward what she safely assumed to be the only gas station for forty miles. Being 5:20AM, the station was closed, but she pulled in anyway, facing that welcome sign. Panic sweats came as she dug into her pocket for her last bits of cash. Twenty-nine dollars and change. She wondered if a real detective would have driven the length of the nation's longest state without making hotel reservations, without knowing anyone for a thousand miles, trusting the address provided by shifty college newspaper boys, all for a chance to catch a lucky break. A chance! Even "lucky break" sounded too solid; she had thrown a Hail Mary pass from the tailgate party.

She shut down the minivan and went to check the hours of operation. Thirty-plus minutes before life began. She stretched and drained the last of her cold coffee into the bushes, trying to ignore the morning chill and the science behind a cigarette's ability to warm her up with only the first inhale.

The welcome sign had been sponsored by the local Lions chapter. Danica saw the emblem for the town police next, likely a force of one. The back of the sign was dark, yet Danica could still make out a couple names from the "Top Tier" donors of Leggett, mostly local businesses and luminaries.

One logo caught her eye: a bust of a man's face, wearing a helmet with a brush top. Trojan Horse Theater. It was not as grandiose as Zeus' Helmet, but it related to Samantha's alma mater. It had to be her.

Danica felt warmer, cigarette or no. The Hail Mary had upgraded to a casual prayer.

The directions took her east, following signs around a

lake. It appeared to be man-made, just off of the Eel River, and along the lake's edge stood a row of cabins, each one with a fence. It shouldn't have surprised her when the phone's GPS gave up on her; satellites didn't hang around these parts. She continued on the last known trajectory.

The road twisted with the water, and Danica struggled to scope out houses without driving off the road. Pavement led to gravel, with hedges and trees set heavy on the road-side. It felt like a ghost town. She couldn't remember the last time she encountered another car.

A flicker of blue steel caught her eye, to the right, and Danica slammed on the brakes. In the driveway, behind some bushes, sat the blue station wagon with Oregon plates. "I'd Rather Be Acting," indeed.

Danica pulled ahead to the next yard, and parked the minivan on the grass. She checked the time and realized it might be way too early to pull off a casual "Funny running into you half a day's drive from Los Angeles" kind of meeting like she'd planned. She could try getting right the point, but Samantha might get scared off, or pissed off, or both.

Danica hopped out of the minivan. She walked back to the entry, to the sidewalk, past the overgrown edges and reached the porch.

She knocked on the red wood door. No answer. She knocked again, double checking the station wagon to make sure it was the one she remembered. Still no answer came. A peek through the window showed no signs of life, which meant there would be little danger of being caught while having a closer look around. Danica stepped off the porch and moved around the side of the house.

A row of short pine trees lined the way to the backyard. She could see a Tuff Shed against the fence, with a pile of wood next to it. An old swing set rusted in the middle of the yard. Danica stood at the corner of the house, her courage leaving her, nervous about stepping into the wide open.

She pulled back to the side of the house again, next to the trees, and faced an open bathroom window. Through the window she could see the white tile sink and the hallway door hanging open. The wall outside the door held a mess of photos, more taped than framed.

Danica's eyes focused immediately on the photo at the top of the mess.

It was the Alberts family portrait. A miniature version of the full version, from the Deaton auditorium. To the left of the Classic Alberts lineup stood the younger Samantha Alberts-Willows. Her hair contained in a conservative bun, yet the artist somehow managed to capture its intrinsic wildness; its desire to burst into a frizzy mop.

Danica pulled out her phone and scrolled back. Even blurry, the poses matched. Mr. Alberts had been upset when the delivery people hung a reminder of his family falling out. It must have set him off to see his sister reinstated, after working so hard to have her removed.

Danica leaned closer to the window to look at the other pictures. Some showed an older Drake III with his arm around his aunt. Another had him with a group of boys of similar ages. Another had him laughing with a dark-haired boy wearing a cape. They all appeared recent, as D3 looked vaguely adult in each shot. Danica couldn't remember a more casual look for the boy, all T-shirts and cut-off jean shorts. The look on this wall had a dorm room feel.

A shadow glanced across the pictures and Danica ducked to the ground. Someone was home after all. Maybe they were asleep when she knocked.

"Hello?" said a man's voice.

Danica's heart ceased pumping blood as she clung to the

siding. This was not the "hello" of someone expecting or even wanting visitors. It held no trace of friendliness. This "hello" was confrontational.

A sprint could get her to the minivan, or to a neighbor's yard. Maybe lose this guy in the morning haze. Her heavy boots stepped as lightly as possible as she crept toward the front yard.

"Hello," said the man again. Same tone as before, but this time from the front porch. The screen door swing open. Danica leaned forward a smidge.

The man looked toward the driveway. He had something dark in his hand. A bat. His grey hair was messy. He wore pajamas, and even though they weren't beige, she still recognized the drama professor from USC. Danica pulled back against the side wall. Keith Beckett had come to clean up his mess with Samantha.

She heard him step onto the sidewalk and move toward the road, toward the minivan. One last glance revealed his non-baseball bat hand held a phone. He lifted it to his face and spoke, low.

Danica ran to the backyard. She scanned the area, desperate to discover protection she hadn't noticed the first time. Still she saw none. Beckett's voice came again, said something like "...one's here... back...." Time slowed down and sped up.

To the Tuff Shed. Its back portion rested tight against the fence, too close to fit behind, though she gave it a serious try. She would have to call for help, and pray that the Leggett police force had earlier hours than the gas station.

Her pocket was empty. Her phone... She must have dropped it by the window. Sixty feet away; might as well be a million.

She tried the Tuff Shed doors. Locked.

Her only option was to keep moving, to climb over the fence into the forest behind, toward the lake.

She jabbed one foot onto the wood pile and the other against the shed wall. Her push knocked over the wood with a clatter, but it got her over the fence and onto the cold dirt of the forest.

Even at dawn, the forest was dark. Gloom clung low on the tree trunks. She charged into the haze, concentrating only on putting distance between herself and Mr. Beckett. The leaves crunched under her feet. The forest played tricks on her hearing. It sounded like more leaves were crunching behind her. Getting closer.

Ahead of her, the mist thinned at the water and the grey beach. She stopped. Dim, brown land sat across the lake, separated by the length of a soccer stadium. Swimming would be difficult, and would leave her vulnerable in the open water. She needed a boat.

Then she saw one. A motorboat. Coming straight toward her, from the land across the lake. Danica calculated the chances of it being a police boat sent to rescue her, settled on the chances being 0.000001%, and ran back into the forest. She tucked herself against a tree.

The motorboat cut through the water, heading straight for where Danica had just been standing. She pushed back to another tree and kept one eye on the boat and another on the forest, looking for Beckett.

The boat made land and its driver set an anchor. Its driver wore a dark green jacket with a hood and carried a phone of her own. The voice was feminine and the removal of the hood confirmed it, letting loose that frizzy grey hair. Samantha Alberts-Willows reached back into the boat and retrieved an axe.

Danica yanked herself back against the tree trunk and listened to Samantha's footsteps running into the forest. She'd been a complete idiot — more than usual. Beckett must have called her. They were a team. Always had been. And now they outnumbered Danica, with no place left to run.

She found the courage to look for Samantha's green jacket. She saw none. After another two seconds, Danica ran out of patience, then ran to the motorboat, pulled up the anchor and kicked away from the beach. The outboard started on the first pull, but gave up a few feet later. She settled on the oars.

When she reached land (and could finally see straight again for all the rowing), Danica stood facing a large cabin, like at a summer camp. On either side of the cabin, as far as she could see, was nothing but forest trees; a wooden island, isolated from civilization. Two large doors hung open, facing the water. She ran past the row of trimmed bushes and inside, hoping for a miracle. Car keys lying around or at least some place to hide. Even tripping the alarm would tell police where to find her body.

Her footsteps echoed, and she could tell the room had high ceilings and little else. A single standing light without a shade accomplished very little other than announcing its own existence.

Danica fumbled around for a light switch by the doorway. What she found turned on a few more low, exposed bulbs, but they were enough to show the rest of the black box theater space. She must have entered through the backstage loading area.

The Trojan Horse theater connected the three of them. Beckett and Samantha could have killed D3 when he wouldn't support their business venture, or tried to extort money from his family, when it all went wrong (probably from Samantha's nerves of glass).

It seemed possible, but unlikely. Samantha could have been a great actress, but her tears at the visitation and at Malcom Fine's office were legit.

Didn't matter at the moment, of course. If Danica could prove any of it (which she couldn't), she would still have to survive the day first and foremost.

One of the lights lit some audience seating, and judging from the dust, they hadn't been sat in for a while. The audience faced a minimum of on-stage props and set dressing: a couch, rug, coffee table and a chair. A book shelf with no books stood like a monolith against no backing wall.

Danica shuffled stage right, to a door on the side and opened it to a small kitchen with waxy floors. Two things came into clear focus in the kitchen: the steak knives on the counter, and the phone on the wall. She tried the phone only to discover it was not plugged in, probably used as a prop and never reconnected. She took a mid-sized knife and continued to search for a wall connection for the phone.

Returning to the stage area, her eyes adjusted and found a narrow flight of stairs against the back-stage wall. She took them and found a ramshackle lighting booth, with more dusty contraptions and buttons, but still no phone. It had a window, though, and through it she could see the lake and her boat.

And Mr. Beckett, walking toward the theater. He still had his phone and bat, and seemed to get more angry up with every step.

The knife in her hand would have to do. She could dodge the bat, fight his phone away, call some help, and maybe hold him off long enough to stay alive. If she could manage a suitable ambush. She rushed out of the booth, down the stairs, and hid behind the stage couch, blocked from the loading doors.

They opened wide, letting more morning light inside along with Mr. Beckett's footsteps.

"H-hello?" His voice trembled this time. From rushing up from the beach, she thought. As he closed the doors behind him, she thought that he couldn't be nervous; such a state didn't seem very becoming of a murderer.

She watched under the couch as Beckett's shadow crept toward the kitchen. Her fingers flexed around the knife handle. For someone who had never been in a fight in her life, a surprise knife attack would be a dramatic step up. She'd read about these moments, where things seemed to slow down as the brain processed millions of thoughts in microseconds. She needed it.

Beckett reached the kitchen doorway, his back to her. He paused. Her moment had come.

She stood, silent and — as she had hoped — her brain fired a million thoughts in microseconds. She stared at the back of the man who killed Drake, who had pinned it on Josue and who had come all this way to kill Samantha.

But he hadn't. Was he partners with her. Danica couldn't keep it straight. What made him so nervous, here and at USC? He had a bat and likely knew the space, yet there he stood, shivering. No. Not shivering. Just a single shudder of his shoulders before opening the door, like a prep ritual. Her million-thoughts-a-minute brain exploded, and finally landing on the Deaton Auditorium, where she'd seen the same maneuver.

She stopped moving and said, "Turn around."

Beckett jumped, and dropped his phone in the process. She repeated the command and he obeyed, dropping the bat when he saw her knife. Fear permeated his face. He never killed anybody.

"Pick up the phone and put it in your pocket."

He did.

She lowered her knife. "Tell me about the Mayor."

CHAPTER THIRTY-SIX

Tuesday, September 2, 2008. 7:35AM. On Stage at the Trojan Horse.

The living room set smelled like a fireplace had been going the night before, with that warm camp-out smell hanging in the rafters above. It built a weird pocket of pseudo-coziness in a vacant room.

Danica instructed Beckett to sit on the couch. He stumbled on a bump in the rug as he did, and clutched his heart when he righted himself. She sat in the set chair opposite him.

"You followed me," he said.

"Sorta."

"You followed Samantha then?"

"This is your theater, right?"

"Samantha and I ran it together."

"How'd you get this theater?"

"It's Samantha's."

Danica twirled the knife in a 'go-on' motion.

"She's had it about a year, after the Bel Air space went under."

"On the cul-de-sac."

"Yes. She was forced out."

"By who?"

"The city," he said. "Bel Air."

"Do you know who she sold to?"

"I do not recall. I know she did it in a hurry, pressured by her dwindling funds."

"Dwindling funds? She's an Alberts."

"Somewhat, I'd say."

"Did Drake have anything to do with the theater across the street from his house? Drake the Third?"

"It was owned by his aunt. I'm sure he visited."

"You and he were tight, huh?

He nodded.

"Like... buddies? Student-teacher? Something more?"

"Mentor-mentee. He, like his aunt, had passion for the theater."

"And he followed her up here, too?"

"Sometimes."

"How often is 'sometimes?'"

"Semi-often, I would say. Sometimes every weekend."

"Odd for a business major, huh?"

Beckett cough-laughed at the label.

"He was only doing the business thing for his parents," said Danica. "That's what I think."

"He and his aunt were very close. He came up here for the same reasons she had: to get away."

She should have brought her notepad, to jot it all down. Samantha forced to sell her theater, Drake being into acting. But the main idea returned: "The Mayor of Bel Air. You know who I mean, right?"

"I believe so."

"Tell me about him."

"What do you want to know?"

"Let's start with a name, and cut out the step-by-step instructions."

Beckett chuckled, mostly through is nostrils. "The man to whom I believe you are referring is Ronald Austin."

"How do you know him?"

"He's a student of mine. In a way."

"Pretty old for USC."

"It was just a side gig. I've moonlighted here and there. Acting coach type things. The city's full of actors and hence full of opportunities."

"So this guy signed up to be an actor?"

"In a way. The focus was on public speaking. Presence and voice, projection, that sort of thing. The tools of the theater translate to a great many life skills."

"He ever tell you why he signed up for public speaking lessons?"

"No."

"Did you ever ask?"

"I meant 'No, he didn't sign up.'"

Danica was confused, and said as much.

"I mean," said Beckett, "that Ronald didn't sign himself up."

He paused, she thought, and then it clicked. "Drake brought him."

Beckett nodded.

"Drake Alberts the Third recommended that this old guy Ronald Austin reach out to you for acting lessons?"

"In a manner of speaking."

"Hey, man, I'm the one with the knife here. So if you could pick a manner of speaking that actually gives answers,

I think we'd both really appreciate it. He must have told you something. Don't you do any kind of class get-to-know-you exercises? Did Drake say anything about him?"

"Only that he was supposed to be authoritative. Suiting his title, I suppose."

Frustration took control of her voice. "Bel Air doesn't have a mayor."

"I remember you now," said Beckett. "You're that young woman who almost killed me with her car."

"I'm also a hairstylist, I'm in over my head here so I'd appreciate the help."

"You're not going to kill me," said Beckett.

She stood up, with gusto, with as much power and intimidation as she could bring. "Maybe not. But I know how to use scissors and razors with professional skill. And I bet you don't like being hurt. So let's just get down to it."

Beckett held up his hands. Danica ignored the condescending grin on his face.

"This Ronald Austin is currently the owner of that former theater house, the one on the cul-de-sac."

The grin left his lips, replaced with an open-mouth look of surprise.

"Recent purchase. One of your former theater students is throwing out the theater lights and seats."

Beckett squinted. "Why would he do such a thing?"

"If you don't know, I sure don't. But I think it ties together somehow." She adjusted herself and spoke at as tender a volume as she could. "How did Josue fit into all this?"

Beckett's eyes trembled.

"You knew him, too. You and Samantha. It's why she changed the news story. To protect him, or his image or something. She's sentimental. You and Samantha knew him, or knew something about him and you wanted to protect him. Even after he was dead."

"He was a good boy," said Beckett. "A fine, fine boy."

"Drake knew him from when he worked at the house."

"Other way around. Drake got him the job."

"Drake got him a job at his own house? Was Drake some kind of job recruiter or something? He brought the Mayor to you, he's bringing Josue to work at the house...." She refocused. "Was Josue a student of yours, too?"

"In a way."

"Dang, dude. You're doing it again. Pushing me a little too much, playing all coy like some aristocrat or something. I'm actually on your side here, Keith. But I can't help you if you won't let me."

He folded his arms and stuck out that stuffy chin. "You?"

She chewed the tip of her tongue and wondered if an old fashioned face slap would do the trick with this guy. Even in the face of danger, Beckett dug in to his holier-than-thou attitude. He didn't even sit on a couch like a human; he perched on the edge, smelling the air with his long, snooty nose.

"Do you smell that?" he said, stalling again and sounding like a real jerk while doing it.

Then Danica smelled the air, too. The camp-out smell had intensified. The dust in the air had grown thicker. With actual smoke.

Beckett stood and ran to the wall opposite the kitchen. He flipped a switch, illuminating an actual, non-prop fireplace. He wiggled a lever with all his might and the fireplace showed no signs of wobbling.

"Flue's closed. They're trying to smoke us out."

"Who?" said Danica. She coughed. The smoke filled her

nostrils. She tucked her hood around her mouth and saw Beckett run to the double doors.

"Wait," said Danica.

She had spoken too late. Mr. Beckett opened the doors and his chest accepted a round of gunshot. The force knocked him back while his legs left him, his lifeless body plopped onto the hard stage floor, knocking out the lamp in the center.

The heat grew around her, and the open door did little to slow the smoke's progress. Danica ran to the kitchen. The far wall blazed red. A quick look around laid out her two crappy options: stay and burn or leave and get shot.

She returned to the stage area, ducked and crawled to Beckett's body. Careful not to show herself in the doorway, she extended her arm into the light, dug into his pockets and pried out the phone. Smoke filled her lungs as she scurried back. She stayed on her hands and knees, with panic setting in. She circled the couch, wondering if standing in front or behind would be a better place to burn.

Her knee dug into the rug, and pain shot through her leg. Something harder than rug bulged out from beneath the weave, the same thing that had tripped Mr. Beckett.

Danica pulled back the corner of the rug and found a hinge. Another yank up-ended the coffee table and revealed a trap door in the floor. Smoke curled around the handle as she lifted it. Only darkness below. The screen light from Beckett's phone revealed little else. She tried to remember seeing a basement entry or a storm door on her way. There had been stairs at the entrance. The building had to be off the ground.

The intensifying smoke demanded a decision. She took a deep breath and jumped into the trap door.

She hit hard dirt and stumbled, tumbling onto her back.

Beckett's phone took this opportunity to escape from her grip.

Back on her feet, Danica ducked to keep her head beneath the floorboards. The open trap door provided the only light, and it was getting more and more hazy with every second.

The phone had to be somewhere, face down, light down. She shuffled her feet, hoping for a fortuitous kick.

The dirt floor built to an incline, and her hands found a brick wall. Danica stuffed her sweatshirt's hood between her teeth and took shallow breaths, then spit it out again, along with the dirt from the fall. The heat had reached the crawlspace. She told herself that the fire would likely burn up before it burned down. This counted as optimism. She had some time. Some.

She traced the wall to her right, then stopped. Following that path would take her back to the kitchen and into the heart of the fire. She turned back, and her feet kicked something. Not hard like the phone, but soft; it gave just enough resistance to declare itself.

A shirt, maybe. Clothing of some kind. Possibly cotton. And a belt. She picked them up and pressed on, coming to another corner that felt warmer than the last one.

Her head hit a pipe in the ceiling. She held her forehead, then the pipe. It felt cool. Likely plumbing, going toward the kitchen.

Danica's eyes stung in the dark. She wiped them with dirty clothing, then flattened out the shirt, wrapped its arms around her face for a mask, and added her hood for extra cover. The light around the trap door gave a point of orientation, even with smoke dropping through. Following the plumbing in the direction opposite as the kitchen could lead her away from the fire, toward the lake.

The pipe made it to another wall, and her fingers pried at the joint for a gap. She followed the horizontal lines of the bricks toward to another wall.

The bricks ended. Still something solid, but not brick or stone. Wood. Through tears, she saw a faint sliver of light cutting through this wooden barrier. It seemed like a doorway, maybe to the side of the building, maybe to the front yard and straight into the crosshairs of the person who shot Mr. Beckett.

After a moment's consideration, she retracted her earlier strategy, deciding that a gunshot wound might be superior to burning alive with smoke inhalation.

Danica shoved against the wood. The sliver did not budge. Probably had a lock on the outside; some kind of hook to keep it in place. Her fingers could not fit through the sliver. She tried the belt, its leather tip.

Danica shoved it into the sliver, blocking off more light and air. She lifted up, and it moved without hinderance. She drug the belt downward in the sliver, hitting resistance after a couple feet.

Her eyes would not stop blinking or crying. She shut them. They weren't helping anyway, just stinging her face and breaking her concentration. Danica followed the sliver down and dropped to her knees. The wood angled back into a narrow triangle shape.

She reinserted the belt, pushing a little deeper, and moved up to the middle resistance point. Her shoulder pushed against the wood and she lifted the belt. Something gave, but the flimsy belt drooped and dropped it. She tried again. Another reinsert, another lift. Another inhale, accidentally taking in smoke through her nose, then she reset and pushed.

The belt won. The resistance moved and the door lifted

with Danica's push. She poured out of the crawlspace and onto the wet grass, swallowing air faster than her lungs could handle. Her throat ached. She rolled onto her back and waited for them to come and end it.

She waited.

And waited.

But no shots — or person — came.

She was either dead or exhausted, and unsure which she would have preferred. The flames behind her picked up, and she watched them reach the front wall of the theater, near the door. But she saw them all by herself.

The dew on the grass soaked through Tommy's sweatshirt. She pulled off her makeshift mask and rolled onto her elbows. It was a man's shirt. A polo, striped; not Mr. Beckett's style of beige/dark beige. The dirt around the torso was old and crusted. The top button poked her finger where it had cracked.

After one last look for a shooter, she stood. Whoever had come to kill Mr. Beckett came only for him. It couldn't have been Samantha. She had every opportunity leading up to five minutes ago; why would she kill him now, as well as burn down her own theater?

The walk to the beach was warm. The sun had burned away most of the fog, and most of the remaining clouds were from the fire behind her. When she reached the boat, she could see across the lake, and saw a black car driving on the road. It moved through the gravel to the asphalt, heading south. She didn't want to admit it was the black Audi, but there was no use denying it. Whoever they were, they'd followed her. Again.

While she rowed the boat across the lake, Danica cried. The burning building and the gunshots and the stalking and all of it built up and ran out. The smell of burning theater stuck in her nostrils. She thought about acting classes, flipping houses, rich butlers, and out-of-luck, out-of-life former grounds keepers. It was too much. Maybe she did need a psychiatrist.

Danica's tears ran out about half way across the lake, leaving her with only aching arms and no answers. Beckett had known more than he had let on, but her guess about him being Drake's killer had been dead wrong. He knew about outside elements, too — the Mayor, Josue and Samantha. He paid for his knowledge in the worst way.

The world felt solid as sand. Danica made land and walked through the forest, meeting nobody along the way. She circled around the fence via the neighbor's yard and found Samantha lying in the backyard, facedown, with a bullet wound through her head. A rifle had been positioned in her hand. Taken in with the theater fire, the scene could be interpreted as a murder-suicide. A perfect package, like Drake III. Everything closed, giving no reason to pursue matters any further.

The tears came again and her breath got short. Two dead, but her alive. For what reason? They knew she was here — they followed her — so why not kill her, too?

Because she didn't pose a threat. Or they needed her alive to pin it all on her. Her phone was nowhere to be found, removed from the premises. Danica gave a feeble attempt at looking for footprints, but the yard was cleaner than she'd left it. Even the woodpile mess she'd made was restored.

She walked to the minivan and drove back into town, to the gas station, all while reliving that vision.

That damn vision. The one from James Van Owen, it returned. The barefoot body of a dead young man. It was as clear as that day in the salon, the green grass, his dark pants, and that birthmark on his ankle. Large for a birthmark. Almost square.

Josue. Drake III. Beckett. Samantha. The Dream House. The Alberts family. A weird DNA strain curled around the names as she ran them over again. She tried to picture their faces. Their images. Their appearances varied, but a harmony struck in them, just out of reach.

The only one she hadn't personally met was Josue. And the only way to get to him was by doing yet another thing she wanted to avoid. But since doing things she wanted to avoid had become her lot, and with two new bodies behind her, and with her phone taken to frame her for those killings, Danica had no choice.

She put a stopper in her tears, asked to use a phone from the gas station attendant. The woman agreed and Danica dialed a number she had memorized but had never called.

After three rings, a smooth, weary voice said, "Frederick Ford."

"It's me. I need you to meet me at the morgue in about ten hours."

CHAPTER THIRTY-SEVEN

Tuesday, September 2, 2008. 4:00PM. Downtown LA.

The drive back to LA provided ample time for Danica to replay, question and regret the way she asked for Freddie's help. She'd always been careful around him. Likely just stupid nerves. They were friends. Just friends.

Freddie Ford stood at the front doors of the LA County Morgue, waiting while she parked the minivan. Tommy's mom's minivan. Combined with Tommy's sweatshirt, it all sent a weird message.

"You doing road gigs now, DL?"

She smiled and motioned for him to come to the van. He adjusted his tie, as though it wasn't already immaculate. He leaned into the open window.

"I've had a long night."

"Heard you took a trip."

Crap. He knew about Leggett, about Beckett and Samantha and the theater. Of course he knew. She always suspected he was not only a good person, but good at his job.

"Are you gonna arrest me?"

"Why? Did you do it?"

She shook her head. "I'm being framed."

His eyes blinked, but were not surprised. "You got any proof?"

"I'm working on that."

"Proof would be real handy about now."

"My car wasn't there," she said. "You can check the mileage. The odometer's off by ninety-four thousand miles, but it tracks."

"I'm not the one you'll have to convince."

"You believe me?"

He did not blush. Remained mercifully professional. "I know you."

"I need a favor."

He laughed. "I bet you do."

Keep it business, she told herself. This was a business transaction. This was a platonic, business relationship, and nobody would get hurt. Citizen to cop. Cutter to customer. No big deal.

"I wanna see Josue Dominic Rodriguez's body."

Freddie maintained his grin, but leaned back out of the car window. He stood for a moment, then opened the door and sat in the passenger's seat. The van's swampy smell gave way to Freddie's tasteful aftershave.

"That would be information related to the suspect of a murder."

"I realize that," Danica said. "But I don't have time to track down his family to get permission, and I thought maybe you could help me out?"

She tried to keep her eye lashes from batting, tried to keep things even. It shouldn't have been so difficult, given the fact that they were friends — just friends — and nothing more.

The words fell out, "It's just a favor. For me."

Her eyes batted. She felt them, and had no control over them. Somehow, they fluttered when they looked at him. And her hand — her stupid hand — how did it get to her neck? She brought it back down as casually as possible while Freddie thought over the request. God, maybe he hadn't noticed.

She kept speaking, trying to make things better and platonic. "I understand it'd be a little weird for you."

He laughed, and his eyes darted toward the stairs and the morgue doors. He spoke in a low voice. "What do you wanna know?"

"I really can't say."

"Oh, of course not." He was still being playful. Still cool.

"He's here, right?"

"I really can't say that either, DL."

She leaned on the steering wheel. "I'd only need a minute. Two minutes tops. And..." the words rose in her mouth, passing her tongue and between her teeth. She couldn't stop them. They just came out: "I'll owe you."

Freddie repeated it back. "You'll owe me?" He scrunched his nose and looked into her eyes. He knew she wasn't a murderer. She could tell he could tell. He knew what she was capable of doing.

His nose un-scrunched and he reached into his jacket pocket, and came back with some folded papers.

"You'll have to do your looking here," he said. "I can't let you make copies, but that's everything."

She opened the papers. Reports, photos and documents on Josue's case.

He guessed at what her silence meant and said, "I put it together before you arrived. Considering where you were — where you should not have been, I might add—" Even his scolding sounded kind "—considering that and asking to meet here, I thought this might be of interest."

The files had heft, printed with detailed details and officious officialness. The time of death, specifics about his body, what he wore, where he was when he was found and killed. It had everything.

Almost.

Her voice trembled. "I have to see the actual body."

"This is everything you need. Every detail. Took a while to put together. It's enough, trust me."

"I do trust you, but I'm serious."

"Hey," he said. More scolding, but this time less kind. "That is a suspect in a murder case you're talking about. All but convicted. It's a high-profile, delicate investigation and not open to everyone with a library card. You're getting more than anyone should."

She looked at the file and back to Freddie's eyes. Even sitting, he seemed tall. He breathed through his parted lips, and looked scared, like he knew what she was going to ask him. Like he knew it would be something he wouldn't want to do, but would have no way to refuse. If she asked, he would say yes.

Because he loved her.

At that very moment, given the circumstances and the rush and the near-death experiences, Danica would have taken advantage of a man who loved her. If it were anyone else in the world, she wouldn't hesitate to ask for what she needed, that one time. The ends would justify the means.

But he was not anyone else in the world. He was Freddie, the man she...

The word 'admired' tried to emerge, through sheer power of denial, fighting off sappy sentiments such as 'loved,' or even the less-committal, junior-high-level cop-out 'liked.' It fell flat, like she was putting on airs, lying to herself to protect herself.

The discomfort of honesty froze her lips together, afraid to let any spill out. She trusted Freddie and wanted to get to know more about him every single moment they had been together, including with this one. She knew he felt the same way about her. She had seen it, every time he came to the shop, in his mind and in the way he looked at her.

Which was why she knew, if she asked him, he would give her what she wanted.

Which she did.

"Please. I have to see him."

Which she felt gross about.

Freddie, the man she wanted to be with more than any other person, looked at his shoes, then back to her. She felt her manipulation working, his affection for her fighting with his ethics.

"Two minutes?" he said.

Something festered in her stomach as he opened the door. "That's all I need."

He opened the door. "Let's go."

CHAPTER THIRTY-EIGHT

THE MORGUE.

Freddie escorted her through the reception area, past a couple dreary-looking cops and a security guard. Nobody said a word while he signed a form, then continued on his way with Danica in tow.

The silence between them burned her ears as Freddie opened a plexiglass door with his security badge, then another, and reached a hallway in the back, dark and smelling like floor cleaner. They passed through a hallway and came to a large door at its end.

Freddie put up his hand to stop them. He pulled out his phone and scrolled for the longest fifteen seconds of Danica's life. He looked at the door's window, then back to his phone, then back to the window.

"Lucky you. Coast's clear." He pushed it open.

The fluorescents buzzed above them, and filled the room with flat light. Before her stood a wall made entirely of metal cabinets and drawers.

"B-5," said Freddie, and got to the metal wall. He dropped his hand heavy on a handle and pulled open the drawer.

The breeze of movement slid the sheet up and revealed the short, black hair of Josue Dominic Rodriguez. A young man with dark, hard skin.

Danica prepared for what would hopefully be her last encounter with a dead body for at least two weeks. He didn't look like the photo cropped by the LAPD and the newspapers. His face appeared even younger, but the bullet wounds on his chest aged him up.

He wore no shirt, revealing a series of tattoos on his torso and arms. Mostly on his arms. The word "FREE" in curly script decorated his left forearm, and spiderwebs covered both elbows.

Danica moved the sheet off of Josue's right ankle.

A small, half-moon shape appeared on his right ankle, near the bone.

A weird sense of relief, fear and excitement came over her all at once. She smiled at Freddie.

"OK," she said. "I'm good."

"That's it?" said Freddie.

"That's it."

Freddie motioned to the door, and Danica followed him into the hallway, back into the silence.

"Send someone to the Alberts Estate," she said. "To wait until they see Mrs. Alberts leave."

"Why's she gonna leave, Captain?"

"I'm gonna tell her to," she said. "Drake had a tattoo removed."

Freddie shrugged.

"Mr. Alberts removed it. Himself. Personally. He killed his own son for the same reason he forced his sister out of the family and why he took the tattoo off: it didn't fit his family image."

"You serious?"

"I can't call her. I might have to do it in person...."

Freddie handed over her phone. At 6% battery, it held enough for a phone call. When he saw her face, he said, "I snagged it earlier. I know you, DL."

"Get someone to the Alberts' house, OK?"

"Just a heads up," said Freddie, catching up with her at the front door. "I'm probably gonna cash in the favor real quick, if you don't mind."

Danica minded a little. She had a rich woman to save and a murderer to help capture, and her lack of experience in achieving such goals didn't make it easy to give a ballpark estimate on her free time. When things were wrapped, he would have plenty of time to call her up and make a move to sweep her off her feet.

"Freddie, I'd love to—"

"Not now, 'course. I gotta get him to the station first."

A curious detail for a proposal. She might have day dreamed their first date taking place at the police station, but not for real, and certainly not with other participants.

"Who... ?"

"A suspect. We got him on a failed hold-up. He's actually part of a ring. We can figure it out later."

Her insecurity flared, trying to protect her from looking like she didn't know what the hell he was talking about, who this suspect was, or where Freddie had learned to ask girls out so poorly.

Her impatience won over her insecurity. "I give up, Freddie. What do you want me to do?"

Freddie cocked and eyebrow, then laughed at himself. "You really gonna make me say it?"

"You might have to. I'm completely lost."

Freddie looked at his shoes, and kicked the side of the step. Like nervous Travis Whatshisname at the Sweetheart Swirl, asking for a dance. She could still tell he was smiling.

"I'd like," he said, looking up again, "I'd like you to tell me what he's thinking."

Danica's insides sunk, like she'd fallen in the ocean, smacked by wave after wave, carried out from under her feet. She lurched back — an actual, honest-to-God lurch! — taking in the totality of Freddie's words.

She'd been so careful for so long. Her mother had made her promise to be careful. She always kept her abilities to herself and had never been careless, least of all around him.

Yet, somehow, he knew. Freddie knew.

He had figured out her secret. Been sitting on it for who knew how long. And in figuring it out, he must have known that she knew about how he felt about her, all those times in the barber's chair. Had he been orchestrating the visions for her benefit? Was he really that shy, or coy? If he knew she knew, how long had he known that she knew? Another ocean wave rolled in and carried her further out to sea.

She met Freddie's eyes, hoping she had misunderstood him. Her mouth opened and closed again, unsure of how to operate.

He was still smiling, and for the first time in her life, she considered coming clean about everything. To really let someone in. Even her mother had never known her completely. Danica had lived her life in a guarded state, trying to keep this secret away from others, too scared to share herself for fear of being exploited or mocked or becoming a circus attraction. She could have been labeled an actual freak of nature or been hunted.

Yet there, as she looked at Freddie in that dim light on

the steps to the morgue, his eyes seemed so full and rich that the idea of an open and honest life seemed possible, even necessary. This man, who she knew was good and decent and kind and cared for her and thought of her and would prize her above anyone else — even dream about her once in a while — and protect her and keep her warm and feed and hold her and love her... if anyone would understand her, it was him. He understood so much already.

But the feeling passed, giving way to habitual anxiety and self-preservation.

"I don't know what you're talking about." The words hit dead and flat.

It was Freddie's turn to lurch. His smile melted. "Are you sure? I could use your help. I mean... DL, are you sure?"

It killed her. Pure torture. Worse than baring her soul was the lying. To him. She wanted to hold him.

But more than that, she wanted to protect him from herself. How would life go for the police officer with a freak girlfriend? He'd bring her in for cases, nab criminals and get mocked up and down. 'Can't do the work for yourself, Ford? You gotta sleep with a psychic instead? Real professional!' They'd rip him to pieces. She'd tarnish him. Just like she tarnished everyone. Being honest with herself, she realized that's what she did. Tommy was a turd, but she still never really let him in. Same with Andrew Luman. Same with her mom, unable to face her in her darkest moment. Danica had so often disappeared when things got bad. Protecting herself. Don't let anyone in, and don't get hurt.

"I'm sorry," she said. "Whatever you thought about me... it's not true. I made it up. I bet you heard it from Carla or something, but... I lied. I'm just a stylist. It's not true."

"Really? So you did all this work and got your leads — the whole idea for looking into this case in the first place —

through normal detective work? Didn't have nothing to do with James getting his haircut from you?"

"I'm sorry. I'm so sorry. I'm a liar. I'm not what you think." At all. All energy went to her eyes, fighting against the tears. "I'm so sorry."

"Me, too."

"I gotta go."

He said, "Sure." Flat as a table top.

"Please send someone to the Alberts' house."

"Heard you the first time, Danica," he said.

She left. He did not stick around to make sure she made it to the minivan.

Danica tried to open her phone, to focus on the mission, but the tears won out. When they dried up, she saw a text message from Tommy:

"Car's at your work. Keys in usual spot. Call so I can get mom's van."

Her eyes burned again as the situation before her settled in. She would top tormenting Freddie with having the most difficult conversation she could possibly have with a grieving mother. She dialed.

"Mrs. Alberts? This is Danica Luman. I have something to tell you about your son's murder."

CHAPTER THIRTY-NINE

TUESDAY, September 2, 2008. 9:36PM. Earl's World of Curls.

The shop had been closed for about a half hour when the taxi pulled into the lot. The cab parked between the minivan and the Accord.

Danica juggled the keys in her pocket, watching from her station, as Mrs. Alberts paid the driver. She approached the locked front door. Danica let her in.

"No chauffeur tonight?"

"Your call implied discretion. I assume this is not concerning a news article in the Daily Trojan."

"Have a seat," said Danica. They went to the chairs. Mrs. Alberts regarded them like a princess being asked to sit in the bleachers at Dodger Stadium. She chose Carla's chair. Danica took her own, and they spun to face each other.

Mrs. Alberts clutched her hands on her purse on her lap. She sat with perfect posture, as always, but with less self assurance than Danica had ever seen from her. She wore a smart sweater, dress capri pants and heels, of course.

"You have something to tell me?" she said.

"We're just gonna wait for the cops to call me."

"I believe you should present me some kind of evidence or case or something. My husband is a respectable man and I do not understand how you came to make such a terrible accusation—" She broke off, like a hiccup, then found herself again. "—about our son." Again, she broke off.

"Your husband is very close to Ronald Austin, right?"

"I suppose so. We're neighbors."

"And he wants Bel Air to become its own city. To separate from Los Angeles."

"Ronald might have his opinions—"

"I meant your husband."

"Well, most of us do. It would be in our area's best interest."

"But your husband has the means to do it. And the most to gain. His family owns land all over Bel Air, and he wants to sell it if it breaks away from LA."

"He doesn't own — we don't own land."

"Not in his name, but he and your butler have been acquiring land for when Bel Air becomes a city.

"I doubt that will ever really happen."

"Not for lack of trying," Danica said. "He's been making speeches and cozying up to the LAPD and building interest in a break for years. And he really ramped it up recently, especially after purchasing the property on Langstrom. On the cul-de-sac. He understands, just like his dad did, that power comes from land and public opinion. If you have both, you control everything."

"I'm afraid I'm absolutely lost," said Mrs. Alberts.

"I was, too. But it's there. It's all there."

Danica adjusted in her seat, and leaned on her knees.

She said, "Your husband has the land that he's ready to sell to the city of Bel Air. He controls everything needed to become a proper city: Space for a police station, a city hall, all that stuff. All he needs, really, is for Bel Air to actually *become* a city. To truly incorporate. He can help that along by acting like it already is. A kind of 'fake it til you make it' thing."

"Like you," said Mrs. Alberts. "And all this detective work."

"Yeah. And that's where this Mayor comes in."

Mrs. Alberts sat somehow straighter, unconvinced.

"I have a friend who's a cop," said Danica, tripping on the words as she heard them. "He said all the cops call Ronald Austin 'The Mayor of Bel Air.' But they didn't come up with the nickname. Your father-in-law did. For himself first. Which is lame, but he did it. He pushed it, repeated it. He got the LAPD to refer to him that way. And when people do that — when people make personas stick — perception becomes reality. They faked it to make it."

Mrs. Alberts titled her head two degrees off of perfect.

Danica doubled down. "If people like Drake the First and Ronald Austin act like the mayor, then people will think they *are* the mayor. And they'll think he has a city to be mayor of."

"And then they'll think Bel Air is its own city?"

"Yes!" said Danica. "Exactly. And soon after that they'll say, 'Well, why *isn't* Bel Air its own city? It's got its act together. Already has a mayor.' They'll see everything is ready to go and it'll seem like such a natural fit that they'll just go along with it."

"Perception becoming reality." Despite her understanding, Mrs. Alberts continued to question. "How does this relate to my son, precisely?"

"I'm getting there. Making Bel Air a city wasn't going to happen overnight. It would take long-term planning, set it in motion years in advance. Drake the First knew this. Knew he might not see it through, too, but believed it was important to his legacy. It would pass on to his son and his grandson if necessary. Drake, er, Drake the Second, I mean... do you ever get them confused? All these 'Drakes?'"

"No."

"Well, I do, so I'm gonna say 'your husband.' So, your husband was groomed by his dad to fake-it-until-he-made-it as mayor, and they did the same thing to your son. It's like a retirement plan for greed. The only problem was that your husband just didn't fit the Mayor Type."

"That's the only problem?" said Mrs. Alberts.

"He's kinda squat and rubs people the wrong way. He started out doing all the handshakes and big-check hand-outs. He could push around money and throw cop-support fundraisers, but his look just doesn't fit. Grandpa's plan depended on someone fitting. Your husband knew himself well enough to acknowledge this. Since your son was too young to fit the part, Mr. Alberts looked for a stand-in. Enter Ronald Austin.

"And Austin totally looks the part. A little snooty, like a duke. Your husband wanted assurances so he used his son to introduce Austin to Keith Beckett. Get Austin trained, quietly, trained in public speaking. So he'd be more mayor-like."

"Is he?"

"Is he what?"

"Good at it? At being this mayor-like thing you're describing?"

"He's not bad. You can see him apply his training, all the way down to this little shimmy move he does before he steps up to perform. It was good enough to keep the plan alive. And while Austin held the spot, Mr. Alberts moved on to acquiring the land. Even forcing out his own sister.

"Samantha was always the black sheep, and probably didn't wanna go along with all this Mayor stuff anyway. Your husband took advantage of her. He encouraged her to buy the house knowing she'd tank it quick enough. She didn't have business sense. She was an artist. He knew it would fall apart. And when it did, he swooped in with Mr. Peters to buy the place — to 'save her' — drove Samantha out of town."

Danica held up her hand before Mrs. Alberts could push back.

"I'm getting to it, I promise. So your husband followed his dad's mission. He had the land, the cops. He had a mayor-in-training who could step away when his son came of age.

"Except Drake — your son — didn't want to be part of it. He was close with his Aunt Samantha. He liked acting. And your husband, he didn't think Drake had the right... stuff. To be mayor."

"I'm even more confused," said Mrs. Alberts.

"Your son, um..." This was no fun.

"Drake argued with us," said Mrs. Alberts. "Of course. What child doesn't with his parents? But as far as wanting—"

"Was your son gay, Mrs. Alberts?"

Her face somehow went paler than normal. Mrs. Alberts wriggled in her seat, sitting rigid as possible, before she said, "I'm sorry?"

"I don't mean to get so personal, but the whole mess is

personal. Your husband's plan has a strict code — a mission. And he needs everything to be perfect, to fit into his father's vision of what a 'Mayor' should be. They had to be male, from a prominent Bel Air family, with no blemishes on their character, good in business or perceived to be. And straight."

Danica rubbed her fingers together, ignoring the tension of outing a dead son to his own mother.

"However Drake identified, he loved Josue Rodriguez, and your husband couldn't take it. It screwed up the whole Alberts family legacy plan. And that's putting it in the nicest light. Again, I don't mean to put it so blunt, but your husband is not the most progressive guy around. He found out Drake was gay — probably while checking up on Ronald Austin's progress with Mr. Beckett. They all shared a teacher. Maybe he found out by accident, or he found out they had the tattoo, but he couldn't take it. And he killed him."

"Drake's tattoo? For USC?" Mrs. Alberts remained motionless. She blinked occasionally.

"No, the other one. On his ankle. Josue has a matching one. Your husband cannot stand imperfection. He found out about Drake and his rendezvous at the Trojan Horse theater in Leggett. Drake had been drawn there by his aunt. Mr. Alberts has a problem with free thinkers. Anyone he doesn't think is worthy of his respect. Samantha was one of those people. He erased her from the family. Probably tore her out of the wills. I know he re-did that family portrait. He lost his mind when he saw it at the LAPD event. He had driven her away, but he couldn't write off his own son so easily, especially with so much riding on him. He had to make Drake a figurehead, one he could use to gain more power and influence. So he followed him to Leggett, for one more try. But he flipped out and killed him. Look."

Danica pulled the dirty polo shirt out of her sweatshirt pocket.

"This is your son's. I found it at the theater. The button's broken, see? Not 'right.' Your husband made him change it to a 'right' shirt, drove him home to Bel Air, killed him, then planted the body on his own lawn — where he could get his own police force to handle it all his way — and pinned it on Josue. A perfect choice: the disgruntled ex-employee, a minority for the LAPD to go after. It all makes sense. Mostly."

Danica took a breath and leaned back in her seat. Mrs. Alberts turned away, processing. Her bottom lip quivered. Danica reached out and took the woman's hand.

"I'm sorry to be the one to tell you," she said.

"I cannot believe it. You figured all this out yourself?"

"I had some help. A lot, actually."

"What are you going to do now?" said Mrs. Alberts.

"My cop friend — who I'm really hoping is still my friend — went to your house after you left to handle your husband. I wanted to make sure you got out safe."

Silent tears ran down Mrs. Alberts' face, onto her perfect sweater.

Danica leaned back, her fingers tracing the broken button on the bloody polo. She considered what a big risk it had been, taking so many hunches, but they'd added up.

Mostly.

That cracked button tripped her thumb's route. Danica justified the shirt changing by throwing around Mr. Alberts' irrational temper. The man had a vision, and obsession. But tickling that button, Danica's insecurity rose again. Was Mr. Alberts so far gone as to change his victim's shirt? And removing the tattoos.

Well, the one tattoo.

Removed with medical precision from his ankle.

Danica looked Mrs. Alberts in the eye.

She'd stopped crying. Her face had focus. She grabbed Danica's wrist tight, and dug her nails into the skin.

"My son is not gay."

The first punch connected with Danica's chin and knocked her back into her barber chair. The next couple punches kept her there.

Danica's brain entered a binary state, recognizing she had been hit, and that more hits had come. She raised an arm to block one punch, only to have another come, then another and another.

She grabbed Mrs. Alberts' hair. There came a scream, followed by a knee to Danica's chest. It drove the wind from her lungs. As she choked, a tightness grew around her wrist. Something metal.

Handcuffs. Pressing into her skin. Mrs. Alberts clasped their mate to the arm of the chair and stepped back. Wiped the sweat from her face.

Danica reached out with her free hand, grabbing nothing.

Mrs. Alberts walked down the hallway toward the backdoor.

The cuffs were tight. Pulling on them accomplished nothing but deeper cuts into her wrist. But she still pulled.

With a grin like she'd just arrived to host another tea, Mrs. Alberts returned. "Back's already locked. Smart girl. Good practice." Her grin faded when she looked at Danica's station, that same disapproving look she had when she arrived. She slid to Carla's station, more to her liking, and picked up a box.

Danica recognized it: her graduation gift.

Mrs. Alberts removed the straight razor from the box and moved to the back of Danica's chair.

Danica's heart slammed into her ribs. Her feet panicked, kicking at the chair bolted to the floor. "Don't you wanna know how I figured it out?"

Mrs. Alberts said, "You made it very clear that you didn't. Not entirely."

"You killed Samantha and Beckett, too, didn't you," said Danica. She was grasping, hoping to hit some kind of trigger word or phrase, something Mrs. Alberts would respond to, to buy time. "Or you arranged it. Your butler or someone."

It bought no time at all. Mrs. Alberts opened the razor. Then she grabbed Danica's free hand and held it down. She pulled the sweatshirt sleeve back and slid the blade across the bare forearm, drawing blood.

"You're a sad girl," her voice a whisper. "You lost your mother and you're all alone in the big city. You struggle to find purpose so you nose around in business that is not your own, only to find solace. You traveled up north and attacked those people, my stupid sister-in-law and her artsy-fartsy friend. The police already have your phone. You had no way out. So you came here, and did this."

The razor cut Danica's other arm.

Her eyes fluttered and the brightness of the room dipped out of focus. Danica squinted, saw Mrs. Alberts move back a few steps, admiring her work and turn into a blur. The sink turned on. Mrs. Alberts washed the razor, then set it on the edge of Danica's sink. There it would stay until Danica bled out, at which time it would surely be placed in her own hand.

The Blur walked around the chair, and reached into the pocket of Tommy's sweatshirt. Danica's eyes traced the Blur's hand, then returned to the light. Something about the light kept them focused, like finding air above water. A jingle. Car keys, removed from her pocket.

Danica lifted her unchained arm above her head. To stop loss of blood. It trickled down her sleeve, down her arm, showed no sign of slowing or stopping. As the depth of the cuts explained themselves, she felt lightheaded. Her balance failed, and she slid out of the chair and thumped to the floor. At least on the floor, with her arm still shackled, she could keep both arms up.

Fingers tingled and wrists grew heavy. Danica tugged on the chain. She couldn't feel it digging into her skin anymore. All she felt something between numbness and nothing. The blood had evacuated her fingers, and her toes were beginning to follow suit. It would not be long.

But she could still feel them, her toes. She kicked her legs to make sure. Her right boot came loose, to her ankle. Her imitation Docs — heavy on a normal day — now felt like kettle bells. And the closest thing she had to a weapon.

Another kick. Her heel came loose, but the boot clung to her dead toes. She told them to wiggle and hoped they listened. She twisted her feet together, prying at one another to loosen the laces, pulling and kicking and spasming on the linoleum.

The boot. Her foot. She could see them separating from each other. More kicks. Then a flick. A pull. Another kick. Her heel. She saw it free. She had to. Focus. The Blur, forget it. Focus on the heel. The boot. Yes. The boot lay empty on the floor.

More blood.

Focus.

Her foot. Move it.

The foot hooked the boot. Pulled it to her free hand.

Fingers. They had to listen. They were still hers. Command them. 'Move. Grab the boot.'

Footsteps? High heels. From the Blur. Somewhere.

No matter. The boot. Focus. Grab it.

The fingers listened. Danica pulled the boot off the floor. Kettle bell. Up to the seat.

A rest.

Her feet. Put them underneath. Push. Hard.

Do it.

Danica raised herself up, back into the chair. The boot next to her, still in her hand.

Blood sprinted from the holes in her arms.

The Blur, by the sink. Looking at her? Maybe. Freaked out? A little. Ready to attack? Couldn't tell. Only a Blur.

Her chained hand. Tried to move it. It didn't. No feeling in those fingers. Danica rubbed the boot on the chained wrist. No response. Nothing. All feeling had spilled on the floor.

Now, to her unchained hand, a clear, simple message: 'Lift the boot.' She repeated it to the hand, to the fingers. Still hers. Still hers to command. Still alive.

It listened. Lifted the boot above her head. Locked upright, pouring more blood down her arm.

The Blur at the sink. Moved back. Never mind.

To her unchained hand: 'Down. Hard.'

The hand smashed the boot onto Danica's numb wrist.

The impact made a sickening smack. Bones broken probably. Danica couldn't tell. If she had more time to think it through...

Danica took another breath, sent another command to her hand to raise the boot again.

Again it listened, and followed with another smack onto her hand.

She slipped out of the seat, crumpled onto the floor, into the lake of her own blood.

Her hand. Had to be broken now. Had to be. If not, she would die in Earl's, like some sort of poem or crappy high school band's original song.

The lights flickered again. A nap sounded like a great idea. A nice cool one, right there on the floor. All her problems washed away.

Her mom's voice called to her. Did she believe in Heaven? Would she see her mother again? It sounded just like her, and closing her eyes let Danica hear her more clearly. Sounded just like her. Her mother's voice got closer and louder.

It said, "Stay awake."

Danica opened her eyes. Bit her lip and shook her head. Her brain spun inside her skull, but she was awake.

"Pull" said the voice.

Danica pushed her feet against the chair and yanked, pulling at her arm away from the shackle.

The mess of what had once been her solid hand slipped through the cuff.

Her body flew back, free of resistance and its own agency. Landing against the other chair might have hurt if she still had the blood to register such things.

The good hand, the one that listened, still listened. And still clung to the boot.

The Blur said something, like from underwater. Danica responded by swinging the boot. She spat and swung and made noises, all the while her mom's words repeated.

"Stay awake."

Danica rolled over, toward the sink wall, toward the mess of the tools on her counter. God, she hoped Carla hadn't tried to clean up her station. She whipped her boot at the pile.

Down came the mess, including her shears. She traded the boot for them.

The Blur made noise and moved back. Vision sagged again. Danica squinted as the world got dark. Where did the Blur go?

A noise. Those heels. Far away, or was that just death coming for her again. Had to be somewhere.

A thump, like wood. Or metal. Like down a hallway. Somewhere else. Outside.

"The desk. The phone." Danica listened to her mom.

She crawled toward the reception area. Yanked the phone cord, pulling the entire phone on top of her.

A dial tone, or just her ears ringing. She hit three numbers. The floor pad under her back felt warm.

The fluorescents above her. It was brighter before. Now, so dim.

Danica closed her eyes. The nap convinced her. The sleep she'd avoided for so long finally took hold.

CHAPTER FORTY

ELSEWHERE.

The light was bright again, almost burning. Obnoxious, really. Danica blinked and held her hand in front of her face. She was surrounded by stillness, and a weird smell like cheap Pine-Sol.

A bed. She was in a bed, with sheets and blankets. Her arms had bandages. One side of the room had a light brown closet and a door, and the other had a grey curtain. The TV on the far wall played some 24-hour news channel, muted.

If this was Heaven, it was underwhelming.

Danica looked at her feet. Beyond the bed stood a woman in all pink with her hair tied up tight. She had her back to Danica, prepping something at the wall, and talking.

She said, "You keep this down, it'll help. But take it slow. You don't gotta jump in to the deep end." Danica watched the nurse pour some liquid in a cup.

"Miss," said Danica. Her mouth dry as the Sahara, giving her a 50-grit sandpaper voice. "Can I... water?"

"Just a minute, hon," said the nurse. She picked up the tray and carried it through the grey curtain.

Danica tried to sit up, but reeled from the pain. Her right hand hid in a cast, the size of a boxing glove.

Pain traded places with panic as her memory returned. Mrs. Alberts. Where did she go? Was she in the bed behind the curtain? Was she recovering from some kind of face-replacement surgery to escape without anyone finding her again? Did she take Danica's face? Was that why they were here?

The nurse re-emerged and picked up the pitcher and cup. "You need a straw for this, honey?"

Danica breathed what sounded like "Uh-huh." The nurse held the cup and placed the straw to Danica's lips. After a couple gulps she found her voice. "What happened?"

"Not sure I can tell you," said the nurse. "You've been here for about a day, I know that much. I'm only starting my shift, but that's what your chart says. Came in last night 'bout midnight. Or just before then."

Danica locked eyes with the nurse. "I didn't try to kill myself."

"You don't owe me any explanations."

"I'm serious. I didn't. Someone did this to me."

The nurse nodded and reached for Danica's pillows, giving them a straightening. "If you need anything else...." She motioned to the call button on the bed then waddled out of the room.

Danica scanned the room again, noticing the flowers on the table next to her. And her phone next to the vase. Pain swelled in her arms, but the left one reached out.

Twelve text messages, five voicemails, and only 4% battery left to check them all.

Mission: accepted.

She started with the voicemail. The first was a scam, calling about being sued for tax evasion (at least, she hoped that was a scam). The second had bad audio quality, with the person leaving the message who sounded like they'd called while standing next to a train. It might have mentioned a car: "—der parts... part. They don't... when cheap... can get use—... —stimate." That 4% looked thinner than ever, so she skipped it.

The last messages were almost all from Carla. "Girl, are you OK? Call me." "Girl, this is Carla. I gotta hear your voice. Call me." "Call me, please!" She sounded justifiably and comfortingly panicked. She had probably arrived at work and thought the place had been replaced with a butcher shop.

One stray call came from Academy Barber School, congratulating Danica on passing her certification. It mentioned an upcoming ceremony while promising exciting networking opportunities. Must have used the same service as the USC Business Club.

She moved to the text messages.

Four from Carla, companion pieces to the voicemails. She had covered all the bases. Seven were from Gabby, and played in similar territory as Carla's, all along the lines of "You OK" and "Carla's calling me— calling, not texting" and "You OK?" again.

The last one said only, "Nice work, DL."

Her heart felt light again. If it took a near-death experience to get back on his good side, she'd take it.

She wrote back, "You saved my number?"

In 90 seconds, Freddie wrote, "You're awake!"

"What did you mean nice work?"

"They got her."

Danica paused to allow Freddie the chance to correct

any mistakes. Maybe he typed too fast. A minute passed, but no correction came, so she wrote:

"Details please. Help a girl out."

She immediately questioned the potential flirtiness, then ignored it.

2% battery.

Then came: "Evelyn Alberts."

For just a moment, the sting in her arms drifted away. She stared at the name on her screen and her lungs filled, fuller than they had been for a week, maybe a month.

"Keep going."

He did: "Whole story — I went to house personally. Found Mr. Alberts. SUPER pissed. He said Mrs. A was going crazy and scaring him.

"Yeah. Scaring HIM. That guy.

"I called for back-up and headed to Earl's. Figured you drew her out and kept it a secret LIKE YOU SHOULD NOT HAVE.

"On way there, I get to Sepulveda and see your car stalled on the side of road. Smoke coming out of the hood. Mrs. Alberts in the car screaming and yelling."

"I'm impressed she got my car to start."

"She looked scary. And rubbing at her sweater. Blood on sweater. Yours, we found out. She saw me and ordered me to help.

"Ordered, DL.

"Or. Drrd.

"I ask how she got your car. No good answer. I call for a squad to go to Earl's. Sorry it wasn't me who found you."

Danica re-read the last line. She felt her cheek and wondered if she had picked up a sudden fever.

"How did you know she killed Drake 3?"

Danica buckled herself up. "Long story: Albertses think

they're better than everyone and need to show it. Want to break Bel Air from LA, make it its own city so they can lord over it. They have the land to sell, and position themselves as even more powerful. They have cops on their side (no offense). All to preserve Their Legacy. When D3 threatened to expose them as anything but perfect — just cuz he was gay and didn't want to rule the world — she flipped. She wanted a prominent family. To her, he didn't fit."

Danica watched the three dots of Freddie composing his response. She expected a lengthy diatribe about taking risks and getting in over her head and not being careful.

Instead he simply wrote:

"Daaaaaamn."

1%. Then:

"But proof?"

"Follow the Mayor of Bel Air. Ronald Austin. He played a part, cast by Mrs. Alberts. Originally supposed to be D2 then D3. He knew Keith Beckett and Samantha. Plus Mrs. Alberts is obsessive compulsive. Like for real. She can't leave anything alone. Showed up to visitation late so she could correct a bush that got trimmed wrong. Cleaned up a mess I made at Samantha's house. Wood pile. Removed her dead son's tattoo after killing him. Prob with a scalpel. She was pre-med. Left the USC tattoo, but not the one matching Josue.

"And attacked me only using 'clean' stuff."

"I'll have to get Austin to talk."

"You'll do fine."

"Still don't get why she did it. They have more money than God."

"Greed always wants more."

The three dots returned, until Freddie finally responded, "Nice work, detective."

And at that, her phone died.

Her head felt like her phone, exhausted from overuse. Also full of the images she'd pulled from Mrs. Alberts. The compulsion to change the boy's shirt, staring at that cracked button, then tossing the shirt under the floor like a diseased rag, unable to stand the sight of such imperfection.

She brought him a new shirt, forced him to put it on, then stabbed him with the knife she'd stolen from the Trojan Theater. With all the buttons intact.

Danica leaned back and grabbed the nurse's call button. Whatever pain killers they had, she'd take more. She owed Andrew a phone call. They could talk about how he had been doing, and reminisce about her mom. Take him up on the offer to fly back to him.

She would get out of town for a couple weeks. Or a month. Just be somewhere else. Somewhere away.

Continue reading for a *sneak peak* of
the second Psychic Barber Mystery...

The following takes place in mid-January of 2009. Danica has returned to LA. In Earl's World of Curls, Carla has explained that they cannot afford to hire her back (yet). She has just left on an errand, leaving Danica alone in the salon....

The morning ticked by, customerless. No money came in, only went out. After a good forty minutes of lonely self-pity and without a better plan to follow, Danica turned off the hallway and bathroom lights. At this point, every buck counted.

She took a big gulp of pride and swallowed it whole. She could act all bad when she had money, or at least had options. But without money or those options....

Phone in hand, she texted Gabby. "I'm sorry. I'm in. For real this time. Won't be late again."

In record time (even for Gabby, an Olympic-level text responder) a message returned: "Will keep eyes open."

Done. Good. It would be good. She could make a little cash and spare Carla the trouble of babysitting her.

A few minutes later, Gabby wrote again. "You can do reality, rite?"

"That's what I do already."

"Reality TV. Like makeup and hair for documentary type stuff."

Danica paused, considering the question. She could do hair, obviously, and perform standard makeup maneuvers. However she'd never done any honest-to-god work in the realm of reality television. She'd barely watched it. She understood enough about makeup to know there had to be subtle differences in application for the variety of performances being filmed (Stage makeup wasn't good for film, film makeup was different from TV, TV wasn't right for dates, all that), but that meant she only knew she didn't know anything.

So she wrote, "Totally."

"Perf," said Gabby. "BRB."

More time slid out of the day. Fifteen minutes became twenty, then thirty, all in the empty Earl's. She'd just started a daydream about styling a drag queen for a global race show when a car parked in the lot. A gray Escalade, clean and new looking. She stood, hopeful this was a walk-in with deep pockets and friends. When the driver did not emerge, she sat back down and resumed her musing.

She weighed how terrible her punishment might be for lying about her reality TV qualifications. Worst she could imagine: they wouldn't hire her again. Which meant she'd be right back where she was, but with a day's pay.

After a minute, a man exited the Escalade. He slipped into shadow while heading to a neighboring door, so Danica could not get a good look at him. He quickly disappeared from sight, but then returned just as quickly, appearing in the window of Earl's. His face at last in full sight, the man's gaze went straight through the glass pane and caught Danica's.

It should be well-noted that Danica was not the type of person to go gaga over anything, let alone anybody. She had gone weak-kneed for a few celebrities here and there (her middle-school commitment to the films of Christian Slater bordered on alarming), but nothing reached beyond her control. She had seen clips from "Ed Sullivan" where girls pulled their eyeballs out over the mere sight of Elvis or the Beatles and never understood it. Sure, she could capably recognize beauty and attractiveness, but that recognition never manifested into a physiological reaction.

That was until seeing the driver of the Escalade. His looks were so classically "good" that Danica's brain system lagged in comprehending the rest of his form. The chiseled chin, sparkling dark eyes and gentle-yet-commanding grin sent beams across the lot, through the door window and straight into Danica's soul. She regarded the face before her with amazement, the kind early humans must have had the first time they saw the Grand Canyon. The man before her was a marvel.

A marvel that walked through Earl's front door.

"Hey there." His voice was neither high nor deep, rather dripping off his lips like chocolate syrup. His smile somehow grew wider when he looked at her.

A second of frozen non-responsiveness passed before Danica managed to speak. "Can I?" She thought she'd added 'help you,' but couldn't be certain of anything any more.

"Can I ask you something?" He leaned against the door frame. Lucky frame.

She might have uttered some form of an answer, anything between "Certainly, sir" and "Muh-m'buhhn."

"Do you know Madame Lorena?"

Full world collapse. Nothing made sense. Why would this apparition of human perfection know of Lorena's existence, let alone sully his alabaster teeth by uttering her name? The grotesquely gorgeous man even pointed toward the neighboring business, toward Madame Lorena's parlor of tarot cards and light chicanery. As if such a motion would help anything to make more (or any) sense.

He moved away from the door and entered the full light of the salon. Once under the unforgiving fluorescents, Danica scientifically confirmed his looks were not a trick of favorable exterior light or window refraction.

"Yes," she said, managing not to drool on herself.

The Grand-Canyon Man nodded. "It's my first time meeting with her. Supposed to be right now, but her place doesn't look open. Lights are off, too." The noontime sun cast a golden glow around the man's head. Somehow this dude knew how to find his light in a strip mall hair salon. That or the light just naturally found him. At this point, anything seemed possible.

With a kind of strength she didn't know she possessed, Danica looked beyond the man's incredible nose and magnificent cheeks to deliver a coherent sentence.

"If I see her, I'll let you know. If you want to leave your number."

Not half bad compared to the prior two minutes.

"Nah, that's okay. I'll just keep waiting. Thanks." He waved and turned away, confirming Danica's suspicions about his backside.

He reached his car and disappeared from her sight, thereby breaking the spell. Her head ached at the mere memory of his looks. His features appeared almost touched up, but in real life! It fractured Danica's brain. His eyes lingered the longest; they'd appeared disappointed at the delayed appointment, but worried as well. Worried about what, Danica could not venture to guess. Good looking people had problems, she supposed. Good-looking problems. Something was distracting this guy.

Her phone buzzed with a Gabby text.

"Tonight," it said.

Danica re-read the preceding exchange before responding, "Tonight like you found a job for tonight? As in today at night?"

"Yep. 9."

"That was fast."

"Online content moves quick. No costumes or blood or fx or anything. You heard of Sofi Starr?"

She had not, but wrote, "Yep."

"Great. Hair n make-up. You in?"

The phone grew heavy, waiting for an answer. Danica typed, "In," and sent it.

Plan, settled. Pride, swallowed. Keep surviving. Keep eating. No drama.

Danica told herself these things as she put her phone away and resigned. She couldn't expect Carla to do everything for her when she had her own stuff to sort out. Gabby sent a follow-up about prep related to some other Sofi Starr videos. The links were all videos with "Sofi Tries" as their first words in the titles. Danica added them to her mental to-do list and took one more glance at the Escalade in the lot. Its tinted windows shielded the world from the radiance in the driver's seat.

She turned from the door to the salon stations just in time to meet eyes with a 60-year-old woman and scream.

The woman wore a thin scarf, a thinner smile and a Member's Only jacket over a flowing dress. She stood beside the reception desk, looked to be about the same height as Carla, but was definitely *not* Carla. This woman had tanner skin, with deep creases in her cheeks. Her hands were out and open, as if to signal 'I'm not here to kill you.' Danica remained unconvinced.

"Easy, dear," said the woman. She wiggled her right hand. A set of keys hung from the forefinger and her bony wrist cracked when she gave them a jingle.

"I entered through the back. Didn't think anyone was here."

Danica's breath finally exhaled as she stared at Madame Lorena Baronette in the flesh.

They'd first met years earlier, when Danica became a full-timer at Earl's. Lorena would often stop by to pick up the rent check, but more often to complain about things like trash not being handled properly. Sometimes she popped over between palm readings, often through the back door. Lorena owned the building and acted like it, much to her renters' chagrin. After a few of these uninvited visits, Danica had made a habit of keeping some distance between herself and the would-be mystic.

Danica held the door handle for support and glanced through the window. "You've got a client waiting for you."

Lorena joined her at the door and peered through the window. "Indeed I do. You've seen the boy, I trust?"

Her voice hissed when she spoke, words sliding through her teeth, transforming into smoke. "How could you miss him? He is dreamy, but I understand he has little cooking in the kitchen, if you follow my meaning." She leaned in for affect: "I hear he's got money."

This last detail explained so much to Danica. "Yeah, well, he's waiting and you're late."

Lorena squinted at Danica's scalp. "You're Carla's girl, aren't you? The one with the trouble last year."

A prickle zapped through Danica's forearm. "I've been out of town for a few months."

"Out of town." Lorena dragged the words through her incisors. Danica sensed no mockery in this mimicry; it was more akin to how a hypnotist might lull victims to sleep by stretching every syllable into a purr. Danica blinked and reminded herself to stay alert and keep her hand on her wallet.

Lorena's scrutiny released Danica. "I apologize for my intrusion. I arrived after my client. And since I prefer to maintain an air of mystery and magic about my person, such tardiness would dilute that aura."

Danica awaited more explanation.

It finally arrived, with less magical affectation. "I did not want to drive up in my Kia and unlock the door like a common troll."

"So you sneak into the salon? You can't do your seance stuff in here."

"And so I shall not," said Lorena, regaining her performance. "Our two businesses share a wall, allowing me to bridge the gap from this business to my own, maintaining my mystic atmosphere."

Lorena delivered the speech with such authority that it took a moment for Danica to realize she still couldn't put it together. "Come again?"

"I'm sneaking into my place so he doesn't see. My back door's jammed up, so I get in through here." Her formality dropped again, loosening her accent. The faintest regionality hung on Lorena's words — her 'into' very nearly become 'inta.'

With a slight bow and without further elucidation, Lorena glided to the rear of the salon, toward the Happy Spatula products area. She nudged the shelf to the side with unpredictable strength, allowing full berth of the closet door.

Another key unsheathed from her robes, Lorena unlocked and opened the closet with ease. The interior was just as Danica remembered: dirty, junky and a little spooky. A dusty floor held old paint cans, long-forgotten sweaters and some old hairspray bottles. There was stepladder that looked way below code.

Lorena stepped inside the closet and gandered at the ceiling. She wiggled the ladder a bit, hitched up her skirt, stepped onto the first rung and reached up. Her bony fingers grabbed a rope attached to the ceiling tile. Under her weight, a trap door opened and an attic ladder telescoped all the way to the floor.

The ladder invited Lorena up and, after pocketing her keys, she accepted the invitation, ascending rapidly through the hole in the ceiling.

"Close that door for me?" Lorena's voice came from the hole in the closet ceiling. Danica had moved closer to the closet, as if in a trance. Witnessing a Grand Canyon man with her own eyes was one thing. Lorena's cat-burglar skills sent her head spinning.

Just as the last swath of silky scarf billowed up through the hole, Lorena popped her head back down, spry as ever.

"It was that Alberts family murder, was it not? The one last summer? The case you solved, I mean?"

More head spinning. "I was... I helped, yeah."

"And," said Lorena, again studying Danica's scalp, "you cut hair as well."

"Sometimes. Well, not 'as well.' I do other things... I'm trying to. Cut hair again, I mean."

Lorena nodded, so Danica nodded back, unsure of the proper response to such an inquisition from a woman hanging through a hole in the closet ceiling.

"I'm gonna have to tell Carla about this," said Danica.

"About what?"

"You sneaking around our— her place. It's not right, Lorena."

The woman held up her ringed pointer finger. "Please. *Madame* Lorena."

With that, she vanished into the darkness.

A minute later, Danica heard Lorena's door swing open outside. The older woman's voice announced her arrival with all the glee of someone who could never be accused of abusing her authority.

Go to www.phillipmottaz.com to get your copy of "The Homicidal Hairstyle of the Viral Video Vixen!"

DID YOU ENJOY THIS BOOK?

You can make a _big difference._

Reviews are a powerful tool when it comes to getting attention for my books. Unfortunately I cannot write them myself, so I'm asking you to help out!

Honest reviews help my books get attention from other readers.

If you enjoyed the book, I would be forever grateful if you could take just five minutes to leave a review. Post on Apple Books, post on Google Play, tell a librarian — whatever you like.

Also, while I try to be a good ally, I recognize that I make mistakes due to my personal biases. Please feel free to reach out and hold me accountable. I promise to do better in the future.

Thanks so much.

MORE READS

<u>More Psychic Barber Mysteries</u>

- *The Homicidal Hairstyles of the Viral Video Princess*
- *Pearls Before Fine* (short story)
- *The Sequins of Events* (short story)
- *The Killer Cuts of the Gutter Punk Band* (coming soon)

<u>The Gallagher Brothers Mysteries</u> (new in 2024!)

Parody series where Noel and Liam — the warring brothers from Oasis — reunite not to play music... to *solve murders!*

- *Deadly Maybe*
- *(What's the Story) Dead and Gory*
- *Be Dead Now*

ABOUT THE AUTHOR

Phillip Mottaz grew up in Illinois' smallest city and graduated from Knox College before studying improv and sketch comedy in Chicago. Since moving to Los Angeles, he has written for YouTube stars, film, television, music magazines and for fun. He has also produced multiple podcasts including the comedy show **Superpunk Radio** and the music tribute show **Ramones of the Day.**

He lives with his wife and son in the San Fernando Valley.

Join the email list at **phillip.mottaz.author@gmail.com,** follow the blog at **phillipmottaz.wordpress.com** and follow on Twitter and Instagram **@phillipmottaz.**

www.ingramcontent.com/pod-product-compliance
Lightning Source LLC
Chambersburg PA
CBHW031612100726
47898CB00006B/1760